ANOTHER WOMAN'S HUSBAND
A SINFUL LOVE AFFAIR

BY: JOHNAZIA GRAY

D1527169

Acknowledgments

Wow! I am so blessed and thankful to be giving you guys another book. Not just any kind of book though, but a book that touched me and I pray that it touches whoever reads it.

I honestly just want to thank God for this! I stayed up so many long nights making sure that I gave my all to this book. I prayed and prayed and asked the Lord to guide me through. When I wanted to push my computer to the side and give up my prayers would always make me fight through and get it done. This book is so powerful to me, and I give that to God.

To my two test readers Earline and Adia… I appreciate you women from the bottom of my heart. Y'all pushed me to the max, and made sure that I gave it my all. Whenever I felt a little discouraged you ladies were right there to remind me on how good this book was. I texted you ladies all times of the night and y'all were right there ready to give me the honest feedback that I needed, and I'm so thankful and grateful. I honestly don't think I could've made it through without y'all. Thanks so much!

To all of my ladies in my readers group "Johnazia's Motivational Dream Chasers" I love y'all to the max! I've met some wonderful women, and some amazing friends and I am so grateful for the connection that all of us have. Y'all motivate me and keep me on my toes, and I love that. Can't wait to meet you all. :: Hugs and kisses:

To all of my family and friends that support me, THANK YOU! Thank you and I love you all so much. This journey have been so amazing with y'all on my side! I love it!

To my publisher, my team, and all of my supporters I just want to thank y'all for the genuine love, and support that I receive. I'm so appreciative. I honestly thank God for y'all. It's a blessing to be a part of such an amazing team.

To everyone that will be reading this book I pray that you enjoy it. I'm claiming that this book will open so many doors for me, so when you're saying a prayer make sure you add me and this book in there. *Giggles* God bless and enjoy!

CONTACT INFO:
Facebook: Johnazia Gray
Twitter:Johnazia_Gray
Instagram: Author_Johnazia
Email: Johnaziagray@gmail.com

Chapter 1

Michelle laid in bed with her sorry baby daddy lying on the side of her. After a session of great sex, she stared at the ceiling and wondered why the hell she allowed his dead beat ass to hit it once again. Charles and Michelle both met when she was fifteen years old. They had a ten-year-old daughter together who they both loved to the moon and back. Charles was only a dead beat because that's what Michelle allowed. But, she was finally tired of it.

He slept comfortably in her king size sleigh bed. Michelle had worn his ass completely out. The only reason Michelle continuously had sex with him was because he was the best that she ever had. See, Michelle birthed her daughter ten years ago. Her mother was so disappointed because she always thought that Michelle was the most perfect child in the world. When Michelle's parents found out that she was pregnant by an eighteen-year-old boy, the first thing her mother hollered was pressing charges. The only thing that saved Charles was Michelle's daddy, Luke. He figured since him and Michelle's mom, Shirley, did the same thing when they were younger, they would be hypocrites to jam Charles up.

Michelle knew nothing about having a baby because she was just a baby herself. She even wanted to have an abortion but her mother figured since she wanted to be grown, she was going to step up and raise a baby like she was grown. At first, Charles was a great father to their baby girl Briana, but after a while, he gave up. He used to go to Boston University but was kicked out after being caught selling drugs on campus. After being arrested and kicked out of school, he turned to the street life, which only sent back and forth to jail. His entire background was fucked up after a while, so after that, he gave up.

Even though Michelle was young, her parents made sure she stayed in school. She graduated high school with a 4.0 grade point average at the age of sixteen due to great grades, hard work, and determination. She received a full scholarship to go to University of Massachusetts. At the age of twenty-two, Michelle graduated and received a Social Work Degree. She worked with kids for a long time, but soon she decided that she no longer wanted to do that, so she went back to school to get her degree in Office Administration. Michelle was always a smart girl and she always took care of her daughter with or without Charles, thanks to her parents, but now she was finally over him and his bullshit.

Michelle was scheduled to graduate from Boston University in two weeks and she needed to focus. She couldn't do that with Charles all up in her ass though. Right now, Michelle was unemployed. She had gotten fired from her job two weeks ago because she kept calling out due to her daughter being sick from her cancer disease. She really enjoyed being the head receptionist at the Cannon Design center, but she knew that her time there was up when they couldn't understand that she had a daughter that was sick from cancer. Briana had been diagnosed with bone cancer last year and it broke Michelle's heart. It hurt Charles too, but he had a terrible way in showing it. Michelle had to fly with Briana back and forth to her doctors in Pensacola, Florida and her managers just couldn't take it anymore. When they laid her off, Michelle was heartbroken. She had given those son of a bitches two years of hard work and they laid her off. Although she didn't need the job, she had finally found one that she loved and got attached to. She could've had her parents to help her, but she figured they had done more than enough, even though they wouldn't have mind helping her with Bri. Her parents didn't know that she was out of work and they also thought that Charles had been helping her at one point, but her father knew better. It crushed everyone when they found out that Briana had cancer, but they had to stay strong for her.

That's exactly why she couldn't understand why she continued to allow Charles to feed her lies. She always loved him and knew that he could be better and do better, but Charles just didn't want to grow up and be a man.

He leaned over and threw his arms across her and she flinched. She was disgusted just by thinking about everything.

"Charles, get up," she said to him.

He heard her but he decided to ignore her because he knew she was about to come with the bullshit. He didn't feel like hearing it.

"Nigga, I know you hear me. Get the fuck up!" she yelled.

"Why the fuck you tripping now? Damn, I was in a good ass sleep." He wiped his eyes. She stood there with a big t-shirt on and her arms folded across her chest. Just the sight of him made her want to punch him in the face.

"This is not going to work. Get your shit and leave. It was fun while it lasted." She flicked the lights and gathered his things for him. He started giggling.

"I guess you're back to being a bitch again, huh?"

That was another thing she hated. He was a disrespectful ass nigga when he got mad. Ignorant was what she'd call it.

"No, I'm just tired of dealing with your fuck ass. Let alone letting you fuck me. Your sex game is good but it's not worth it. I can't even believe I've tried with your ass for so long." She shook her head.

He walked up to her with pity in his eyes. He always did that when he wanted his way. She wasn't falling for it this time though.

"I'm gonna do better bae. I promise," he lied.

"Do better with someone else then Charles. I'm over this shit. I've been laying there this entire time thinking how dare I even lay up with a nigga who won't even take the time out to take his daughter, who has cancer, to the doctor. I've been struggling with my baby Charles, and you don't even care." She started to cry. "I've lost my job, hell, I can barely pay the bills and you're not helping me. I feel less than a woman to even let you walk foot in my house. You act like you don't care about Bri and what she's going through. I'm just sick of this." She broke down.

"How the fuck you gone tell me I don't care about my lil mama? I do care about her. What the fuck?" he snapped. He did care about her but not enough. He probably didn't even know if she was living or dying.

"Okay, if you love her so much, she has to be to Pensacola in two days at 3:00p.m. She has to get her chemo and she has to get blood drawn. Can you book a flight and take her while I stay here and look for a job?" She already knew what the answer was going to be, she just wanted to point out to his ass that everything she was saying was right. He was never going to get his shit together for his daughter.

"That's my father's wedding rehearsal day. I can't miss that, Chelle."

She couldn't even say anything. Her stomach was doing flips and she wanted to throw up. The tears silently escaped from her eyes as she shook her head at him.

"Please just leave, and don't ever come back. I don't wanna see you, don't call me or my baby, nothing nigga. Just leave. If something was to happen to her right now, I know that I'd only have my people. Get the fuck out." She started fighting on him. He ignored it though. It hurt him because he knew that he wasn't being a man. He didn't know how to deal with his daughter having cancer. Even though he was a deadbeat, his heart was really aching that his only child had to deal with something so terrible. He didn't love Michelle the way he claimed and he knew it, but he kept playing her just so she wouldn't move on. He would go crazy if she found someone better than him.

Charles jumped into his Dodge pickup truck and sped off. He called this broad up he had been messing with for about three months. She didn't answer, so he figured that she was busy with her nigga. Instead of heading over to her house, he decided to go to his sister's house. He just knew that visit was going to go left.

When Charles pulled up to his sister's apartment in Bowdoin Manor, he dreaded going on the inside. Michelle and his one and only sister, Ciara, had been best friends since they were kids. That's how the two of them hooked up, it was Ciara's idea, but boy did she regret hooking them up now. Her brother disgusted her. The way he treated her niece and her best friend wasn't acceptable. She didn't even converse with him.

He knocked on Ciara's door as he stood back and waited for someone to open the door. He was puffing on his blunt filled with loud to ease his nerves. Michelle had run his blood pressure to the fucking sky and he just needed to calm down.

His eight-year-old nephew, TJ, opened the door.

"Uncle Charles! What's up man?" Charles roughened him up. He missed his nephew. He hadn't saw him in a few months since his mama was always tripping and shit.

"What's up man? Where your mama at?" Charles asked him as he took a seat on the black leather sofa in the living room of the apartment.

"She's in there sleeping. You want me to go and wake her up?"

"Yeah. Handle that for me."

TJ ran to the back and knocked on his mama's door. Ciara was yelling and cursing because she had just got into a good deep sleep.

"Get away from my damn door TJ!" she yelled at her son.

She walked to the front of the house patting her head. Her thick hair was in a bonnet. She wore a cheap silk robe and her face was turned up. When she locked eyes with her brother, she rolled her eyes and went to turn around.

"Come on Cici, don't be like that," he said to her.

"Why are you here Charles? Take your deadbeat ass on somewhere!" she fussed.

He laughed and shook his head. He couldn't believe that he and his sister had turned out the way they did. They used to be so close. Sometimes it broke his heart that they hated each other. They were full blooded brother and sister and instead of her being there for him and understanding that he wasn't perfect, she treated him worse than anybody.

"I need your help. Michelle's done with me." Charles dropped his head. He was really hurt. Despite all the bullshit that he had done, he really did love his baby mama and his daughter. The nigga just had some serious issues when it came to manning up.

"TJ baby, do me a favor and go to your room for a second, please?"

TJ mumbled under his breath while he stormed to his room. He couldn't believe that his mama and uncle would ruin his game of 2K the way they did.

Ciara sat in the love seat across from Charles and looked him dead into his eyes. Ciara was so beautiful, but those angry facial expressions she was making made him think about their mother. Ciara was identical to their mother, Loretta.

"Your ass want me to help you?" She laughed at him like he was a joke, well, in her eyes he was because she wasn't helping a damn thing. "Nigga, I would be less than a woman to reach out to my best friend, another woman at that, and talk her into staying with you. Hell, I've been begging her to leave your ass alone for years because you don't mean her any good. You're disgusting. You know that my niece has cancer and you don't even try to help Michelle with her. You're a disgrace and I'm really ashamed to say that you're my brother. Look at you, you're dressed down to the fucking tee, three hundred dollar pants on, and I know those shoes cost close to five hundred dollars, but you can't even buy a plane ticket to go with Michelle to Briana's doctor's appointments. You have your priorities fucked up big brother, and I'm even shocked that your ass came and asked me, out of all people, for help."

As much as Charles wanted to slap the shit out of Ciara for talking to him the way that she did, he just stood up to leave. Even though everything Ciara said was true, Charles figured that through it all, he was her brother, so she wasn't supposed to treat him like a random nigga. But Ciara didn't give a damn, she always gave it to you straight with no chaser.

"Fuck you Ciara! You can't look down on me when you didn't have your shit together either. Let me remind you that mama had TJ for five years while your ass was out in the streets acting as if you didn't have a son. You ain't perfect either, shit," he snapped.

That triggered Ciara off. She stood up and walked up on him. "Nigga, it don't make a difference! The only reason why I didn't have my shit together was because TJ's father raped me. That shit wasn't intentional and you know that." She tried her best to whisper. She didn't want her son to know that the man he thought was perfect was really a monster from her nightmares.

"Your ass was still off the chain. Fuck you mean? You were seventeen and out of control. That nigga probably didn't rape you. I don't believe shit that comes out of your fucking mouth," Charles said. That cut Ciara really deep. Tears fell from her eyes. She couldn't believe that her brother would say something like that to her.

Ciara was raped by her baby's father, Trey. They were together but during the time, she was still a virgin, and she wasn't interested in having sex. Trey slipped a drug into Ciara's drink one night when they were out having a good time, and he used that time to take advantage of her. She was only seventeen at the time. She didn't want to believe that he did it, so for years, she told everyone that the baby was planned. She also didn't want

Trey to go to prison because she was really in love with him, and she didn't think it was that serious at the time. She simply thought that her boyfriend wanted to spice up their boring relationship. At least that's what she made herself believe. When she turned twenty-one, that's when she decided to accept the fact that Trey was sick and really raped her. Then he confirmed it one day when he got drunk and mad with Ciara because she wouldn't give him any ass. She couldn't overlook it anymore. She told her mother, Michelle, and Charles only. Their mother was crushed when Ciara told her. Loretta knew that her daughter wasn't lying because she knew her child, but Charles had a hard time believing her. Michelle never liked Trey. She always told Ciara that Trey came off as weird to her.

How can you go so long knowing someone raped you without saying anything? Charles always wondered.

Since Ciara was still young and still had a lot of living to do, her mother took TJ in like he was her own. She didn't have a problem with it at all because she always loved kids and she didn't want her baby girl to miss out on life how she had done when she had Charles. Ciara was a hot girl after she had TJ. The streets where her life, but she did graduate high school and get her diploma through all the drama she had going on in her life. When TJ turned five, Ciara decided that her time was up in the streets. She wanted to be an amazing mother to her son and she wanted him to love her the way that he loved his grandmother. She really knew she had to get herself together when TJ would call her by her government name and would call Loretta, mama. That used to break Ciara's heart. But, it was her fault because she chose that. When she got herself together, she decided that she was going to go to Boston

University and received her degree in social work with Michelle's help. Ever since then, it was like her past never existed. She was a social worker at the *Beth Israel Deaconess Medical Center* and she loved her job to the fullest. All of the families that she helped loved her. She was made for that job because she made so many people happy. Ciara didn't know it, but Charles was clearly jealous of her. She had bounced back from so much and she got herself together for her son. Charles couldn't do that if his life depended on it, even with a daughter who had cancer and that fucked with him.

But, he did not believe that Cici got raped. That just didn't make sense to him.

"So, you still think that's a lie, huh?" Ciara wiped her tears.

"Fuck yeah, I do."

"Well, I don't give a fuck what your ass thinks. I don't owe you shit. At least I got myself together for my child. Maybe you should try it, and move on from Michelle because she don't want your broke 'can't get a job' ass."

She tried to hurt his feelings and she was succeeding. He waved her off and left out the house, slamming the door behind him.

He was pissed and so was Ciara. Ciara wanted a drink and he wanted some weed. She picked up her house phone to call her mother and tell on Charles. Loretta was his teaser, and Ciara knew that if she called her mother and told her the things that Charles had said, she was going to curse his ass slap out.

***

Michelle stood in the alphabetical order line at graduation. She was super nervous and her knees where weak. She couldn't believe that she had made it this far. She had a child at fifteen and here she was, about to receive another degree, her Office Administration Associate in Science Degree. It was so many times Michelle wanted to give up from the stress and heartache she's had for years, but she always thought about her daughter. That was who motivated her to do better and go harder. Her line started moving. When they walked on the stage, she could hear her loud, ghetto family showing major love, especially her uncle Tall. He was the loudest one out the crew.

When the Dean of the school called Michelle's name, she began to cry. It had finally hit her. She made it through the struggle and that was something to be thankful about. She strutted across the stage with her head held high. She was proud of herself. From that day forward, she told herself that if it wasn't about her daughter, her family, and her career, it didn't matter to her. She wanted to focus strictly on finding a good paying job and her daughter's health. Everything else would come last, especially a man. She needed to find herself first before she even took that route.

After sitting through the rest of the ceremony, Michelle said her farewells to everyone then went to go and meet with her family on the outside. When she saw her family standing outside of the building waiting on her, she couldn't help the tears that fell from her eyes again. She looked at her daughter who was clearly in pain, but through it all, she smiled. Briana was proud of her mother and she just wanted her mother to be the best in life. Briana was a strong little girl, and she hated when people felt sorry for her. She wanted her life to be normal, how it was before she was diagnosed with cancer.

Michelle ran into her daughter and hugged her tight. She broke down and started crying. She just wanted her daughter to know that she did all of this for her. Their family crowded around her hugging and kissing her. They were proud of Michelle and they wanted her to have a good time.

"Stop all that crying girl. Your ass made it," her uncle Tall said to her. She wiped her tears and smiled. She took her best friend, Ciara, in for a hug. Ciara had been there through it all and everything was solid in their friendship.

"I'm proud of you, sis," Ciara whispered and kissed her friend on the cheek.

"I know. I need a strong ass drink too," Michelle said.

The entire family retired and went to the Boston Dance Room Ball Room where her auntie Christine had rented out the ballroom for her graduation party. Everyone was ready to turn up and have a good time. One thing about Michelle's family was they knew how to have a good time and be there for one another. When they got there, all of the older people partied and had a good time. Michelle danced with her father, Luke, on the dance floor. Her father was her everything. She wished like hell that she could find a man like her father. Wealthy, handsome, honest, and loving he was. She admired that. She always had to tell her mother how lucky she was to have such an amazing man. Michelle's happy spirit went down the drain when she saw her daughter sitting off to the side. She could tell that Briana was weak from the look in her eyes.

She stopped dancing and went to sit next to Briana.

"Bri, if you're in pain, we can leave right now and go home," Michelle told her.

"This isn't about me mommy. This is your big day. Enjoy it." She smiled.

Michelle didn't want her daughter to see her cry, so she got up from the table and headed towards the lobby. Everyone was drinking and calling her name to take shots, but she ignored them. Her heart was heavy and her head was hurting. She couldn't stand to see her baby like that. She just needed a little time to herself.

When she stepped in the lobby, she quickly turned around when she saw that Charles had the nerve to show up. He was full of shit for even trying that.

"Wait, Michelle!" He ran behind her and grabbed her hand. "Just hear a nigga out for a second," he begged.

Michelle rolled her eyes. "Please leave Charles! I don't want to be around your ass!" Michelle said through gritted teeth.

"Right fucking now before I call mama and tell her you're trying to ruin her day." Ciara came out of nowhere, ready to curse her brother out. Ooh, they couldn't stand each other and right now, she was pissing him off for blocking. If Ciara wasn't in Michelle's ear so hard, he probably would've gotten back in with Michelle with absolutely no problems.

"Mind your fucking business Ciara!" he told her. "Look, I brought you these flowers. I'm not sure if you think I'm not proud of you because I don't say it all the time, but I am. I'ma get better Chelle. I promise."

"How the hell are you going to get better and you haven't even saw your daughter in two weeks? I bet you don't even know what's going on with her health. Take your stupid embarrassing ass on. You make me sick!" Ciara yelled at her brother. She really hated him.

"That's what I'm saying. You haven't called me or Briana to check on her, this isn't about me, Charles. Me and you are done, over, finished! There is nothing you can do that can make me change my mind. I've been dumb for the past few years but I'm over that. You need to leave." Tears dropped from Michelle's big brown eyes. Not because she was finally done with Charles, but because she really couldn't believe that this man didn't care about their sick daughter.

"I'll call her," Charles said, embarrassed. He turned to walk away but like always, Ciara had to run off at the mouth.

"Nah, don't leave. Bri is right in there. Go and show your face. At least try to make her feel good," she said.

"Nah, he can leave. I don't need his ass feeding lies to my baby," Michelle said.

"Whatever man. I'm gone." Charles left.

Ciara looked at Michelle and shook her head. She tried her best to stay out of their business and let Michelle handle her own, but she got sick of the way Michelle acted when Charles came around. She could look Michelle right in the eyes and tell that Michelle was still in love with her brother.

"What?" Michelle asked, looking down at her nails.

"You're doing well with moving on. Charles means you no good friend," Ciara told her.

"Yeah, I know. I still love him, but I won't turn back to his ass ever again. I can promise you that."

"That's my bitch!" Ciara and Michelle slapped hands. Michelle went back in the ballroom to join her family. It lightened her mood when she saw her daughter dancing and having a good time with the other kids. That eased her nerves just a little bit.

"Come take a picture with me Chelle," her uncle Tall said to her.

Michelle and her Uncle Tall had a relationship that was unexplainable. Tall was her father's little brother, but he treated Michelle like she was his own child. Since Michelle was his brother's only child, he always spoiled her rotten. The three-bedroom condo that Michelle lived in was purchased by her uncle Tall as a graduation gift when she first graduated college. He always told her that if she did what she had to do, she never had to worry about money. Tall was the rich one out of the family who made sure that everybody had what they needed.

Michelle took plenty of pictures and had enough drinks to make her feel good.

"Mic check, one two, one two!" Her uncle Tall got the mic from the DJ and stood in the middle of the floor, while everyone stood to the side.

"I wanna give a special shout out to my baby girl, Michelle. My niece is more than amazing, man. It's amazing that I watched her come out and now she's this successful beautiful mother, niece, and daughter," he slurred. Tall was for sure fucked up. He had been drinking Hennessey straight all day. "Michelle is twenty-five with two college degrees. She gets mad when I share her story, but I don't give a damn." Michelle laughed and covered her face because she knew the story her uncle was about to tell. He told it every time when he would brag on her to everyone.

"Michelle got pregnant at fifteen and when I heard the news, my heart crumbled. I didn't want my baby to be a teen mom and I damn sure didn't want her to lose focus on the important things in life. But, when I had a talk with her when she was getting ready to have Briana, she told me that she wouldn't let having a baby come in between her success. She always told me that Briana was going to be a reason why she went harder in life, and she wasn't lying. She graduated high school at sixteen with high honors and went straight to college. Now, we're sitting here today celebrating another damn degree. That should motivate anybody. Hell, my old ass probably is gonna go back and get another degree after this shit here." Everyone laughed. "But, this is for my niece Michelle, I love you and continue to be great. It only gets better from here." Everyone raised their glasses. "Cheers to new beginnings." Everyone threw their wine back and continued to have a good time.

Michelle and Ciara sat down at the table in the far back. It wasn't that loud and that gave them a little time to chat and gossip about every one that was there looking a hot ass mess.

"I didn't even know that Shara started back coming around," Ciara said as she rolled her eyes at Shara.

"She don't come around me. My mama be inviting her ass to everything. Come to think about it, her ass didn't even tell me congratulations but she has the nerve to be walking in here like she's the baddest bitch."

"She looks a hot ass mess too." Ciara and Michelle shared a long laugh because she damn sure did look a hot ass mess. Shara was Michelle's first cousin on her mother's side. Michelle and Shara was close coming up, but Michelle always knew that Shara was the jealous type. Shara went behind Michelle's back and tried to fuck Charles. Surprisingly, Charles told Michelle everything. When it first happened, Michelle gave Shara an ass whooping that she'd never forget. That was two years ago and Michelle still didn't fuck with Shara like that. The only thing she would get from Michelle was a hi or bye. Michelle's mama, Shirley, would always tell Michelle that she should be ashamed of herself because they were two sisters' kids at the end of the day, but that didn't mean shit to Michelle. If you weren't loyal, you couldn't be around her. Michelle honestly didn't deal with any of her female cousins because they were mean and hateful. She always told them that she didn't need that type of energy around her.

Ciara smiled as she looked down at her phone. Michelle smiled at her and tried to look at the phone.

"What's the tea bitch?" Michelle asked her.

"Come on and you'll see." Ciara took Michelle's hand as they went outside.

"Who driving that nice ass Audi?" Michelle asked Ciara.

"Shut up and act like you got some sense. I invited my boo here to celebrate with us. You've been begging to meet his ass, so now he's here." Michelle smiled.

When she saw the two men who stepped out of the car, she almost dropped her Styrofoam cup of liquor. She couldn't believe who it was. Ciara had been really holding out on this one.

Ciara walked up to Terrance and pecked his lips, but Michelle was still at a loss for words. The two men were the most successful lawyers in Boston, Massachusetts. Terrance Shield and Timmy Ralph. The only thing Michelle wanted to know was how in the hell Ciara got with Terrance. This was a big shock to her and she couldn't wait to get Ciara by herself and drill her sneaky ass with questions.

"Michelle, this is Terrance and Terrance, this is my best friend, Michelle." Terrance hugged Michelle and passed her an envelope.

"Congratulations on everything. I've heard some amazing things about you." Terrance smiled.

"Thank you so much."

"This is my best friend, Timmy," Terrance introduced his right hand man.

Timmy wasn't quite as friendly as Terrance was, but he looked so much better than Terrance. He wore a serious facial expression on his face that Michelle couldn't read. She almost drooled out of her mouth as she looked him over. He was tall, standing 6'3" at height. His shoulders were wide and he was muscular. He was the most beautiful man that Michelle had ever seen. He looked like he was mixed with something. His low Caesar cut was curly and the beard on his face was trimmed nice. He was dressed down in some slacks, black Versace loafers, and a business collar shirt that had their law firm logo on the pocket. Michelle's heart fell to her feet when she glanced at the beautiful ring on his finger, the nigga was married.

He smiled at Michelle, showing off his beautiful pearly whites. At the bottom, he had a shining iced out grill. She wasn't sure if that was a flirtatious smile or if he was just being nice. Either way, Michelle had to look over his married ass.

Ciara cleared her throat, snapping Michelle out of her glance she had on Timmy.

"Y'all can follow us on the inside where everyone is," Ciara told them. She grabbed Michelle and whispered in her ear, "He's married, bitch."

"I know. Damn." Michelle shook her head.

They walked on the inside and joined the family. Everyone was standing in line waiting to be served for dinner that was prepared.

Chapter Two

When Michelle and Ciara walked into the ballroom with the two men, all eyes were on them. They couldn't help but to notice how all of the women were staring them down. Everyone was surprised that the two lawyers were attending Michelle's party. Michelle walked away from them because she didn't need anyone to think that Timmy was there with her. She didn't even know this man personally.

"Whoa shit! Timmy and Terrance! What's up man? Y'all know my daughter?" Luke walked up to them and shook their hands. Luke and Shirley knew the two men personally. Shirley and Timmy's father, Serri, used to be a part of the same church over at Tremont Temple Baptist church, but he left when he and his wife, Reece, moved back to Dubai.

"What's up Mr. Luke? Nah, I don't know her. I didn't even know that this was your daughter. I'm here with Terrance and he's here with Ciara," Timmy told him.

Timmy knew Mr. Luke from the law firm. He had helped Luke out with his businesses.

"Yeah, Michelle's my baby. I'm glad y'all are here. Get comfortable and have a good time with us. I had no idea that Terrance and Cici were fucking around. That's surprising."

Michelle walked up behind her daddy. She laughed at the language he was using. Luke only cursed when he was feeling good on his Apple Crown Royal. He wanted to be young again so bad. He was even dressed in a young gear.

Michelle and Timmy locked eyes again, but she quickly turned her head. It was something about the look he gave her. It was like he was undressing her with his eyes.

Luke walked Terrance and Timmy around introducing them to everyone, like everyone didn't already know who they were.

Michelle sat next to her daughter who was playing on her iPhone 6 plus. Despite having cancer, Briana was a beautiful little girl. Briana had lost a lot of weight due to receiving so many treatments of chemotherapy but she was still chubby. Well, Michelle called it thick. She had hair that hung down her back, but it was slowly falling out. Her caramel skin was smooth and it had that glistening look to it. She had big hazel eyes just like Charles, and the braces she had on her teeth had her mouth looking fabulous.

"Are you enjoying your day, mama?" Briana asked her.

"Only if you're enjoying it." Michelle smiled and grabbed Bri's nose, shaking it from side to side. That tickled Bri. She was a really goofy little girl too, goofy and full of life.

"I'm having fun. Just a little tired. Look at this."

Bri passed Michelle her phone. Charles had sent her a text message. As much as Michelle didn't want to read it, she did anyways.

I love you with all of my heart. Never feel like I'm neglecting you. I'm just trying to get used to everything. You're my everything Briana. Always remember that. ☺

Michelle shook her head. There was no way that she could hide that Charles wasn't shit from Bri, so she always kept it real with her. She never bashed Charles to Briana but she did always let her baby know that her father had some fucked up priorities. But Briana was old enough and smart enough to realize that herself. She used to be crazy about her father until she overheard her mother crying and begging him one night to go with the two of them to one of her doctor's appointment. She told Charles she just wanted Briana to have both of her parents just that one time. He made every excuse and every time Briana heard her mother cry, that made her dislike him even more. She would never disrespect him because that was still her father, but she didn't care for him that much. At the end of the day, her mother was the one making everything happen for her and that's all she cared about.

"He'll get better one of these days Bri," Michelle told her.

"Yeah. I hope so." Briana smiled. "You look so beautiful and sexy in your jump suit mama. You need to find you a good man." Michelle covered her mouth and burst out into laughter. Briana was picking up on too much.

"Mama do look good, huh?" Michelle smiled.

"Sure do." Briana winked.

Timmy walked over to where Briana and Michelle were sitting, and he joined the two of them. Ciara and Terrance were busy being all lovey dovey. They weren't even keeping poor Timmy company and Michelle damn sure didn't want to be the one to have to do it. That man was too sexy to be around alone.

"You don't mind me sitting here, do you?" he asked Michelle.

"Oh, nah... this a free country," Michelle said, which caused Timmy to laugh.

She smiled and looked confused. "What's funny?" she asked him.

"Nothing." He waved her off. "Two degrees at the age of twenty-five huh?" he asked her, catching her off guard.

"Yes," Michelle said proudly, sticking her pierced tongue out.

"That's what's up, man. I didn't even know that Luke was your pops. That's a cool ass old man."

"How do y'all know each other?" Michelle questioned.

"I've handled a few things for him and his business. That's all."

Michelle nodded. She tried not to look at him so hard, but that was so hard to do. His voice did something to her.

"This your little mama?" he asked Michelle.

"Yes. Forgive me for being rude. This is my baby Briana, Briana, this is Timmy. Your auntie Ciara's friend." Briana waved her hand.

"I'ma go over here and bother granddaddy, ma. I'll be back." She smiled at her mama. She thought she was slick.

"Is that your only child?" he asked Michelle.

"Yes. I had her at the age of fifteen. I was too busy trying to get myself together. I didn't have the time to make another one." They laughed.

"Damn. That's good man. Most women would've gave up." He nodded his head. He was impressed.

"Thank you. The shit wasn't easy. I'll tell you that." Michelle nursed her drink. Timmy paid close attention to her. The way she licked her lips made his dick jump a little bit. He knew that he was wrong for lusting over another woman besides his wife, but it was hard. Michelle was just so pretty to him. Her light skin was so smooth and clear, and her lips were full and plump. The way her breast sat up in her jumper was unexplainable. She was thick in all the right places and beautiful was clearly an understatement.

"Do you have any kids?" Michelle asked him.

"Nah. My wife doesn't want any kids," Timmy said in a low tone. Michelle frowned her face. She could tell that his wife not wanting kids fucked with him.

"You want them?" she asked him.

"Yeah. I want a soccer team, but if she doesn't want them, I'm comfortable with that. Whatever makes her comfortable." He shrugged. Michelle didn't want to say too much because she didn't know much about him or his wife, but just hearing that made her roll her eyes. She could tell that he was a good dude, but for him to put his wishes on hold just for her was just stupid to Michelle.

"Why you looking like that?"

"I'm just stuck on the part when you said you're comfortable with putting your dreams on hold just because she doesn't have the same dreams."

"You're putting words in my mouth," he told her.

"Nah. You said that you wanted a lot of kids, but she doesn't want them, so you're comfortable with not wanting kids if that's what she doesn't want. I said that just in a different way." He giggled.

"I mean to each his own. You're married and that's amazing that you're considering her feelings like that, but damn… I hope she changes her mind so you can get that soccer team, especially since you're so understanding. That should make her want to give them to you."

"You know something, huh?" he laughed.

"I know a lot." She smiled.

"So, what's your plan since you're done with school?" he asked Michelle.

Just that fast, they had gotten caught up in good conversation. All of her nosey, messy ass cousins were staring at them, but she figured that nothing was wrong with just conversing with him. He held great conversation.

"I'm just looking for a good paying job. I was laid off a few weeks ago for calling out too much. Those bastards didn't even care that I was taking my daughter back and forth to the doctors to get chemo."

His eyes widened. "Chemo? She has cancer?" he asked, shocked.

"Yes. A year with bone cancer," Michelle told him. Her voice cracked up but she wasn't going to cry in front of him. Most people would feel that she needed to toughen up, but that was easier said than done.

"Wow. I am sorry to hear that. She looks so strong though. I would've never known that if you didn't tell me."

"Yeah, but enough about me. How long have you been married?" She tried to change the conversation, but dip in his game room at the same time.

"Next month will make it a year."

"That's beautiful, and how old are you again?"

"I'm thirty-three."

"That's great. I hear so many great things about your law firm. Keep up the great work. You don't find too many successful black men like you and your friend these days."

"That's real shit, but if they want it, they can make it happen. They don't want it these days. That's the only problem."

"True." Michelle nodded her head, while agreeing. The first person she thought about when he said that was her dead beat ass baby's father.

Michelle's phone rung and notified her that she had a text message. When she read the text message, she had to giggle at her daughter.

He's the one mama. He even looks better than daddy.

She stuffed the phone back into her purse. Terrance and Ciara walked back up. Michelle smiled at the two of them. They actually made a great couple, but Michelle couldn't lie to herself and say she didn't feel any type of way. She wanted to know why Ciara left her in the blind about Terrance for so long. They never kept secrets from one another, so she had to know what was up with that.

"Michelle, come over here and take these final pictures before everyone leaves baby," her mother called out to her.

"Yeah, we have to get back going to the office anyways, so I'll let you go. It was nice talking with you and congratulations on everything." Timmy and Michelle hugged. He smelled so damn good and being in his strong arms felt even better.

"Thank you so much and good luck with the soccer team you want." She winked at him and walked away.

When he left the facility, she could finally breathe. Lord, that man was the truth. He had better be glad that he was married, otherwise Michelle would've one night stand his ass. He looked fuckable, and she could bet her last dollar that he had a big dick.

After taking what seemed to be a thousand pictures with her family, everyone gathered their things to leave and go their separate ways. Michelle had so many gift envelopes until it wasn't even funny and she couldn't wait to see how many checks and how much money she had in all.

Michelle, Ciara, Michelle's auntie, and her parents stayed back to clean up the ballroom. It was a complete disaster, but if everyone worked as a team, they would be out of there in no time.

"So, when the hell were you gonna tell me that you were in love with the damn rich lawyer of Boston?" Michelle stared at her best friend.

"It's not even like that Chelle. Terrance and I met one day when I was at the court house with my mama, and we exchanged numbers. Hell, I didn't wanna do anything but fuck him, but that turned into something bigger than what it really was supposed to be. We've only been seeing each other for two months." She shrugged.

"But damn, you could've at least told me when y'all first started fucking around. Hell, I felt like your ass was keeping a secret."

"Well, I wasn't friend. These last couple of months we barely saw each other or talked because you were so busy with your finals and preparing for graduation, so get out of your damn feelings," Ciara told her. "Your ass better leave that married man alone too." Ciara squinted her eyes and smiled at Michelle.

"Oh, girl please. I don't want that damn man. He looks good as hell though, but I wouldn't dare mess with a man who's married," Michelle told her. She was serious too. Messing with a married man was a no go for her.

"I'm not even going to lie though. I had been checking y'all out from afar and that nigga was almost lusting over your ass. His eyes were glued to your breast. He even kept licking his lips at you."

"Yeah, I caught that shit. I felt very uncomfortable too."

Michelle's cousin, Shara, strutted to where the two of them where. Michelle sighed really loud to let her cousin know she wasn't in the mood for her and her shenanigans.

"Hey cousin." Shara waved.

"Your ass has been here all this time and you're just now speaking to me? What's up Shara?" Michelle asked her.

"Oh nothing. I didn't know that you and Timmy were friends. I'm really good friends with his wife, Patrice."

"Girl, take your nosey, messy ass on somewhere. They're not friends. They just met today and he was here with me. Now, if your ass is fishing for answers to go back and tell his wife, you've failed. Now, take your ass home and brush that hair," Ciara snapped. Michelle was glad that she did because she didn't feel like going off on Shara. She was having a good night and she didn't want anyone to ruin that for her.

"Ugh. You're always talking when no one is talking to you." Shara rolled her eyes and walked away, but she knew to talk shit why she was leaving. Ciara never had a problem with busting a bitch in their mouth when it came to her bestie.

"That's just why I don't like that bitch now. She's so fucking messy," Michelle said.

"Her ass just wants answers to go and tell that man's wife. But, she has nothing to tell. She's such an idiot." Michelle had to agree.

After they were done cleaning the building and packing all the gifts and left over foods in Luke's car, everyone got in their cars and left. Briana was staying the night with her grandparents since it had been a while and

Ciara decided that she was going to stay the night with Michelle, so that they could catch up with everything. The reason why Ciara hadn't been telling Michelle everything was because Michelle was so focused on graduation and she didn't want to distract her friend with nigga problems. She wanted Michelle to finish out strong, just as much as Michelle wanted it for herself.

***

Timmy walked into his five bedroom, three bathroom mini mansion quietly. It was after eleven o'clock that night, so he already knew that his wife, Patrice, was dead asleep. After leaving Michelle's graduation party, he and Terrance had to go back to the office and finish working on a case they had been assigned too. Honestly, both he and Terrance were scared shitless about cracking open this case.

T&T Criminal Law Firm was owned my Terrance and Timmy. Over the years, they had worked their asses off to make sure that their business was successful and working hard got them a successful law firm. They were the most known lawyers in Boston, Ma and they couldn't be touched. Terrance and Timmy had been best friends since they were nine years old, ever since they were just kids selling drugs together. They were from the hood and coming up, they did whatever it was they had to do to make sure they made something out of themselves. With plenty of drug money saved up, they went to law school then started their own law firm. It was the best thing they could've ever done too.

After taking off of his shoes, he went into the kitchen. Like always, there was no food cooked, not even a sandwich made. He did notice that there was a sticky note on the refrigerator. He snatched it off and read it.

Hey babe, I have a business conference tomorrow morning, so try not to wake me up. LOL. Love you and I hope you had a wonderful day at the office.

He sighed then blew his breath. Honestly, Timmy wasn't happy in this marriage. He had only known Patrice for two years and he married her in no time, which he was now regretting. Honestly, he didn't even know how he ended up with her because they were the total opposite, and they shared nothing in common besides both being lawyers. Patrice was just another lawyer who was beautiful, smart, and wealthy. She wasn't down to earth at all and he hated her uppity attitude. When Timmy first married her, he knew she was the one simply because she was a chick who had her head on her shoulders, it was like he fell for her for all the wrong reasons.

He went into the fridge and pulled out everything to prepare him a ham and cheese sandwich. He got sick of coming home to no home-cooked meals, especially after a long hard day of working.

When he finished making his sandwich, he went into the living room, turned on his 70" inch Samsung TV, and changed it to the sports station. He took a bite out of his sandwich and thought about his miserable life being stuck here with ol' boring ass Patrice. Honestly, they barely fucked. Most of the time, he wished that he would've listened to his mother when she begged him not to marry Patrice, but like the hard headed ass son that he was, he did it anyways. His mama knew that things weren't right in their relationship, but he wouldn't dare tell her that.

His mind went back to none other than Michelle. No lie, he was really attracted to her. He loved how strong she was. He liked her even more when he learned that she had her first child as a teen and got so much done in her life. She was very down to earth, beautiful, and funny. That's just how Timmy liked his women. He really believed that he was going through a phase when he married Patrice. It was true that he did love her, but he wasn't in love with her and that's what fucked up the entire marriage. It wasn't his fault though. She made it boring.

When he was finished eating, he went upstairs to their master bedroom where Patrice was sleeping peacefully. He tiptoed to the dresser and pulled out some night clothes. He went into the shower and let the hot water run over his entire body as he thought about a lot. He hoped and prayed that their marriage got better because he couldn't take too much more. He told himself that he was going to talk to her about how he was feeling and she was going to either get with it or get left. He was still a young man and miserable wasn't something that he wanted to be.

After his shower, he stepped out and dried off. He put on his Polo pajama pants and a plain white tank top. He pulled the covers back and climbed into bed. Instead of doing the normal and turning on his side and going to sleep, he decided to wrap his arms around his wife and cuddle under her but of course, she moved around and mumbled for him to move. That pissed him off even more than he was before.

"Babe… I was trying to sleep," Patrice complained.

"Then take your ass to sleep then," he snapped.

Patrice was used to his attitudes when he couldn't have his way, so she wasn't even sweating it. *He'll get over it.* She thought to herself.

The next morning, Timmy woke up to a wonderful smell of food. He looked at the clock and it was ten o'clock, meaning he had over slept.

"Shit!" he whispered. He got up and handled his morning hygiene then went downstairs. He couldn't believe that his wife had prepared a huge breakfast. He was almost excited to have breakfast with her, until he heard on the phone handling business and almost in a complete rush to leave the house.

"Thank you Alina, and can you please make sure that lunch is ordered ahead of time so that my clients can eat as soon as they come in? Thank you. Is my coffee and muffins already there?" Patrice spoke to her assistant over the phone. She was asking Alina a thousand questions at one time. Hell, even Timmy couldn't keep up with it all, so he could only imagine how Alina was feeling.

Patrice hung up the phone and smiled at her handsome husband. She pecked his lips then rubbed her hand up and down his built arms.

Timmy looked her over and she looked good. Patrice had smooth chocolate skin like a snicker bar. Her round brown eyes fit her beautiful fat face perfectly. The dress that she had on was sexy and it screamed business. It hugged her juicy ass and her curvy hips. Her freshly shaved skin shined. She looked absolutely gorgeous.

"I made breakfast for you, babe. I'm meeting with two clients this morning, so I won't be able to stay here with you. I love you." She kissed him one last time before she grabbed her trench coat and left the house. She didn't even give him enough time to tell her that they needed to talk. She was just that busy and this was an everyday thing.

He grabbed a plate from the counter and made him a plate of sausage links, eggs, and cheese grits that she had prepared. He checked his phone and he had three missed calls from Terrance and three missed calls from the office. It must've not had been that important because he didn't call the house phone, nor did he send any text messages. He dialed Terrance's number and he answered on the third ring.

"Damn nigga. Miss prissy must've put that good pussy on your ass last night." Terrance laughed into the phone.

"Nah nigga. I wish she would've though." Timmy shook his head and so did Terrance.

"Yo', I don't see why the fuck you married her bruh. You're a married nigga. You're supposed to be able to get in them guts whenever the fuck you want too. Damn, she's boring as fuck. I don't see how you do that shit," Terrance fussed.

Timmy giggled and shook head. "Get off my wife man. What's up?"

"This case is what's up nigga. You need to get your ass down here and let's work. Plus, I got to tell you about Ciara's wild ass last night man. Shit got real."

"What she do? Lick your ass or some?" Timmy died from laughter, but Terrance didn't think that shit was funny.

"Nigga, I will fuck you up if you ever say some shit like that to me. She just sucked my dick and my balls at the same time, but you don't know shit about that, do you? Ole married ass nigga don't get no pussy, no head, nothing. I bet she don't even let you touch her ass huh?" Now it was Terrance's turn to laugh, but Timmy joined him.

"Fuck you man. I'll be there in thirty minutes."

"Hurry up, nigga."

Timmy hung up the phone and finished his food. After he ate, he went upstairs and pulled out his outfit for the day. Timmy was an original street nigga before he was anything else, so he always had to throw his street taste in his business look. He wore an all-black suit with a baby blue and white shirt underneath. His white tie set the entire suit off. He put his 10k gold earring in his ear and his all-white Versace loafers on his feet. He checked himself out in the mirror and thought his bottom grill would only set the look off. Patrice hated when he wore that to work, it was so unprofessional. He grabbed a file out of his office and went to his garage. He decided that he was going to drive his black 2015 Hummer H3. He jumped in and hooked his phone up to the aux cord. He turned the volume all the way up and allowed *Future's Where I Came From* song to blast loudly through the speakers. He vibed and did his own little dance the entire ride to the office. He was determined to have a great day. When he pulled up into the office, he sighed when he realized that their clients where already there. They had been running Terrance and Timmy crazy. The guy, Carmelo Hurnez, was a part of the known cartel in Boston but he was facing a lot of serious time after being set up by some cats from across seas. Carmelo's father, Bishop, was the head man over the Hurnez cartel and whenever anyone was in trouble, they always came to Terrance and Timmy. The two of them were complete beasts in the courtroom and they beat every case, but this one was tough and scary. No matter what; they were determined not to lose this. Besides, the prosecutors didn't have enough legal information on Carmelo to send him away from life.

Timmy walked into the office and Carmelo stood to his feet and shook Timmy's hand.

"We've been sitting here waiting for you all morning, Timmy," Bishop said to him.

"Yeah, I overslept. That's my bad, man. Why are y'all asses here?" he asked them.

"We need to know what the hell is going on. The trial takes place in exactly one month, and we need to know that Carmelo is going to be fine. I can't lose my son to the system, Tim. You know how I feel about this."

Bishop had a personal relationship with Timmy and Terrance. When they were younger, Bishop was their connect. In reality, Bishop was one of the reasons they were sitting there in that huge luxury law firm.

"Bishop, I have a question," Terrance interfered.

"What is it?"

"How many cases have we cracked open for you?" Terrance asked him.

"I don't know, about ten of them." He shrugged.

"And out of all those ten cases, did we ever lose?"

Bishop and Carmelo shook their head no.

"Okay man. Ease up a little piece and let us work through this shit. Nothing is gonna happen to Carmelo's fat ass. We got him covered, but we can't focus with you sushi eating mufuckers coming in here every five minutes standing over us while we get shit together.

"Alright man. Maybe we're just nervous. We'll let the two of y'all do y'all," Bishop said as he got up. He grabbed his hat and put it on.

"Thank you!" Terrance said to them.

Terrance went into his office and saw all the papers and files stacked over his desk. He seriously needed an assistant because that shit was starting to get a little too hectic. The assistant that they had moved to Hawaii with her husband and newborn daughter, and they were missing her something terrible. Shit had been crazy since she left. They hadn't bothered trying to hire anyone new assistant because at T&T Law Firm, they ran shit totally different than other law firms. They didn't need anyone in their circle who they couldn't trust, so for that moment, they decided they were going to have to deal with all the chaos alone.

***

After working non-stop, responding to emails, setting up meetings and more, Timmy was tired and needed a meal and a nap. The second he pushed his keyboard to the side, Terrance was paging him over the intercom, telling him to come to the lobby for lunch. He wanted to say fuck the food and take his nap, but he just went along with the flow.

When Timmy walked up front, he was shocked when he saw Michelle sitting there with Ciara. Michelle looked so beautiful, better than she did the first time he saw her. She had her hair wrapped and her face was made up. He couldn't help but to notice her thick thighs and wide ass that was hugging the tights she had on. He licked his lips and bit on his bottom lip.

"Damn nigga. Are you here?" Terrance snapped his fingers, which caused all of them to laugh.

"Man, fuck you. What's up ladies?" He hugged Ciara and kissed Michelle's hand. Yeah, he knew what he was doing when he did that.

"They brought us lunch, nigga," Terrance told him.

"Is that right?" Timmy asked sarcastically.

"No, she brought Terrance some lunch and decided to get you something too. I didn't bring you anything," Michelle said, flippantly.

Timmy laughed at her. He loved her feisty attitude and he loved the way she rolled those big beautiful eyes when she went to talking shit.

"I don't think it's anything wrong with you bringing a nigga lunch. You're a friend," Terrance said to her.

She smiled and waved him off. "I just met Timmy," she said.

"That don't mean shit." Timmy smiled.

"Ciara, let me holler at you in my office for a minute," Terrance said to her. She smiled and bit her bottom lip. She already knew what he wanted and she was ready to give it to him. Again, they left Michelle and Timmy alone. Michelle felt uncomfortable as Timmy stared at her.

"Why are you looking at me like that? Don't you have a wife?" Michelle bluntly asked him. She got up and walked around the building. She admired how nice it was in there. She stopped at his office door and took a look at his desk.

"Wow. You're messy," she told Timmy.

"I know man; I need an assistant so fucking bad. I'ma get it together though," he told her.

"How much do you pay your assistants?" she asked him.

"Whatever meets their needs." He shrugged.

"Well hell, hire me. This is what I do. Assist." She winked.

"Yeah?" he asked excitedly.

"Nigga, I'm not saying hire me to flirt with me and watch my ass and my breast. I'm telling you to hire me so that I can help this place out, and I need the job."

"When do you wanna start?" he asked her.

"Hell, I'll start tomorrow, but I must let you know that I do have to take my daughter to her doctors in Florida a lot." He waved her off. That didn't matter to him.

"That's nothing, man. From here on out, I'll make sure that you and your daughter get there and back, first class trips." She smiled. So much for a married man.

"I don't need you to do that, but I do appreciate you giving me a chance to work. Hell, I didn't think I would find a job today. Look at God!" She threw her hands up and playfully shouted.

Timmy laughed at her. She was goofy.

Chapter Three

Michelle stood in the mirror admiring her shape. A lot of people didn't know that Michelle had just gotten that banging body that she had. She used to be a little over two hundred and fifty pounds. Now she was a nice one hundred forty-five pounds, standing at 5'3". Her legs were sexy and they went perfectly with her curvaceous body. She was more than excited to be starting work. She just hoped and prayed that Timmy stayed in his lane and let her do what she came there to do. No matter what the circumstances were, she wouldn't dare go there with him. Michelle wasn't a fool though. She knew that Timmy wasn't happy and she only knew him for two days. The conversation they had at her party was enough to read him. Her phone rung and snapped her out of glance.

She rolled her eyes at the screen. It was Charles.

"If you're not calling me for your daughter, then hang up right now," Michelle said. She was aggravated with him and she definitely didn't have anything to say to him after he sent his daughter that weak ass text message.

"I just called you to let you know that my uncle got me a job working with him. It's a trash collector's position, but it's better than nothing, right?" Michelle could tell that Charles was excited. She wouldn't dare talk down on him for having a trash man job because something was always better than nothing.

"Wow. Congratulations. Did you tell Bri?" Michelle asked him.

She wanted him to know that he should've been doing it all for their daughter. Charles didn't believe it, but Michelle wasn't lying when she said that she was done with him. If it wasn't about Briana, she wasn't interested, not even interested in having a simple conversation.

"Nah, I'ma call her when I get off the phone with you. I just wanted to share the news with you."

"Yeah, I'm proud of you. Keep it up."

"When can I see you?" he asked her.

"Um yeah, I gotta go, getting ready for work. I'll talk with you later." She hung up on him while he was still talking.

Michelle walked out of the room and into the dining room where Briana was sitting at the dining room table, braiding her manikin doll's hair. Briana only did that to motivate herself. For Briana to only be ten years old, her braiding skills were off the chain. The only thing that got in the way was the sharp pains she would get in her hand. Having bone cancer sucked really bad but no matter what she did, she continued to strive through it. She always told everyone that she was going to kick cancer's butt.

"Hey, Bri. You know what would've been cute. If you would've took that braid you have in your hand and braided it over the zig zag one," Michelle suggested. Briana loved that idea.

"Like this?" Briana asked her mama to make sure that she was braiding the doll's hair right.

"Yeah, just grip the other piece of hair next to that braid," Michelle instructed

Bri was happy. She had learned something new.

"You took your medicine this morning?" Michelle asked her.

"Yep. I'm ready to go now." Briana was spending the day with her grandma and grandpa. They promised her that they were going to take her to Macy's to get her a few Michael Kors items. Since Briana was the only grandchild that Luke and Shirley had, she got whatever it was that she wanted from them. They also treated her to anything because of her cancer disease. They wanted her to feel normal. Briana seemed to be the only one that accepted the fact that she had cancer. That should've been motivation for the adults, but the whole cancer thing was scary to them. They got into Michelle's Audi and headed to her parent's home.

When they pulled up, they saw Luke outside washing his car. Briana and Michelle looked at one another and laughed. It was forty degrees outside and he was washing up his Benz. He didn't even have on a coat.

"Grandpa, you gone be sick as a dog out here like that." Briana ran up to him and hugged him. She loved her grandpa something terrible. In her eyes, Luke was her father.

"Nah, I ain't. It ain't even cold out here. Y'all women are just extra." He kissed Briana's cheek and she retired in the house.

"How you doing daddy?" Michelle kissed her father's cheek.

"I'm just fine beautiful. How you doing?"

"Couldn't be better." Michelle smiled and showed off her pretty deep dimples.

Luke dropped the water hose and stared at Michelle. She was happy and glowing, and he hadn't saw her like that in a while. "Why are you so happy? You and Charles must be on good terms?"

Just that fast, Michelle's smile faded away. Hearing that name even did something to her good mood. "No, I'm not worried about his ass." Michelle rolled her eyes. "I just got a new job that I'm starting today." She smiled.

"Really, where?"

"T&T Law Firm. I'll be their assistant." She smiled.

To say that Luke was excited for her was an understatement. Timmy and Terrance were some good guys and they had a wonderful name in the streets for themselves. He was happy to know that his daughter was a part of one of the most successful law firms in Boston.

"You're lying," he said to her.

"No, I'm not. I went and checked the place out yesterday and they were in a complete mess. I was only joking when I told him I could assist them, but he wanted me to work for real. I wasted no time with accepting the offer either." She smiled.

"When were you going to tell me and your mother that you were no longer working at the Cannon center?"

That caught Michelle off guard, she had only been gone from there a month. She should've known that her daddy was going to find out though. That man knew everything.

Michelle dropped her head. She was ashamed that she had kept something like that from her parents. She just didn't want them to stress about that. She wanted to get everything done on her own.

"I'm sorry, daddy. I didn't want to aggravate y'all with my problems. Y'all have helped me and Bri out enough," she apologized.

"What happened though, Michelle? You know your mother and I live for you and Briana. If you needed anything, why haven't you told me?"

"I don't know." She shrugged. "They just got tired of me calling out when it came to Briana's doctors' appointments, so they laid me off." It made her mad just talking about the situation.

Luke shook his head. It was amazing that some people didn't even care about people these days. "Fuck them. Your mother doesn't know though. I didn't tell her." He winked.

She smiled. Luke was always looking out for Michelle.

"That nigga can't be helping you though. What's up with that? Has he been going to Briana's doctor's visits with you?" he drilled her with questions.

"I'm gonna be late for work daddy. We'll talk about that later. Let me go say hey to mama before I leave. I love you." She kissed him then walked fast.

"Yeah. Don't think you're gonna get off that easy!" he yelled.

Michelle walked into the house and the smell of her mama's homemade famous chili filled the air. Michelle's stomach growled. It smelled so good.

Shirley and Briana were already sitting at the island eating a big bowl of it. Briana flicked through her pictures on her phone and showed her grandmother the braids she had done it her doll's head.

"You're so flaw, mama." Michelle shook her head.

Briana and Shirley laughed in unison. "Why y'all laughing?" Michelle asked.

"Cause I was just telling Briana how you were gonna come in here calling me flaw. I told Briana to tell you that I was cooking chili this morning, so she's the flaw one."

Briana smiled and lowered her head. She wanted that chili all to herself. Michelle fixed her a bowl to go and then she left. She didn't have to be to work until twelve, so she had an hour to spare. She went to Starbucks and ordered up coffee and muffins. She wanted to show her appreciation of her new job the right way. After riding for thirty minutes, she pulled up to the law firm. She looked in the mirror to make sure she still looked good. She stepped out of the car and grabbed the coffee and her chili. She was ready to start the day.

When she walked inside, nobody was upfront, but her new desk was decorated nice with flowers and welcome cards. She smiled. She thought that was sweet. Minutes later, Timmy's door swung open and a mad woman stormed out with Timmy behind her. She wasn't sure if the woman was his wife or one of his clients, whoever the hell she was, she was pissed off.

"Hello!" Michelle smiled and spoke.

"Hi! I'm Timmy's wife, Patrice," she said as she eyed her. Michelle stuck her hand out to shake it, but Patrice just smiled. Michelle didn't let that bother her though. This was her first day and no one was going to ruin that for her. What Timmy and Patrice had going on wasn't Michelle's problem.

"It's nice to meet you. I'm the new assistant here," Michelle said to her.

"Yeah, I see," Patrice said flippantly.

She's one of those kind, Michelle thought to herself.

"You can get settled at your desk, Michelle. I'll be back to step you through everything," Timmy told her. He grabbed his wife's hand and walked her outside. As soon as the door closed behind them, she was going off.

"You didn't think to fucking tell me that you had a new assistant? A woman assistant at that! What the fuck is your problem? You're keeping secrets?" she snapped. She was pissed, but this was nothing new. Patrice had lost a case in court and of course, she had to come to her husband and take all of her frustrations out on him. Seeing a beautiful female assistant only made her more furious. It was just too much going on in one day for her.

"Man, calm your ass down. Every fucking time you lose a case in court, you come with the dumb shit. I'm not keeping no fucking secrets. I didn't tell you about the last assistant and you didn't trip, so why are you tripping now?" he asked her. Now, she was pissing him off and when Timmy got pissed, all hell broke loose.

"Why the hell did you buy her flowers and shit? It doesn't take all of that for a simple welcoming."

"I didn't buy her those damn flowers, Terrance did. When have I ever disrespected you and this marriage like that, Patrice?"

"Never," she admitted.

"Okay then. Like I said, she's an assistant just as well as Kelly was. That's why I never told you."

Even though Timmy wasn't happy and was clearly attracted to Michelle, he wouldn't do anything stupid to hurt Patrice. He wasn't raised like that. Actually, he had hoped that things were going to get better for them.

She crossed her arms over her chest and poked her lips out. She wasn't going to let her husband know that she was insecure and didn't want such a beautiful woman working around him.

"Whatever Tim. That was different," she said to him.

"No it wasn't. Now, what happened in court?" he asked her.

"I don't even want to talk about it right now. I just need to go home and get some sleep."

Timmy shook his head. That was the shit that he was always talking about. No type of communication was in their relationship and he couldn't get with that.

Sure enough, he was pissed, but he wasn't going to let that interfere with his day. He had a lot to get done and worrying about his spoiled ass wife wasn't on his TO-DO list.

He walked back on the inside and his eyes almost popped open when he saw Michelle bending over and fixing something behind her desk. Her ass was so big and round. Patrice had nothing on her.

Timmy cleared his throat and Michelle jumped.

"I didn't even know you were standing there," she said to him.

"Yeah… I just walked in. Is something wrong with your computer? I saw you messing with it."

"No, everything is fine. I just didn't like how the cords were sticking out of the back though."

He smiled and nodded his head. "Sorry you had to see my wife like that. She gets very upset when she loses a case in court." They shared a laugh.

"I didn't even know that she was a lawyer. She's beautiful too."

"Thank you." Timmy smiled. "Everything here is pretty much simple. I'll email everything to you that I need you to do. The main thing I'll need is for you to make sure that appointments are set and make sure to respond to every email."

"That's easy. I got you." She handed him a cup of coffee and a muffin from Starbucks.

Terrance came out of his office and smiled at the sight of Michelle being there. Terrance was glad that Timmy had a distraction from his nagging ass wife. Just like Timmy's mother, Terrance begged his boy not to marry Patrice. He didn't like her nor did he trust her.

"What's up, sis?" Terrance hugged Michelle.

"Hey, Terrance. How are you?"

"Happy now that we got some fucking help in here."

She laughed. "Yeah, I'ma get y'all together." She smiled. "Have you talked to Ciara today?" Michelle hadn't talked to her since the night before.

"Yeah. She's supposed to be on her way here now, so we can go out for lunch." He smiled.

You could tell that he really did like Ciara and in Michelle's eyes, that was amazing. Ciara was always messing with bum ass niggas, so she was just excited for her friend.

"Y'all are too cute for me." Michelle smiled.

"She don't wanna make the shit official though."

"Nigga, can you talk about relationships some other time? Come in this damn conference room, so we can discuss this case," Timmy interfered.

"Well, excuse the fuck out of me boss." Michelle and Terrance laughed. "He's just a little salty because his wife ain't gave him no pussy. That's all," Terrance whispered. Michelle's mouth dropped open.

They begin to work and like always, they were ready to go in that courtroom and shut shit down. It was only right.

***

Ciara blushed as she stared into Terrance's eyes. He did something to her that she couldn't put her finger on. He was so damn handsome that it was crazy. He was light skin with the most perfect, charming smile. His built, buff body was covered in tattoos, and that was just the way Ciara liked them. His hair was cut low and his waves looked damn good. Even though Ciara was feeling him, she refused to commit to him. It wasn't because he wasn't any good to her but it was because she had serious trust issues. Ciara hadn't been in a serious relationship since her baby's father, so she just had a few flings here and there.

Ciara also thought that she wasn't worthy enough for a man like Terrance. She still lived in the ghetto and she was a ghetto girl. Even though Terrance was from the ghetto, Ciara always wondered why her, out of all women, and he sure as hell didn't carry himself like he was from the ghetto. Ciara did though. She couldn't help it. She was just a chick from the hood and the hood was all she knew. Ciara was beautiful though. Despite her ghetto girl ways and her slick ass mouth, she was beautiful and she was very intelligent. Terrance liked her because he was able to be himself around her. When he spent time with her, she didn't make him feel like the rich lawyer, like all the other gold digging bitches did. He felt like the normal dude that he was and wanted to be at all times. Ciara reminded him so much of the lady he always told his mama he wanted to marry when he met her. He just wanted a chick who had their head on their shoulders, down to earth, and trustworthy. The last two months he spent with Ciara pulled them in close together. He didn't think he was moving fast either. His mama had always told him 'when you find the love of your life you will know it because you can feel it.' He was really feeling the love.

They sat at their reserved table at Marliave Restaurant and scanned the menu. Terrance wasn't a big seafood fan until he started seeing Ciara. This was her favorite restaurant. For their appetizers, Ciara chose the Lemon Raw seasoned oysters and Terrance had the Cocktail Sauce Little Neck Clams. Once the server brought them their food, Ciara wasted no time. She sucked the oysters out of the shell and licked her lips. Terrance laughed and shook his head at her.

"They're not even all that damn good. You're just being dramatic." They laughed.

"Boy, you're sleeping on these oysters. They make you wanna slap your mama. Hell, and your grandma too." They both shared a laugh.

"You off the chain, man." Terrance shook his head.

He loved spending times like this with her. It was relieving.

"How's everything coming along at the office?" Ciara asked him.

"Everything is everything, man. I have a lot of faith in this case we're on, but Timmy's ole scary ass sweating it."

He wasn't lying. Terrance always had faith in their cases. Timmy was the one that panicked every time.

"I have faith in y'all too." She smiled.

Every time she licked her lips, Terrance wanted to reach across the table and suck on them. They were big and glossy. He just pictured her wrapping her full lips around his thick meaty dick.

"Thank you baby. You need to have faith in me, and let's go ahead and make this shit official."

She looked at him then looked back down at her oyster. She slurped her last oyster up before she said anything. Terrance laughed at her. She was wild as hell for that one.

"Why me?" she asked him.

"What you mean?"

"Exactly what I said. Why me? Out of all the women that you've been dealing with, why me?"

She really needed to know. It wasn't a secret how she felt about Terrance, but every time she fell for someone and gave them her heart, she ended up hurt. Her heart couldn't take any more heartache. She had been through enough with men and she just wanted to be happy. It had gotten to a point where she just accepted the fact that she would never take a man serious, relationship wise. If being lonely meant bringing her inner peace and happiness, then she was fine with that.

"I'm feeling you, ma and that's no secret. You're amazing. You're beautiful, smart, funny, and you're like a breath of fresh air. When I'm with you, it isn't about the money, it isn't about the fame. You just make a nigga feel like himself and ever since I blew up, it's been hard to find a chick who loves the normal life. I love the fact that you love the simple things. Nights when I want to take you out on a fancy date, you would rather to stay home and watch movies and eat cheesecake. You're a very positive, real, blunt ass chick and I don't come across that often."

Ciara couldn't help but blush. A man hadn't made her feel that good in a long time.

"What about my son? Can you deal with me having a son, a baby's father?"

"Look, when I accepted you into my life, I accepted TJ too. You don't ever have to question the love I have for you or your child, and as far as your baby daddy, I don't have a problem with him because I don't know him. As long as you're good, that's all that matters to me."

Ciara was so happy. She wanted to jump into Terrance's arms. She wanted to go against it, but something in her heart told her that Terrance was the one. He was the one that she had been looking for over the years. "Just don't fuck me over Terrance. That's all I ask for."

"That ain't nothing you have to worry about. I'm a grown ass man who doesn't play games, and you should know that by now."

Ciara nodded her head as she agreed.

"So, how does it feel to be my woman?" He smiled at her.

"Nigga, we ain't been in a relationship but for two minutes. Go on somewhere." They died from laughter. It was quite refreshing that Ciara was now in a relationship. She felt good. Him being a rich lawyer meant absolutely nothing to her, she was just happy that a man like Terrance wanted to be with her. Just when she had given up on love is when God sent her that somebody.

***

TJ sat in his father's lap on his grandmother's couch. Trey was in town just for the weekend and he figured that he would stop by and see his son. Trey was almost like Charles. He never spent time with TJ, but he did send Ciara money for him all the time.

"How come you never come and get me, man?" TJ asked his father.

"I'm always busy, man," Trey marked him.

Loretta rolled her eyes. She couldn't stand Trey, ever since she found out that he raped her daughter. Hell, she didn't like him before she found out about that.

"You should never be too busy for your son, Trey!" Loretta yelled. She was in the kitchen washing dishes. She decided that she was going to give the two of them some alone time, but she had to say something when she heard him say that.

"I know, Ms. Loretta." Trey rolled his eyes.

"Check this out, lil' Trey. I'll be back to take you to the movies or something before I leave. I need to go and handle a few things. Okay?" Trey said to him.

Loretta shook her head. She knew that was a lie.

"Alright daddy. I'll see you later."

Trey reached into his pockets and gave his son two twenty dollar bills. TJ loved money so that made him happy.

On his way out, Ciara was walking through the door. She was taken back when she saw him. She and TJ hadn't saw him in about five months. She didn't like how he just popped up either.

"What's up Cici?" Trey smiled.

"What's up? How many lies and excuses you done told my son this time?" Ciara asked.

"I don't lie to my son."

"Boy please." Ciara tried to walk off, but Trey grabbed her arm.

"I still love you." He blew her a kiss and she yanked away from him.

She really hated him.

***

"Oh shit, Solem. I'm about to cum all over your face," Patrice cried out. She was riding her side piece's face, and that nigga was giving her life. He sucked on her clitoris and flicked his tongue up and down her entire hole. All of her frustrations she had earlier where gone now.

She bounced up and down on Solem's thick long tongue and grinded from side to side. She was always amazed at how he used his tongue on her. He was so nasty with it and when he would stick his thumb in her ass, that would take her over the edge.

"Shit! Here it comes!" Patrice screamed and came all over Solem's face. He had already put a hurt to her pussy earlier, so the head was just a plus. She climbed off top of him and kissed his wet, pussy juice covered lips.

"That was so good Solem." She let out a breath of relief.

Solem was a forty-year-old probation officer. Patrice wasn't really in love with Solem, but she did have love for him. He being ten years older than Patrice meant a lot to her. She learned a lot from him and she was just amazed at how damn good he looked at such an older age. He was a dark skin man with very skinny, neat dreads in his hair. He had a few grey pieces in there, but that didn't matter. Not only was he a ten in the looks department, but this old man fucked and sucked Patrice's pussy so good. No, Timmy wasn't bad in bed, actually Timmy fucked better than Solem, but it was just something about Solem that Patrice loved.

It was true that Patrice loved her husband, but something about their relationship had died. Things were much better when they were just in a relationship and not married. Patrice felt like she was in a box her entire marriage, and she hated how hood Timmy was. He was so intelligent and smart, but he acted as if he got his degrees from the hood. The only reason she married him was because her mother loved him, and he was a successful, rich, sexy black man. The reason Patrice hadn't been fucking her husband was because she was too busy fucking Solem. She couldn't fuck two men, she felt like that was the nastiest thing to do. In her eyes, she wasn't a whore; she was just a married woman who was still having fun.

She really enjoyed having Solem on the side. He was smart, funny, and wiser. Not only that, he was professional twenty-four seven.

"I booked our flights for Jamaica next month baby." Solem kissed her forehead, which made her smile.

"I'm ready baby. I have my bathing suit already ready." She smiled.

Her phone rung and alerted her that she had an incoming text message.

I'm home early today. Where u? We need to talk.

She rolled her eyes and threw her phone down on the couch. Solem already knew who that was. She did that same thing every time Timmy texted her.

She began to put on her clothes. Solem was sitting there staring her beautiful body down. Solem was glad that he had Patrice in his life. Even though he was on the side, he knew that he had her heart more than Timmy did. He couldn't wait for their getaway.

"That's hubby?" Solem asked.

"Yeah. He's home early. I got to get going," she mumbled.

She was somewhat upset because she had planned on spending the day with Solem. Out of all days, this would be the day that Timmy chose to come home early.

Once she was dressed in her clothes, she fixed her rough hair. She grabbed her keys and was ready to go. Solem was still naked with his nine-inch curved dick hanging. He stood up and walked Patrice to the door. She turned around and slowly tongue kissed him.

"I love you. Call me later, okay?" Solem gripped her ass.

"I love you too," Patrice lied.

She got into her Toyota Highlander and drove home. She wondered what the hell did Timmy want to talk about where he had to get off of work early. Honestly, she didn't even want to talk. She just wanted to shower and crawl into bed.

"Here we go," Patrice sighed as she turned into their driveway. She got out of the car and went into the house. Timmy was sitting at the kitchen island, drinking coffee and talking on his phone. It was his mother who Patrice hated with her whole heart. She rolled her eyes and threw her purse on the counter as she went into the counter and pulled out a bottle of red wine.

"I'ma call you back, ma. Yeah. We'll talk about that later. Alright bet." He hung up the phone.

"The fuck you got your nose turned up for?" he asked her.

"What do you want to talk about Timmy? I'm not trying to argue with you," she said to him. He laughed at her and shook his head.

"What's your problem, Patrice? This shit is getting out of hand and too be honest, a nigga tired of it," he snapped. He wasn't about to play with her.

"What's getting out of hand Timmy? Communicate," she had the nerve to say.

"Communicate? That's what the fuck I've been trying to do with your ass. Every time I try to communicate, you shut me out and shit. What the fuck have I done to you?"

"Nothing. I've just been tired from work lately. That's all babe," she lied.

She straightened up quick because she knew when Timmy started cursing and getting loud, he was very pissed. She didn't need that.

He walked closely to her and kissed her. She smiled.

"You be giving a nigga a hard ass time," he told her.

"I'll get better."

Timmy bent down to plant a kiss on her neck and noticed a red bruise, a passion mark. He immediately frowned up.

"Where the fuck you get a hickey from?" he asked her.

Michelle quickly rubbed over the mark. She hadn't even noticed that Solem had gave her one. She came up with something quickly.

"What the hell you mean? Your drunk ass can't remember the things you did to me the other night?"

"Nah, refresh my memory," he told her.

"We just had some wild good ass sex." She licked her lips.

For some reason, Timmy didn't believe her. For the first time, he was questioning his wife's loyalty for him. Timmy was for sure a wild ass nigga in bed when they were having drunk sex, but he never left passion marks on Patrice. He wasn't that type of nigga.

"Oh okay," he said. He tried to push the idea of her being with another man in the back of his head, so he quickly changed the subject. "Let me get some," he told her.

"Maybe later, babe. I'm a little tired right now."

"Bet." He walked away from her and left the house.

When he left, Patrice rushed to her phone. She was about to curse Solem ass out. For him to leave a hickey on her neck was totally disrespectful and she didn't think the shit was funny. She could really lose her husband behind some shit like that. Her heart beat fast as she waited for him to answer. She was livid.

Chapter Four

Charles used the key to go into his mother's house. He had promised his nephew, TJ, that he would come and get him so that they could spend the day together. It would only be for a few hours since his mother wasn't aware of it, but that was okay with TJ. He loved his uncle and when his mama kept them away from one another, he would be very upset.

"Mama!" Charles called out.

"I'm back here in the laundry room!" Loretta yelled.

He walked to the laundry room where his mother was. She was washing and folding clothes. He kissed her on the cheek and passed her a box of chicken that he had picked up from *New York Fried Chicken*. She smiled. That was her favorite chicken spot and she hadn't had any in a few weeks.

"Thank you. You know your mama like a book because I've been craving this chicken all week." Loretta smiled.

"It's all good mama. Where's TJ at?"

"He's in the den playing on that damn game."

"TJ, come on before I leave you little nigga!" Charles yelled to the back.

Loretta sat down on the couch and dug into her chicken basket.

"Alright. Let me finish this last game and I'm coming!" TJ yelled.

Charles laughed and shook his head.

"Come sit down and let me talk to you for a minute, Charles," Loretta said. He sat down and took off his cap. His mama had all of his attention.

"Why, son?" she asked him, which caught him off guard.

"What you mean?"

"Come on Charles. Don't play with me. Your sister told me everything. I didn't raise you the way that you're carrying yourself. What's up with you and this relationship with my granddaughter? Ciara told me how you haven't been helping Michelle. Why the hell not?"

Charles rubbed his hand over his head. He didn't know what to say, and he didn't want to lie to his mama.

"You don't hear me talking to you?" she snapped.

"I've been distracted, ma. I don't know what the hell has gotten into me. I got a job though. I'm getting it together."

"For my grandbaby or for her mama?" He frowned.

"For my baby. What you mean?" he lied.

What he was doing was not for Briana. He only got a job because he knew that was the only way he could get Michelle back. At first, he thought she was just talking shit, but the way she was treating him made him realize that this shit was not a game.

"I'm never in the blind. Your sister tells me everything that's going on. You need to leave Michelle alone and focus on getting your life together. If it isn't about Briana, I don't wanna keep hearing your damn sister's mouth about you harassing Michelle and all that other bullshit."

"I don't know why Ciara just don't mind her business, dang. She's so miserable, it's ridiculous. She got a whole baby daddy and all them niggas she be messing around with, and she's worried about me and my baby mama." He couldn't stand Ciara. She was always snitching and starting shit.

"Chile please." Loretta laughed. "Ciara and Michelle are just that close. You know that. Blood couldn't make them girls closer."

"Yeah. I guess so," Charles said.

"Alright Unc. I'm ready." TJ came from the back.

"Make sure you have him back before five o'clock. I don't wanna hear his mama's mouth."

"She'll be alright." Charles and TJ hopped into his truck and headed to Charles' apartment.

"Yo Unc. How come you and my mama not close how y'all used to be?" TJ asked.

He really wanted to know because it was a time when Ciara and Charles were inseparable. Ciara didn't fuck off when it came to her brother back in the days, but now it was like they hated each other.

"Yo' mama just always tripping on me. She loves me though and I love her, but I just try to keep my distance so we won't have it out."

TJ nodded his head. "She got a new boyfriend. I like him."

"Oh yeah?"

That was shocking news. Ciara hated relationships and Charles couldn't remember the last time she had been in one.

"Yep." TJ nodded his head.

They pulled into Charles' driveway. He had to remind himself to feed his dogs before he took TJ back to his mama's house.

When they got in, Charles went to his room and unplugged the PlayStation 4 to take it to the living room.

As soon as he got comfortable in his seat in front of the TV, someone started banging on his door. He already knew who it was and honestly, he didn't have time for her and her bullshit today. He snatched the door open.

"Why the fuck are you here?" he asked Shara.

She stood there on the porch and looked sad. At least, she had gotten a new hair due because the one she had at Michelle's party was horrible.

"I need to talk to you," she said sadly.

He sighed and stepped to the side. She walked in the house.

"Hey! That's the girl that my godmama fought a while back," TJ pointed out.

Charles messed up big time because he had forgot that TJ knew who Shara was. He was just going to give his nephew a couple of dollars and tell him to keep his mouth shut. If Michelle found out that he was fucking her first cousin, all hell was going to break loose.

"Shut up, nigga." Charles went into his pocket and gave TJ a twenty-dollar bill. TJ smiled and covered his mouth with his hands.

Shara and Charles went to his bedroom. He closed the door then gave her a look that was so evil.

"I should slap the shit out of you. Why the fuck are you just popping up at my house? What's so important that you had to come here unannounced?" he asked her, as he balled up his fist.

She went into her big yellow unnamed brand purse and pulled out a piece of paper. She handed it to Charles and he looked at it. His face frowned up as he balled the paper up.

"You're not keeping that fucking baby," he told her.

"Nigga, you must be crazy," Shara said while she crossed her arms over her chest.

"What the fuck did I say?" Charles said through gritted teeth.

Shara had tears in her eyes. She didn't understand why the hell Charles could be with her behind closed doors and not in public. She didn't give a damn that he was her first cousin's baby daddy, hell she never liked Michelle anyways. She just wanted Charles and she hoped that this baby could help her get him.

"But this baby is going to make us work, baby?" She rubbed him on his arms.

"If the baby ain't coming from Michelle, I don't fucking want it," he said to her.

That cut Shara deep. For him to throw his feelings for Michelle in her face made her blood boil. "That's how you feel?"

"Fuck yeah. Get an abortion," he told her.

"I'll let Michelle know what's up before I get rid of my fucking child."

Shara turned to walk away, but Charles snatched her back and jacked her up against the wall.

"What the fuck did you just say?"

"Let me go Charles." She was scared.

He let her go and followed her as she walked out of the room. There was a loud knock on the door and Charles' heart dropped. He didn't need anyone to know that Shara was here.

"Open up this fucking door Charles. I know you got my son in there."

"Shit," Charles mumbled.

It was Ciara. But, what the hell was she doing there that early? She was supposed to be working late.

"He coming!" Charles yelled out.

He really went crazy when he heard a key unlocking the door. He panicked. Ciara still had the key that he had given her to the house. They were for sure caught.

When Ciara walked into the house, her mouth dropped open while Shara smirked.

"What the fuck is this Charles?" Ciara pointed to Shara.

"Huh?" Charles asked.

"It's exactly what it looks like. Now, excuse me. I was just about to leave," Shara said. Before Charles could say anything else, Ciara pounced over on her. She sent a blow straight to her jaw, which caused her to fall to the ground. Ciara grabbed a hand full of Shara's new weave and punched her over and over in the face. Poor Shara couldn't stand a chance with Ciara. Charles tried to pull Ciara off of Shara, but she turned and punched him in the nose.

"Fuck man!" Charles called out.

"Get the fuck off of me, you hood rat bitch!" Shara yelled.

"Chill out Cici! Let her go!" Charles yelled.

Ciara was livid. She was breathing heavy, and she had ripped her brand new work shirt. Her hair was messed up too, but that didn't matter to her. She couldn't believe the two of them. She got off of Shara and kicked her dead in the face. Shara held her nose and cried out in pain.

Charles didn't give a damn about Shara and how his sister had beat her ass. He was just wondering what Ciara was going to tell Michelle.

"You're a fucking dog. A broke, nasty ass dog!" Ciara yelled at him.

"Please don't tell Michelle, Ciara. Please man," he begged.

"Nigga, you must be crazy! TJ, bring your ass on!" She snatched him up and smacked him upside the head. "Who the hell told you to leave mama's house and go with him?" she yelled at TJ.

"Grandma said it was okay, ma." TJ was scared. This wasn't his first time seeing his mama in action. He didn't want her to take her frustration out on him.

"Let's go!"

Charles followed them outside and left Shara in the house. If he thought that she wasn't going to tell Michelle, he had another thing coming.

"Go back in the house and check on that slut bitch," Ciara told her brother.

"You don't have to tell Michelle. You just like starting shit. You make me fucking sick," he snapped. Ciara's phone started ringing and surprisingly, it was Michelle. She called at the right time. She waved the phone in Charles' face and he wanted to smack her.

"Hello?" she spoke into the phone.

"Why the hell it sound like you just came from running?" Michelle asked on the other end.

"I just whooped your whore ass cousin's ass."

"What? Who?"

"Shara. She and Charles are fucking. I'm sorry to have to break it to you, bestie. I came over here to get TJ and the bitch was in there with them," Ciara told her.

"You're a fucking lie Ciara!" Charles lied.

"Really Charles? Swear on grandma's grave then."

Ciara knew he wouldn't do that and that was all Michelle needed to know. Michelle was quiet on the other end.

Ciara got into her car and sped off with Michelle still on the phone.

"Michelle, you there?"

"Yeah," she said quietly

"Are you okay? Where are you?"

"I'm not okay Ciara, but I'm about to head to my auntie's house. I'll call you later." Michelle was hurt and Ciara could tell from the tone of her voice.

The love that Ciara had for Michelle was so genuine, her heart hurt for her best friend. She actually had tears flowing from her face. Michelle couldn't catch a break and she didn't deserve all of this she had been going through. It was already bad enough that her daughter had cancer, but to continuously get hurt by the people close to her was just too much to deal with.

"You okay mama?" TJ rubbed his mama's back.

"I'm okay son. Don't worry about me," she lied.

She sent Terrance a text and let him know that she needed to see him. She didn't want to go to the office in front of his clients with her drama. When he texted her and told her he would be to her house in a few minutes, she felt better.

***

Michelle wiped the tears from her eyes. She looked into her mirror and her face was full of smeared mascara. She was going to get herself together, but she didn't feel like being fake today. She wanted everyone to know how she felt. For so long, she had been hiding her real feelings. She had been quiet and overlooking shit because she was always peaceful, but at this point, she didn't give a damn about peace. She stepped out of her car and walked towards her auntie Sally's house. She had an hour before she had to go back to the office, and she was going to use that time wisely. She knocked on her auntie's door, and she came with her other daughter, Sami, in tow. She opened the door and her eyes almost popped open.

"Michelle, baby, what's wrong?" her auntie Sally asked her.

As much as she wanted to snap and take all of her frustrations out on her auntie, she wouldn't dare. Sally was a good woman and she didn't teach her daughter to do the things that she had been doing over the years. Sally and Shirley also had a great sister-sister relationship, so Michelle wouldn't come in between that.

With tears running down her face, she walked in and sat down in her auntie's family room. Before she said anything, she broke down and started crying. She wasn't just crying about what Shara had did to her, but she was crying about everything. Low self-esteem, her daughter suffering from cancer, she just was in a mess. Her life was a mess. She wasn't happy and she had no peace in her life. Sometimes, she found herself questioning God. She just wanted to know what had she done so wrong to be so hurt. Whatever it was, she couldn't take anymore. She was drained emotionally and mentally.

Her aunt Sally rubbed her back and wiped her tears off her face.

"Auntie, Shara has been sleeping with Charles," Michelle blurted out.

"WHAT?" Sally stood to her feet.

"Ooh! She ain't lying either mama. Terri told me he saw them together a few times, but you know she's always keeping up mess, so I never believed it," Sami said, referring to her best friend. Sami and Michelle was always cool. Sami was off the chain, but she wasn't just about as terrible as her big sister.

Sally sat back down and shook her head. She didn't know what to say about her oldest daughter. She was a mess. Embarrassing was what she was. Sally felt like that shit was a slap in the face because she had not raised them to go around and be whores. Her heart beat fast and her head hurt very badly.

"Sami, go in there and get my blood pressure medicine please," Sally said.

Sami shook her head. Now she was pissed because her selfish ass sister had her mama's blood pressure high. Sami couldn't believe that Shara would stoop that low. Having a man wasn't that serious.

"Michelle baby, I am so sorry. I am. I apologize. I don't know what the hell is wrong with Shara. She must've got that shit from her daddy's side because I've never did shit like that." Sally wiped the tears from her face.

"I'm just tired, auntie. No matter how much I try to be humble and peaceful, the devil just takes over. I'm tired. I just wanna be happy." Michelle wiped the tears away.

When Michelle looked up and saw Shara walking through the door, her first thought was to jump up and kill her. It wasn't even about Charles; it was about how disloyal she was. She couldn't believe that her first cousin was her biggest enemy. She had never done anything to Shara but love her and treat her like family, and she hated her so much that she would do anything to see her hurting.

Sally stood up. "You are full of shit. You know that, Shara?" Sally walked towards her.

Shara waved her mama off. "Ma, you don't even know what's going on," she said to her.

"Then you tell me. What's going on Shara?"

"She sleeping with that girl's man. That's what's going on." Sami came from the back of the house. She loved her sister with all of her heart, but wrong was wrong, and she was dead wrong for doing Michelle like that.

"Shut up Sami." Shara rolled her eyes.

"What have I ever done to you to deserve this, Shara? I just wanna know," Michelle asked. She felt like a weak bitch for crying and letting Shara see her cry, but it was what it was. She wanted Shara to feel like shit. Shara kept her head down. She began to play on her phone until Sally knocked it on the floor.

"Answer her fucking question!" Sally yelled.

"Why would you do that?" Shara yelled back.

When Sally walked away and went to the back, Shara thought about leaving and going on about her business but she couldn't move, for some reason. Sally came back into the family room with a wooden broom. Without a second thought, she started beating Shara with the broom.

"You think this shit is a game?" She beat her with it. Sami nor Michelle moved. Shara tried to block the broom licks, but Sally was putting one good whooping on her ass.

She swung the broom so hard, she hit Shara in the face. That's when Sami stepped in.

"Mama, you need to calm down before you have a stroke."

"Back up off me, Sami!" Shara cried and held her stomach.

"I'm sick of your shit, Shara. This has done it. I'm tired of your ass. Why would you sleep with Charles? You're pathetic. Leave my house right now!" Sally yelled.

Sally was upset that she had to treat her daughter the way she did, but she needed it. She had given Shara too many passes, but she was over it. She hurt her sister's child in the worse way and that fucked with her.

"I'm never coming back here," Shara said.

"If you say something else to mama, I'm gonna beat your ass and it won't be with a broom," Sami said and pushed her out.

Sally probably felt sorry for Shara but Sami didn't. She knew how her sister got down, and she was happy that her mama finally saw it with her own eyes. For a long time, Sami had been trying to tell her mama how slimy Shara was, but in Sally's eyes, Shara could do no wrong up until now.

"I am so sorry, Michelle. I don't know what to say about her." Sally shook her head.

"It's okay, auntie. You handled that just fine. I just have to keep my distance away from Shara and Charles. I hate that I have a child with Charles because I have to deal with him regardless, but I hate him so much. He doesn't even do for me or my daughter."

Sami and Sally shook their heads.

"I'm gonna leave. I have to get back to work." Michelle stood to her feet.

"Sorry again, Chelle. I hope things get better." Sally hugged her.

"Thank you, auntie."

Michelle got into the car and headed back to the office. Even though she wasn't in the mood to work, she had to get shit done and she had to make her money. She wasn't going to focus on Charles or her cousin. She had to take Briana to Florida in the next two days, and she was trying to focus on her baby's health.

She fixed herself up then walked into the office. She didn't know what the problem was but it seemed like all eyes were on her. It was Terrance, Timmy, and another guy that she wasn't familiar with. She felt uncomfortable.

"Hey. Why y'all looking at me like I'm a damn ghost or something?"

They all laughed.

"They're just admiring your beauty, sis," Terrance said to her, which made her smile.

People didn't know but the simplest things could change Michelle's mood. Even though Michelle was beautiful and she knew it, she had very low self-esteem. She didn't feel worthy. Well, at least not worthy when it came to keeping a man. No matter how fabulous she was, Charles never treated her like the queen that she was. He treated her like shit. So, that's what she felt like, shit.

"Thanks Terrance," Michelle said. "Have you talked to Ciara?"

"Yep and she told me everything." He shook his head.

"She's always had a motor mouth." Michelle shook her head.

Any other time, Michelle would've been mad that she was telling her business but she didn't give a damn anymore. She might as well tell the truth and stop living a lie.

"Are you alright though?" Terrance asked her.

"I'm fine," she lied.

"Alright, well, I'm leaving for the day to go home with my woman. I emailed you a few things to handle for me. I need them done before tomorrow noon. Looks like it's just you and Tim in the office this evening." He winked.

Something about just the two of them being in the office did something to Michelle. She didn't feel comfortable being around Timmy alone, but she was a big girl and she could handle herself. She would go home and finish the work from her home office before doing anything stupid.

"I'll see you later." She giggled.

Timmy stared at her and licked his lips. Her pussy was wet. He needed to leave her alone. He went into his office and closed the door.

"Jesus, don't let me go there with that man," she mumbled.

***

Michelle jumped when she felt some big hands on her shoulder shaking her. She looked over her shoulders and it was Timmy. Obviously, she had gotten a little tired and fell asleep at her desk.

"You were out, ma. Come on. You can finish that shit in the morning," Timmy said to her.

"What time is it?" she asked.

"1:00 a.m."

She shook her head and wiped the sleep from her eyes. She checked her phone and she realized that she had several missed calls from her parents and her daughter. She knew that her parents were worried because she hadn't talked to them all day and she knew that her auntie called and gave her mother the devastating news. She sent her mother a text and let her know that she was fine, and she had been working late. She wasn't going to get Briana that night because she needed a little time to herself. She needed to sob in peace and she didn't want her daughter to be worried about her.

"You coming or are you just gone sit there?" Timmy asked her.

He had his coat, his briefcase, and his phone in his hand, ready to lock up the place and leave. Michelle gathered all of her things and walked outside with Timmy.

She tried to walk off from him but he caught up with her.

"Why you running from a nigga? I'm not gone bite you, Michelle. Damn."

"I'm not running nigga, its cold out here, and I'm ready to go home and get in my bed. The same thing your married ass should be doing." She smirked. She loved putting Timmy on the spot when it came to him being married.

"Fuck all of that. Let's go and get a drink. I think we both need them," he told her.

"Timmy?" she said to him.

"What? Shit?" he asked her.

"You are a married ass man. I will not be caught in a bar with you at one in the morning. That shit would probably be all over the news," she said to him and that made him laugh.

"I'm a married man and my wife is probably somewhere fucking every chance she can get. Just get in the car and let's go. I'll drop you off home after we leave the bar. I won't bite."

Michelle's mouth flew open. She couldn't believe what he had just said about his wife. She looked at her car then looked at his. She could definitely use a drink or ten. She got into Timmy's hummer and the heater felt so good as it blasted in her face.

"I love this truck so much," Michelle complimented.

"Thanks beautiful." He smiled.

"So, you should already know that I'm nosey as hell. Your wife cheating on you?"

Michelle wasted no time. She wanted to know everything. If she was cheating on him, she wanted to know why. *Maybe he had cheated first*, Michelle thought.

He laughed. "I didn't want to believe the shit, but yeah, I believe her ass is," he said nonchalantly.

"Why do you think that?" she asked him.

"Because she had passion marks all over her neck. I don't leave hickies and shit, so I already know what's up." He shrugged.

"Wow. Did you call it out?"

"Hell yeah. She gave me these bullshit ass lies saying when we had some drunk sex I was wild, and all type of dumb shit."

"Damn. What have you done to make that woman cheat? She doesn't even look like she'd be the cheating type."

He laughed. "Why did I have to do something to her? I didn't do shit but love her ass. Love her and put up with her shit. I don't know why she stepped out on a nigga. Then, what makes me feel like she's been cheating even more is every time I try to fuck, she pushes me away."

Michelle's mouth dropped open. Timmy didn't even seem like the type of nigga to not get any pussy. He just looked to good, he was built too perfectly. Lord, she hoped and prayed that his fine ass didn't have a small dick.

"She ain't fucking you? Damn, Timmy. Don't tell me your sex is whack," Michelle joked.

He looked at her like she was crazy.

"I don't mean to come off as cocky ma, but you see me? You can reach over here and feel my dick if you want to. My sex game is A-1 and I always make sure my lady is satisfied in bed. Patrice is just one of those women who takes a good nigga kindness for a weakness, but I got to show her better than I can tell her."

Michelle couldn't even lie, she loved Timmy's vibe and his honesty. He was so open with her and that made her feel very comfortable being around him.

Michelle shook her head. Women like Patrice made it hard for women like Michelle. Here she was wanting and needing a man like Timmy, and an ungrateful bitch had him. Not only did she have him, but she had his last name.

"What happened with you earlier?" he asked Michelle.

She wasn't going to tell him, but she figured since he had been honest with her then she was going to do the same thing.

"My best friend caught my first cousin coming out of my baby's daddy house." She looked out of the window.

"Damn ma. I'm sorry to hear that. Y'all still fucking around?"

"Nope. We were, but I had to let his ass go. He doesn't do anything for my baby. He doesn't even care to fly to Florida with me to take my baby to her doctor's appointments. I used to make excuses for him and that's what made him think he could do all that shit he has been doing to me and my baby, but not anymore."

"I hate a dead beat ass nigga, man."

"Me too. I can't even believe that I've been settling for that all of these years. He's so pathetic, man. I just really wish that he wasn't my baby daddy."

"Yeah, you definitely don't have to settle for him, not if he's not even taking care of baby girl. Any nigga with a heart gone make sure his baby is straight. Then for her to have cancer, that nigga supposed to be moving mountains for her."

"Exactly," Michelle agreed.

They pulled into *Grill 23*. That was Timmy's favorite spot, but Michelle had never been. He got out and opened the door for her. She was impressed. He was a gentleman. A married gentleman. She would always remind herself.

They went into the bar and ordered up a few shots of Hennessey and Cîroc on the rocks. Michelle trusted Timmy so if she got too fucked up, she was sure that he was going to make sure she was okay.

"How does it feel to be a famous, rich lawyer?" Michelle asked him.

He shrugged his shoulders. "My life is still normal. I don't let the shit get to me. I remain humble through it all and I pray a lot to make sure I stay focused through it all.

"Praying man huh? I like that." Michelle sipped on her water.

"Oh yeah. The man in charge have to get all the praise."

Damn. Why couldn't he be my husband? She thought in her head.

He stared at Michelle and she stared back at him. When he licked his lips and bit that bottom one, a cold rush went down her spine. She crossed her legs.

"Stop looking at me like that, Tim. You're married. Let's just enjoy this night as coworkers and go on about our business," she told him.

"You right."

When they got their drinks, they wasted no time with throwing them back. Michelle made Timmy laugh a lot.

"This is strong as shit. Count to five then I'll throw it back," Michelle said.

Timmy counted down and Michelle threw two shots of Cîroc back. She licked the salt off the rim then sucked on the lime. She wasn't fucked up yet, but she was getting there. She needed to have those drinks because it made her forget all the bad things that was going on. At that moment, she didn't feel the heartache that she had every day all day.

One cup of Cîroc and five shots later, Michelle was feeling good as shit.

"I'll tell you one thing. Patrice will miss you when you're gone. Like you told me in that truck, you don't have to settle for that bullshit," she slurred. "I'm not settling anymore. I'ma go out and have me some damn fun. Live a little and find me a real man."

You got one right here, Timmy thought to himself.

"Yeah, you're still young. Live a little bit."

She laughed loud. Timmy knew it was time to go when she kept trying to drink from the empty glass. Any other nigga would've thought she was tripping, but Timmy thought it was cute and funny. He was glad that she was enjoying herself. He just hoped she could control all of that.

He pulled her up from her chair then walked to the front. After he paid for their drinks, he put her in the truck.

"Timmy?" Michelle called out.

"Yeah? You alright?" he asked her.

"I'm fine, but I do have a question."

"What's up?"

"Have you ever had a one-night stand?"

He giggled. "I've had a few in my life. What about you?"

"Nope. I wanna have one though."

Hearing her say that made his dick stand straight up. She turned and looked at him.

"You wanna fuck me, huh?" she asked him. His eyes widened. She was already blunt, but she got super blunt when she was on the drink.

"Chill out, Michelle. You drunk," he told her.

"I'm not drunk, boy. I'm tipsy. I know you wanna fuck me. I watch the way you look at me. You lick your lips at me and you're always staring at my breast, and your dick is hard right now." She licked her lips.

"So, what you saying?" Timmy asked her.

"I know that you're married, and I know I'm going to hell for this, but I want you to make love to me. I want you to take your time with my body. No one ever have to know about this."

"You brave on the liq' huh?" He laughed.

"Just for you, though. I know in the morning I'm going to be embarrassed because I came on to you, but I just wanna try something new. I've never done anything like this before, and I've only slept with one guy and that's my baby daddy."

"Damn. That's the only dick you had in your life?" he asked her.

She laughed. "Yep."

"Well, I'ma handle that tonight. You wanna get a room?" he asked her.

"No! No room. I'll feel like a whore then. We can just go to my place. You don't have to stay either."

"Yeah. I'ma fuck the shit out of you, then wake up next to you in my arms. I won't leave you, but I must say that I don't wanna just fuck you. I wanna know more about you but right now, we gone focus on fucking." He laughed.

"881 E 2nd street unit 15," Michelle told him the address. He put it in his GPS and pulled up in no time.

When they got upstairs to her unit, she placed the key in. Timmy looked around and he was impressed. Her condo was laid out. It looked like her all the way too. When he thought about her all the time, this was what he imagined her living in.

She kicked off her Gucci heels and kicked them in the corner.

"Don't walk on my white carpet with those big ass shoes on," she told him.

He laughed and kicked his kicks off. She grabbed his hand and went into the master bedroom. She sat at the edge of the bed and stared at him. She bit her bottom lip and leaned back.

Timmy took off his shirt and walked close to her. She slowly took off her shirt and exposed her beautiful big breasts. He took one hand and stuck it into her bra feeling her big round nipples, and he did the same with the other one. He planted soft kisses on her neck then licked her neck from the left to the right side.

"Mmm..." she let out a soft moan. She was hot and wet. He was doing all the right things. That was what she wanted and needed.

He rubbed his index finger over her pretty lips. She sucked on his finger and made his dick stand again. He unzipped her skirt and pulled it down over her legs. Her skin was so smooth and pretty. Her pretty fat pussy sat up in her black and pink lace thong. He kneeled down and kissed her warm juicy pussy through her panties. Then he kissed her inner thighs.

"Spread your legs," he told her.

She spread them as wide as she could. She wasn't that flexible and she was more on the stiff side, but Timmy could work with that.

He took her panties off and admired her pretty tiny pink pussy. He stuck his tongue inside of her hole then he slowly nibbled on her clit. Sucking her clit, pussy, and ass, she had a tight grip on his head with her legs locked around his neck.

"Oh shit! Tim! Shit!" she screamed out.

She never had a feeling like the one that Timmy was giving her. He was sucking on her vagina like a baby would suck on its bottle. He took his finger and slowly finger fucked her. Her clit was swollen, so he made sure that he continued to show it mad attention.

"Oh shittttttttttt. I'm cumming Tim!" Tears slid down the side of her face. Her body shook as she had the biggest orgasm ever. She was ready to go to sleep.

"Hell nah. Don't tap out now. Ain't this what you wanted?" He freed himself from his pants and Michelle felt like she was immediately sobering up.

"How big are you?" she asked him. He laughed but she was serious. She had never saw a dick so long and pretty before in her entire life.

"Stop talking," he whispered in her ear. He slowly pushed himself into her small, wet, tight opening. She didn't know it was going to hurt so good. But, she was willing to take it.

"Fuck!" He bit his bottom lip. He went in and out of her slowly, as he pressed on her clit and watched her juices cover his dick.

"I'm cumming again," she cried out.

He sucked on her ear and her bottom lip. The faces that she was making turned him on more. Her pussy was bomb. Better than Patrice's.

"Fuck, Michelle," he moaned.

"I wanna ride you," Michelle whispered. He leaned over on his back and held his dick in his hands.

She lowered herself unto him. She couldn't sit down all the way because she was scared. She didn't want his big dick ass to bust her open.

"Man, go all the way down." He pushed her down. It didn't hurt too bad, but she could feel him in her stomach.

She rode and bounced on his dick. She felt herself getting ready to come again, so she got on top of him and did squats. He gripped her ass, then smacked it.

"Fuck me like you really want this dick."

Ooh, when he said that, that was motivation. She leaned to the side and let her fat ass clap on his ten-inch anaconda.

"Oooohhhh shitttttttt! I'm cumming really hard this time Timmy!" He stabbed her wet pussy and she squirted for the very first time in her life. They shared a kiss that was so passionate and sincere, it was almost scary.

This nigga married, Michelle thought again. She didn't care about that anymore though, not at the moment, at least.

"Get on all fours and arch your back," he demanded.

She arched her back and he roughly fucked her from the back. He knew exactly what to do because she didn't want the slow strokes from the back. She wanted her shit straight pounded and that's what he gave her.

"Shit!" He slapped her ass. "This my pussy now, Michelle. You hear me?" He pulled her hair.

"Yes!" she cried. She caught another orgasm and it was unbelievable. Michelle couldn't believe that his dick was so good. She didn't even believe dick that good existed in the real world.

"I'm ready to bust," he told her.

She threw her ass back on him hard. He gripped her waste and hurriedly pulled his dick out. He shot all of his seeds out on her ass. The nut that he caught was just what he needed. He wasn't just talking when he told Michelle that her pussy was his, married or not. Her and her pussy belonged to him.

He grabbed her towel off her bathroom door and wiped her off. The both of them was full of sticky sweat, but they didn't care. Michelle turned and looked in Timmy's eyes. She kissed him and he kissed her back.

"What the fuck just happened?" Michelle said out loud.

Chapter Five

Michelle tossed and turned in bed. The smell of bacon filled the air and her stomach growled. She sat up in bed and looked at herself in the mirror that was sitting on her wall across from her bed. Her hair was all over her head and she was naked. She remembered everything that had taken place the night before and surprisingly, she didn't regret any of it. She laid back and in bed and sighed out loud.

Minutes later, Timmy walked through the bedroom door with a breakfast tray in his hand. He looked so good. His muscles stuck out and his chest was gorgeous. He wore no shirt, just his same pants from the previous night. Michelle sat back up and smiled. She felt good when he smiled back at her.

"I whipped you up something." He handed her the tray.

It was filled with scrambled eggs, cheese grits, sausage, bacon, pancakes, and strawberries.

"Thank you. It looks good."

Timmy reached over and ate one of her strawberries.

"How you feeling this morning?" he asked her.

"Great." She stuffed her mouth with food and gave her plate all of her attention.

He laughed. "Yeah, well, I feel great too." He laid back in bed and grabbed the remote.

Michelle felt really comfortable around Timmy. At the moment, she didn't feel like she was lying in the bed with a married man. She felt like she was lying next to her man. Well, a man that she had been dreaming about. She wanted Timmy but she knew that she couldn't have him. If her mother knew that she was messing around with a married man, she would get beat, just how her auntie had beat Shara with that broom.

She knew it was a little too early to feel the way that she was feeling, but it was fun for her.

Timmy's phone rung and rung after he powered it on. Michelle was convinced that it was Terrance and his wife. She gave him a look to let him know that he could handle whatever it was that he needed to handle.

"That's Patrice," he told her.

"So, go in the living room and answer it," she told him.

"I don't want to though. Fuck her right now."

She continued to call and call until Timmy got tired of it.

"What, man?" he yelled into the phone as he walked out of the room.

Michelle took that time to power on her phone. She finished her food and sat the tray to the side. She had a million text messages from her mama, her daddy, and even some from Ciara.

She panicked. They probably had been trying to call the house phone but she had unplugged it the week before because Charles wouldn't leave her alone. She called her mother and she picked up on the third ring.

"Michelle Marie Salson!" her mother yelled into the phone.

"Yes mama? What's wrong?"

Michelle was already in her closet, pulling something out to put on.

"We've been calling you since five this morning. Where are you?"

"I'm home mama. My phone was off. What's going on?"

"You need to get to the Shriners Hospital now, Michelle," her mother said sadly.

"Is it something wrong with my baby? Where's Bri?" Michelle drilled her with questions.

"She's in the room. Just get here now." Her mother hung up the phone.

Michelle didn't know what was going on but she already had tears falling from her eyes. She pulled out some stretchable pants and a simple black turtleneck Nike T-shirt. The more she thought about something being terribly wrong with her child, the more her heart broke. She started sniffing and crying harder.

Timmy came into the room, unaware of what was going on. When he heard Michelle crying, he walked into the closet.

"Chelle? What's wrong?" he asked her.

"It's my baby. My mama said something is wrong with Bri." She cried uncontrollably. "I'll be to work later. I have to go be with my baby."

Timmy looked at her and his heart began to hurt. Seeing her like that did something to him.

"I'ma go with you," he told her.

She wiped her tears then looked into his eyes. "You don't have to do that. Get home to your wife, Timmy."

He grabbed his shirt and keys. He leaned down and kissed her forehead. "Let's go check on baby girl," he told her. She looked at him and nodded.

They got into Timmy's truck and headed to the hospital. He texted Terrance and let him know that he was with Michelle, and he was going to be late coming into the office.

Timmy: Long night with Michelle. Headed to the hospital with her and her baby. I'll be to the office a little later. Peace.

Terrance: I'm at the hospital with Ciara waiting on y'all. Shit isn't good my nigga.

Timmy: We're on the way.

Timmy glanced over at Michelle, who was still silently crying. He hoped things wasn't as bad as Terrance had just made it.

"Everything gone be alright, Michelle. God won't let you down on this, ma." Timmy tried hard to motivate her.

"She's just so little. Like, her body can't take this cancer shit. I just wish I was the one that was dealing with it. If something happens to my baby, I wouldn't be able to deal with myself. There will be no purpose for me to live. That little girl means the world to me. Everything I do is for her." She wiped her tears.

"I know and God knows, that's why she's going to fight through this."

Michelle nodded her head. At this point, her faith was gone. She was tired of making herself believe that everything was going to be okay. Every time she made herself believe that everything was going to be okay, things seemed to get worse. She couldn't deal with that anymore.

They went into the hospital. Once they got on the third floor, they went into the waiting room where all of her family was. Ciara and Terrance was sitting off to the side. Like always, Charles was nowhere in sight, but their mother Loretta was there. Michelle was cool with Loretta, but they weren't close. Michelle always felt like Charles was the way he was because of his mother. Loretta was the type to defend her son, even when he was wrong. She could guarantee that Loretta had made up the biggest lie as to why her son wasn't there.

"What's going on mama?" Michelle asked.

"Late last night, Briana started coughing up blood, lots of it. So, we bring her here and then they're telling us that things are looking really bad." Shirley eyes got glossy.

"So, where's the doctor? Where's Bri?" Michelle started crying.

"They're running a few test on her. She needed to get some scans and X-rays done."

Michelle shook her head and started crying harder. She couldn't deal with all of this at one time. Her uncle Tall walked up to her and pulled her to the side. He couldn't take it either. It was bothering him that all of this was happening to his favorite nieces.

"Look at me, Michelle." He lifted her chin. "Everything gone be alright baby." She shook her head no.

"Nah, uncle T. It's not gone be okay. I'm tired of this," she said.

The doctor walked down the hall and Michelle rushed to him.

"Hi doctor. I'm Briana's mom. Can you please tell me what's going on with my daughter please?"

"Well, Ms. Salson, we've been trying to get in contact with you for hours," the doctor said.

"It don't make a damn difference how long y'all been trying to get in contact with her. She's here now. Tell my baby what's going on with our baby," her uncle Tall went off.

The doctor seemed scared. "In private or in the family room?" the doctor asked Michelle.

"The family room please," she told him.

They walked into the room and everyone came close to hear what was going on. They were hoping that it was something simple like pneumonia.

"Well, we've done some chest X-rays on Briana and a few scans. We found a few blood clots in her longs, which is not good at all. After we done a few scans on her, we found not only blood clots in her lungs, but we also see cancer."

When Michelle heard that, her head started to spin and her head was very light headed. Shirley couldn't deal with the news, so she got her purse and left. Briana already had bone cancer, so to have bone and lung cancer was horrible.

"So, what does that mean? Is she going to be okay?" Ciara asked the doctor as tears rolled down her face.

Ciara loved her niece and she hated what was going on. She had tried to call Charles a million and one times, but he never picked up.

"We're going to try our best to make sure that she's okay but right now, things aren't looking good for her. I have to be honest with you and let you know that if she makes it out alive, we will be surprised. But, right now, we have her on a few medications so she can sleep and be in less pain."

Michelle broke down and started crying loud. Timmy held her in his arms as she cried and thought about everything that the doctor had just told her. Ciara rubbed her back and cried with her friend. Loretta sat there with a broken heart. Briana wasn't as close with Loretta as she was with Shirley, but Loretta still loved her grandbaby with all of her heart.

"Look at me, Michelle. We gone get through this. You hear me? Stay strong," Timmy told her. Terrance didn't know what to say. He just sat there and tried to comfort Ciara. Michelle's father and her uncle stepped to the side with the doctor.

"Y'all need to do everything to make sure she's okay. We can't lose her man," Luke told the doctor.

The doctor placed his right hand over Luke's shoulder. "We're going to try, sir."

The doctor walked away. They went back into the room. Michelle had calmed down. Timmy was on the phone with one of his important clients, but he wouldn't dare leave Michelle at a time like this. He wanted to be there for her and hold her hand through it all.

"Let me have a moment with my daughter, please," Luke told everyone. They walked outside in the lobby, but Loretta sat there. Luke looked at her and turned up his nose.

"What's up Loretta? That was for everyone."

"Excuse me, Luke but the last time I checked, Briana was my grandchild too. What's the problem?"

Luke sighed. He really wasn't in the mood to deal with her and her fucked up attitude. He damn sure wasn't about to argue with a bitch who barley did anything for Briana. As far as Luke was concerned, he and Shirley were her only grandparents.

"I don't give a damn that you're her grandma. I wanted to have a conversation with my daughter. Now leave before I call my wife back in here to remove you for me," Luke snapped.

Loretta wanted no problems with Shirley, so she grabbed her purse and stormed out of the room. That caused Michelle to giggle a little bit and seeing Michelle giggle made Luke smile.

"I'm glad someone got her together," Michelle said.

"She get on my damn nerve."

"What if she doesn't make it through, daddy? What if I lose my baby?" Michelle asked. Her eyes got glossy again.

"Michelle, mark my words. If we have to spend our last dime with getting a doctor that can fix this, then that's what we're gonna do. Briana will whoop's cancer butt as she always says." The both laughed.

Michelle nodded her head. She felt a little better, but she wanted to see her baby. She just wanted to rub her beautiful little face.

"Put your big girl panties on and let's think positive. The devil ain't gone win."

"You're right, daddy."

After talking with her daddy for a few minutes, her blood began to boil as she saw Charles walking in the room. She wanted to pick up the vase full of flowers that was sitting next to her and throw it at his stupid ass. Then the nigga had the nerve to walk in there with a dozen of roses and a card.

Everyone must've knew that it was about to go down because everyone walked back into the room. Like always, Ciara was ready to go in on her brother and give him the business.

"Where's Briana?" he asked.

Everyone looked at him like he was crazy. Tall never liked him, so the unit that was on his face explained it all. If Charles knew any better, he probably would've left that hospital when he first walked in.

"She's in the back. They haven't allowed us to go back and see her yet," Michelle said.

He sat next to Michelle and tried to put his arms on her back. She snatched away from him.

"Please, Charles. Don't touch me. Go talk to the doctor, so he can update you on what's going on," Michelle said to him

"Why you can't tell me?" he asked her.

"Because nigga, she don't wanna talk about it no more. Go find the doctor," Tall fussed.

"Chill out, Tall. Let them co-parent. Now isn't the time for this," Luke told his brother.

Tall grabbed his coat and left. He knew if he stayed in that room, he was going to do some damage and they didn't need that.

"Son, let's just go," Loretta said to Charles.

"Nah mama. He don't need to go anywhere. He need to stay right here and be here for his daughter for once," Ciara fussed.

She was tired of her mother too. She raised a weak ass man and he was no better than their father.

"Ciara Brundage, are you talking back to me in here?" Loretta asked.

"No, I'm not. I'm simply saying let your son be a man."

"She always does that shit, mama. She'll go against her own blood for these folks," Charles went off.

"It's a lot going on. I don't think this should be the topic right now," Timmy said

"What the hell the lawyer doing up here?" Charles asked.

"He's here with me," Michelle said flippantly.

That pissed Charles off to the max. He didn't know that Michelle was fucking around with another nigga and he damn sure didn't know that it was the Timmy that she was fucking around with.

"Oh. This your nigga?" he asked her. She laughed.

"Nigga, you're pathetic. You need not to worry about me, Charles. Worry about Briana, who's probably not gonna beat this cancer shit. You're worried about the wrong things."

He waved her off, as if what she said didn't matter.

"A hot ass mess," Ciara said.

"Chill Ciara," Terrance told her.

"I'm just saying. This shit doesn't make any sense."

"You got one more time to open your big mouth and I'ma bust you in it. Now, try me Ciara," Loretta said.

Ciara looked at her mother as if she was crazy. Ciara loved her mother to death, but unlike Loretta, Ciara was real and she was going to call it how she saw it. She wasn't about to be fake just because Charles was her brother.

"Let me go." Ciara grabbed her belongings.

"I don't know why you're acting like you're a good ass girl all of a sudden. You ain't shit," Charles said to his sister. Before anyone could stop her, she was beating on Charles. She slapped him so hard that he had to slap her back. Terrance picked Charles up and slammed him on the ground. Without thinking twice, Timmy was helping Terrance give Charles the ass whooping that he needed. Charles was trying his hardest to fight back, but he couldn't stand a chance with those two. They were punching, stomping, and kicking Charles.

Luke tried to stop it, but he couldn't handle the wild men.

"Get off my son!" Loretta jumped on Terrance's back and scratched his face from the back. He gently put her down. He didn't want to knock her off of him because she was still Ciara's mama, and she was still a lady.

"Ole fuck ass nigga putting his hands on women and shit!" Terrance yelled. He was pissed. He couldn't remember the last time he had to actually lay his hands on someone. Charles hit every nerve in him when he basically bitch slapped Ciara. She had a red mark on her pretty face and her eyes were red from where she was crying.

Michelle sat there and cried. The security came in and told everyone that they had to leave. People were standing around the room recording everything and it was a bit embarrassing.

"I can't leave my daughter," Michelle told them.

"Ma'am, you have to leave," the security told her.

"Nigga, she don't have to fucking leave. Her child is underage and she is the parent. Move the fuck out of the way." Timmy got in his face.

Timmy knew his rights. They were talking to the lawyer of the year.

"Come on Michelle. She's sleep anyways. We'll come back in a few hours," her father told her.

Michelle shook her head and prepared herself to leave.

One girl that was recording had her phone all in Michelle's face. Michelle grabbed her phone and bashed it in the ground.

"What the fuck?" the girl said.

"Bitch, you shouldn't have had it in my face," Michelle barked. Now she was ready to fight. The girl walked off.

Everyone was outside. Terrance and Ciara got into his car and hauled off.

Timmy ran to Michelle. "You good?" he asked her.

"I'm fine. I'll call you later," she told him.

She caught up with her father. She looked back at Timmy and mouthed, "Thank you."

Timmy didn't want to be apart from her though. He wanted to be with her every second. He walked to his car with a thousand things going through his mind. How the fuck could he be feeling her this much and he had just met her? He had to talk to his mama, ASAP!

***

Timmy walked through the front door of his house as he talked on the phone with Terrance, ignoring Patrice's presence. They were both laughing and talking about Michelle's baby daddy. It actually felt good to release a little stress on him. It had been a while.

"Yeah. Ciara good? Alright, bet. I'll be back to the office in about an hour or two."

He hung up the phone and looked at Patrice, who was looking like a mad woman.

"Where have you been, Timmy?" she asked him.

"Who gave you that hickey?" he asked her.

"Are you fucking serious? You know you gave me that fucking hickey. Are you really going to accuse me of cheating?" she asked him.

"Girl, you better remember who the fuck you're talking to. We're not in the courtrooms and you can't get over on me how you do those folks. I'm not fucking stupid. Your ass is creeping and I'm not fucking with it. Don't question me about my whereabouts until you come clean about who you been cheating on me with."

He was already prepared to have this argument with her, but the more she tried to play on his intelligence, the more it pissed him off.

"I know you were with her." Tears fell from her cheek.

"With who?" Timmy asked as he played dumb.

"That assistant bitch. I know you're fucking her. Her cousin told me that y'all were at her graduation party and you were all in her fucking face."

Timmy laughed and waved her off. "Michelle? Nah man. She got a nigga."

"What does that mean? People can easily cheat."

"Oh, you know 'bout that cheating shit, huh?" Timmy laughed. He walked past her and went upstairs to their bathroom. He turned on the shower and prepared to take a shower that he needed. Patrice stripped and prepared to join him. Timmy sighed. He didn't feel like being bothered with her, not today.

"All the time your ass could've took a fucking shower and now you wanna come in here and nag me. Damn man."

Patrice ignored him. She pulled the shower door back and got in. He laughed and shook his head. They got into the shower together and she kissed him. Timmy was surprised that she was trying so hard to get his attention. Lately, she hadn't been doing anything to make sure her husband was satisfied in their marriage, but now that she knew Michelle was a threat, she had to do whatever it was that she needed, to make sure her husband wasn't going anywhere anytime soon. She grabbed his dick and massaged it up and down. She took her hand and traced over his six pack. He gripped her ass and planted a kiss on her neck.

"Turn around," he told her. She smiled and bit her lip.

She turned around and held the wall. She bent over and waited for him to enter her. Even though he wasn't Solem, she still wanted to put it on him so he could remember that marrying her wasn't a mistake.

He entered her and wanted to laugh. He hadn't had sex with her in a few weeks and she felt loose. Her pussy didn't grip his dick the way Michelle's did. Since he was horny and he wanted to hurry and get it over with, he fucked her hard while he grabbed her hair. She leaned back and moaned loud.

"Shit Timmy!" she yelled.

"You like it rough like that, huh?" he asked her.

No words were spoken, she just threw her ass back on him. Fucking her was starting to get boring, so he slowed down and played her.

"You're done?" she asked.

"Yeah."

She smiled like she had done something, but really she hadn't done shit. She washed him off and he was ready to run away from that house.

After dressing down in his Dolce and Gabbana grey and black suit, he brushed his wavy hair and put his grill in his mouth. Patrice stormed into the room.

"Timmy, what the hell is going on?" She turned on the TV, and there was his and Terrance's face and videos of them fighting, all over the news. He knew it was going to come to that but he wasn't worried. He giggled.

"What the fuck? That's not funny. What the hell were y'all at the children's hospital fighting like wild animals for?"

"Some shit went down," he said nonchalantly. She walked over to him.

"You have an image to uphold. You think it's okay for you to go around fighting and carrying on? That's not what's real babe."

"You ain't my mama, Patrice. Chill. I know all of that already." He grabbed his briefcase.

"When will you be back? I wanted to do dinner tonight."

"You'll have to do it alone tonight. I will be at the office a little late, and then I'll be having drinks with the guys at the bar tonight."

Patrice felt a little hurt. This was not like Timmy. She had to find a way to fix this. When he left, she grabbed her phone and called Solem.

"Hello?" he spoke into the phone.

"Hey babe. He just left for work."

Solem could hear the hurt in her voice and that pissed him off. He always told her that she didn't have to deal with that but since she was in love with her husband, she stuck it out.

***

Two weeks later, Michelle was back at her desk and ready to work until she couldn't anymore. The fact that Briana was strong and in a good spirit made her feel really good. Timmy and her had been spending a lot of time together whenever they could. Timmy was really attracted to her and he wanted her to himself.

Michelle set up two meetings for Terrance and Timmy. They had been real busy since the videos of them fighting in the hospital went viral. Instead of that putting a strain on their business, a lot of people had been coming to them for them to work for them in the court. Michelle answered her office phone.

"Where's my husband?" Patrice snapped.

Michelle laughed and transferred her call. Patrice was pathetic in her eyes and she wasn't a threat to Michelle.

Ciara walked into the office with Terrance following her. She had a frown on her face and all Michelle could do was shake her head.

"She disrespected me. Period!" Ciara yelled.

Two clients that Terrance was waiting on were staring at them. Ciara was loud as always. Terrance just laughed and shook his head.

"You think it's fucking funny. But, I don't."

"Ciara, you're loud!" Michelle told her.

She sighed and walked over to Michelle's desk. She was ready to go off but Michelle stopped her.

"Let me send this last email and then we can go for lunch," Michelle told her.

"Okay," Ciara said.

Ciara was playing on her phone. She wanted to call her mother because she hadn't talked to her since all of that went down at the hospital, but she wasn't about to apologize for being honest. She honestly didn't have time to be kissing her mama's ass.

Michelle and Ciara both looked up at the same time when they saw Patrice step in with food in her hand. She looked nice. She was dress in a fusion pink Bodycon dress that showed off her perfectly shaped body. On her feet where a pair of gold Giuseppe stilettos. She was for sure rocking her outfit. She looked at Michelle and rolled her eyes. Michelle giggled. She sat in the chair close to the exit door.

"Can you page my husband for me, please?" she asked Michelle.

"Tuh," Ciara mumbled.

"Am I missing something?" Patrice asked Ciara.

"Girl, find you somebody to play with it," Ciara told her.

Patrice laughed and covered her mouth. "A hot ass mess," Patrice said under her breath.

"I've heard that's what your husband thinks of you." Ciara smiled.

Michelle's mouth hung open and that for sure hurt Patrice's feelings. She didn't have anything else to say to her.

"Cut it out, Ciara. Let's go," Michelle told her best friend.

She didn't want Patrice to say the wrong thing to Ciara because she knew that Ciara would slap her and not think twice.

Timmy came out of his office. Michelle licked her lips at him, not caring that Patrice was standing right there looking at him.

Patrice walked over to her husband and slipped her tongue in his mouth. Michelle wouldn't have felt disrespected if Timmy wouldn't have kissed her back, but he did. Michelle was pissed off and she needed a breath of fresh air. Ciara knew her friend was mad, but neither of them showed that they were pressed about the situation.

"How long will you be gone, Michelle?" Timmy asked her.

"An hour," she told him.

"Bet."

When Ciara and Michelle were out the door, he pulled Patrice in the first conference room and snapped.

"Why didn't you call me before you came?" he asked her.

"Since when have I ever had to call before I came here Timmy? What wife has to call their husband and ask for permission to bring them lunch?" Tears fell from her eyes.

He shook his head. "I'm not fucking her so stop with your fucking insecurities. That shit is turning me the fuck off," he snapped.

"I saw the way she licked her lips at you. Did you fuck that bitch Tim?"

"No," He lied.

She shoved the bag of food that she brought him in his chest and walked away. Timmy wasn't going to stop her either because he didn't want to be bothered with her ass in the first place. He pulled out his phone and texted Michelle.

Timmy: Sorry
Michelle: Fuck you!!!!!!!!!

He laughed and put his phone in his pocket. He went back to his office to finish his meeting with Bishop and

Carmelo. They had exactly two weeks until Carmelo had to make his choice on whether he wanted to take a two years mandatory prison sentence or take it trial where he wouldn't have to do any time, no probation, or no house arrest.

"So, what you wanna do, Carmelo?" Timmy asked him.

Carmelo looked at his father then looked back at Timmy.

"You said we can win this shit, right?" Carmelo asked Timmy.

"We can but you also have to be prepared. Right now, we see nothing they have on you to dry and lock you up, so you're good. We just have to keep the faith that we have right now."

Bishop nodded his head. Bishop had already had a talk with Timmy and Timmy assured him that he and Terrance would beat the case. Bishop just wanted his son to sweat. Carmelo was a busy man and he didn't think before he did some of the things that he was sitting in that office for. Bishop hated that he wasn't a thinker, so when this came about, he figured this could be a way to slow his son down.

"Let's take it to trial, man."

"Alright. Let's go! Two months, man!" He shook Bishop and Carmelo's hand.

They left and he took that time to go and sit at Michelle's desk. Terrance came out of his office. He shook his head. Both of them seemed to be having a rough day.

"Why you looking ugly nigga and why you sitting at Michelle's desk?" Terrance asked him.

"Patrice's dumb ass came up here and started some shit. She fucking kissed me in front of Michelle, now she's pissed." Terrance fell out laughing.

"Aww man. That's some funny ass shit. You're on punishment with your girlfriend because of your wife?" He laughed harder.

Timmy laughed with him. "Shut your dumb ass up man. She told me fuck me and everything, man."

Terrance shook his head. "Well, my mama hate Ciara," Terrance said.

It was Timmy's turn to laugh. "How did I know it was going to be like that?" Timmy asked.

Terrance's mother was one of those women who wanted to pick the way her son lived his life. Terrance was always a mama's boy but his mama was not about to ruin what he had with Ciara. He was feeling her and that's all that mattered to him.

"Man, when Ciara told her that she stayed in the hood, she almost had a fit. I was mad as fuck." He shook his head.

"Cat need to chill out. You're a man now."

Michelle and Ciara walked through the door laughing and talking. Terrance and Timmy looked at each other and smiled. Timmy went to Michelle and tried to kiss her.

"Tim, I wish you would try me like that." Michelle rolled her eyes.

"Bae, it wasn't my fault. She caught me off guard and I didn't want to cause a scene in here in front of the clients," Timmy explained to her. He wasn't lying. She really had caught him off guard.

"Yeah, whatever." Michelle sat at her desk.

"Your mama is evil as hell. I can't deal with that shit Terrance," Ciara went off on him.

"She'll come around Cici."

It was quite funny to Michelle and Ciara how both men were trying to get out of the dog house. They were going to make sure their asses begged their way back into their good graces.

Chapter Six

Charles hopped out of his truck and shook his head. When he saw Shara sitting on his porch, he couldn't do anything but make himself believe that this chick was stone crazy. He had told her if she came back around him, it was going to be consequences, but he guess he had to show her better than he could tell her. He went into the backseat of his truck and grabbed the few grocery bags that he had. He walked on the porch and she stood to her feet.

"I thought I told you not to come over here?" He looked at her.

She looked pretty pitiful but he didn't give a damn. Shara was only there to share her happiness of the baby that they were having together. Last week they had a good week together, but that was only because he needed someone and she was the only one that was willing to give him the attention that he needed.

"You say that all the time and don't mean it," Shara said to him.

"Well, I meant it that time."

He opened the door and they both walked into the house. Charles was so frustrated and aggravated. To know that Michelle was fucking with that nigga made his blood boil every time he thought about it. She changed all of her numbers, and she even had Briana's number changed. Charles was still patched and bruised up from where Terrance and Timmy had beat his ass, so of course, he was still mad about that as well.

Charles put the food up in the refrigerator. He turned around and Shara was standing there in his face.

"You can't fucking comprehend? Leave!" he yelled at her.

She started to cry. "You're all I got at this point. My mama and no one wants anything to do with me right now," she cried.

He waved her off and walked upstairs. Again, she followed him. He went into his room and kicked off his work boots.

"I'm keeping the baby, Charles."

When she said that, his mind went blank. He snatched her up by her hair and pushed her to the ground.

"You keeping what!?" He hit her in the head.

"Charles stop! You're hurting me!" she cried

He pulled her to the hallway by her legs. She screamed and kicked.

"Stand up!" he told her.

She cried hard. She was scared. It was times when Charles got upset and would slap her around, but he never did anything like that before.

"Please Charles! Please! I'm pregnant!" She crawled.

"Do what the fuck I say!" he yelled to her.

He was going to show her not to fuck with him. He was tired of dealing with her and her shit. When she stood up, he pushed her down the fifteen stairs. His heart stopped when he realized what he had done.

"Oh shit! Shara!" He ran down the stairs.

She was unconscious and the back of her head was bleeding, but she still had a pulse. Charles fucked the house up and made it look like the place had been robbed. He checked her pulse one last time before dialing 911.

"Someone is dying, man. Hurry," he said before he hung up the phone.

He jumped into his car and left. He hit his head numerous of times as he realized that he fucked up. He just hoped and prayed that the shit wouldn't fall back on him. Hopefully, Shara wouldn't snitch on him. The only person he could call on was his homie Young. He needed to hide out until shit blew over.

***

Timmy held the door open for Michelle while she walked in. They were taking a tour around the new *Neighborhood Ralph Apartments* complex. The apartments had been under construction for two years, and they were well worth the wait. The apartments were beautiful. They looked like condos to Michelle. They walked around the apartment building and admired all the work that had been put into the place.

"Man, whoever owns these apartments is really blessed. I bet people can't wait to move in. I gotta tell Ciara about these, so her ass can leave the hood," Michelle complimented.

"Yeah, they are nice huh? You think Ciara would want to live out here?" Timmy asked her.

"Hell yeah, she would," Michelle said excitedly.

Timmy nodded his head. They walked towards the office and Timmy held the door open for her to go in first.

"We're closed!" The thick white woman said as she popped her gum. She wasn't the average type of white girl. She was actually bad. She had her hair cut into a feathered bob and her face were beat for the gods. From the look of her eyes, Timmy could tell that she had been smoking on some loud.

"What's your name miss?" Timmy asked her.

"Samantha."

"I'm Timmy Ralph. The owner of these apartments," Timmy told her.

Both Samantha and Michelle were shocked.

"Oh my God Mr. Ralph! I am so sorry!" Samantha said.

"It's all good ma. You're doing your job, but please spit out that gum. That's not professional and that's definitely not how you handle business." He winked at her.

She spat the gum out and smiled. "Is this your wife?" Samantha asked as she pointed at Michelle.

"Soon to be," he told her.

Michelle wanted to smile, but she didn't know how she felt about that. Here she was, out with a married man. She hoped and prayed that Samantha didn't ask any more questions about his real wife.

"She's pretty." Samantha smiled.

"Thank you, but I'm just his assistant." Michelle smiled back.

"Yeah, whatever." Timmy waved her off.

Seconds later, the door opened and a tall light skin man walked in. Michelle looked at Timmy then looked at the man twice, and she could tell that they were related. Michelle couldn't lie though; the dude was more than handsome. He was dressed professionally and he even rocked his bottom grill how Timmy rocked his. He had a fade like the rapper *Lil Boosie* and it looked right on him.

"What's good my brother?" Timmy slapped hands with him.

"Ain't shit man. You met Samantha, huh?" He smirked at her.

"Yeah, I met her. That's you?" he asked his brother.

Samantha stood to the side with a smirk on her face. They were definitely fucking and it didn't take a blind man to see it.

"We'll talk." Timmy nodded his head.

"This is Michelle. Michelle, this is my little brother Silence."

Michelle smiled and shook his hand. "It's nice to meet you Silence."

"Nice to meet you too, beautiful. You haven't taken my brother away from Ms. Piggy yet?" Everyone fell out laughing, but Michelle couldn't believe that Silence felt comfortable enough to disrespect Timmy's wife like that.

"That is not funny. Y'all need to cut it out," Michelle said to them.

"Chill man. He's just being goofy." Timmy kissed her cheek.

"Let me holler at you in the back," Silence said to his brother. He needed to run a few things by him and he also wanted to see where his head was with his phony ass wife.

They walked to the back where his office was set up and Timmy took a seat. Timmy invested into the apartments because on that side of town, it looked a mess. He wanted to give back to the community so he had the apartments built. They would be for people with low-income. They grew up on Portland Street and back in the days, the place didn't look half as bad as it did now. Timmy and Silence were their parents only two kids, and they never went without. Their mother, Reece, was a teacher and their father was a doctor. Timmy and Silence always hung with the kids from the hood. That's how he and Terrance became so close. Timmy never had to live the life he did when he got into the drug business but because he was so down for his boy, Terrance, that's what he did to make his nigga feel comfortable about his life. When Timmy's parents found out that he was dealing drugs, they almost had a fit, but they never turned their back on him. After all, Timmy was a man and he didn't want to continue to live from his parents' handouts, so he went and got it on his own. It made his parents extremely proud when he went to school, got his degree, started his law firm, and became successful. It made them even happier that he wanted to give back to their community. Even though his mother was originally from Dubai, Boston was always considered her second home.

Timmy didn't have the time to look over the apartments because he was too busy being the great lawyer that he was, so he put his brother in charge of everything. Silence had moved back to Dubai with his parents, but he enjoyed Boston. It was just original and more down to earth.

"You feeling her huh bruh?" Silence asked his brother.

"Yep, and as soon as I get rid of Patrice's ass, I can have her the way that I need to have her."

"So, you're really gone leave her?"

"Yeah, I'm leaving her ass. She's been cheating on me and I'm not even happy with her. I'm still young and I still have time to walk away from her ass."

Silence reached across the desk and slapped his brother's hand. Silence was happy that Timmy had finally started to see everything that everyone had been trying to tell him. Patrice meant Timmy no good and he deserved better than her.

"What's up with you and snow bunny? You fucked her before you hired her?" Silence chuckled.

"I like her little white ass, but nah, I fucked her after I hired her."

Timmy shook his head. His baby brother always been wild. "Be careful man. Those white chicks almost crazier than the black girls from the hood once you give 'em that good dick."

Silence laughed. If only his brother knew that Samantha had already bust his windows out and flattened all his tires before, he would be clowning him. Silence was the weird one though. It was something about a crazy ass woman that he loved.

"I'll see you tomorrow. Be on time at the airport nigga," Silence said as he hugged his brother.

The two of them were flying to Dubai for their parents' anniversary. He hadn't asked Michelle if she wanted to go, but he was going to and he was hoping she would say yes. His mother hated Patrice so to see another woman around would probably make her happy, so he thought.

***

Patrice laid in the bed and sobbed. The last three weeks of her life had been absolutely terrible, and she hated it so much. She had been losing all of her cases in court, her husband wasn't worried about her ass, and she felt alone. Even Solem was starting to get on her nerves and that wasn't usual. Timmy had left and went to Dubai that morning, and he didn't even care to ask her if she wanted to join him. It was true that his mother hated Patrice but it was the thought that counted. Patrice wasn't one hundred percent sure but she had a gut feeling that Timmy took that bitch Michelle with him. Just the thought of it pissed Patrice off. It was fine that Timmy wanted to be slick though. She was popping up in Dubai on his ass and she was ready for whatever.

Solem called her phone and she rolled her eyes to the back of her head. She just wanted everyone to get the picture and understand that she wasn't in the mood to be bothered. Her sister and her mama had been calling her, but she'd ignore them too.

"Yes?" she spoke into the phone.

"What's wrong babe?" Solem asked.

Sometimes, he was just too damn nice. That's what the problem was, he was too nice and sometimes, way too sensitive.

"I'm depressed," she said truthfully.

"He did something to you?"

"Left me in America while he went to Dubai to have a good time with that bitch," she snapped. The tears fell from her eyes again. She knew that Solem would feel some type of way about the way that she had been feeling about her husband lately, but she didn't care.

"Well, I'm here and we can leave America and go have some fun if you want to."

"I don't want to," she said.

"Okay well, can I come and see you?" he asked.

"Sure."

She hung up the phone and went to the shower. She got in and cried her eyes out. Once she was done washing herself off, she got out and got back into the bed naked. She didn't even have the strength to rub her body down with some lotion.

Solem came in less than thirty minutes. He was knocking like he was the police and that made her super nervous. She stormed to the door and snatched it open. She was so caught up in her own world that she didn't even notice that it was storming outside. He held his jacket over his head and Patrice stared at his swollen handsome body.

"Are you going to stand there or let me in?" She shook her head and stepped to the side and allowed him to walk into the house. He snatched his wet shirt off and threw it on the floor. His muscles were flexing and it made Patrice's pussy ache. She wanted him in the worse way, and right now was the time for some of that good love making he would always put down on her.

He stepped close to her and kissed her neck. Then, he sucked it. Patrice tried pushing him back but he wouldn't let up off of her. She didn't fight it any longer. She threw her head back and allowed him to do him. He picked her up and took her to the master bedroom. Did she care that she was fucking another man in her husband's bed? No! Did she regret falling for Solem? No! At that moment, nothing mattered to her. She just wanted to feel better.

Timmy sat in the Massachusetts General Hospital and smiled at his phone. Patrice was so stupid; she didn't even know that he had surveillance cameras installed around the entire house. He knew he couldn't trust that bitch and what he was seeing was confirmation. As much as he wanted to be upset with her, he wasn't because he didn't give a damn about her. He was keeping everything for when he would take her before a judge for a divorce. He handed the phone to his brother. Silence's skin turned red.

"Hell nah, man!" he said, almost yelling. Everyone looked at them.

Timmy shook his head. He should've knew that was a bad idea. Michelle's family looked at them with confusion written across their faces.

"Sorry about that y'all," Timmy apologized for his brother's rudeness.

Michelle stood on the side and rubbed her auntie Sally's back. Instead of them leaving that morning for Dubai, Michelle got a call that her cousin had been pushed down the stairs at Charles' house. Instead of Michelle hating her cousin for what she did to her, she was there for her because she felt her pain. Luckily, Shara made it out alive. She had a broken left leg, but that was it. She didn't even lose the baby that was inside of her. She was extremely blessed because she could've been paralyzed for the rest of her life and childless. The only person who knew about her being pregnant was her mother and deep down inside, Sally was devastated and embarrassed.

Shirley stood on the side of her daughter and her sister, assuring them both that everything was going to be okay. Sami was upset. She was upset because Shara was actually trying to cover for Charles and say that he wasn't the one who pushed her down the stairs. She said that it was a home invasion but everyone knew better than that. It was nothing they could do, though. Without her word, the police could only go by what she told them. She was that in love with him.

Sami walked into the room and walked right back out. She couldn't deal. She couldn't believe her sister was so stupid for a nigga. Her cousin's baby daddy at that. All of that shit was too crazy for Sami to process.

"I need to go mama. Your daughter is crazy." Sally shook her head because that was the truth. Shara was crazy.

"Let me go and talk to her, auntie," Michelle spoke up.

"Baby, I don't think that's a good idea. Let her rest," Shirley said.

"I agree with your mama," Timmy interfered.

Shirley cut her eye at the two of them. She still hadn't got around to asking her daughter what the hell was going on with them because it was so much going on, but she was going to get to the bottom of it.

"I'm not going to argue with her. I just want to check on my cousin," she told them.

"Its fine y'all. Let her go in. Shara owe her so many explanations," Sally said.

Michelle got up and walked towards Shara's room. She took a deep breath and pushed the door to Shara's room.

"Please leave," Shara said.

"I'm not here to argue with you or start anything. I just wanted to talk to you, Shara."

Michelle really felt bad for her. She always knew there was something wrong with Shara mentally, but she just wanted to see exactly where her head was.

"You should really have him arrested. You could be dead right now, Shara."

Shara began to cry. "I can't have him arrested. He has to be here for our baby."

Michelle was taken back on what she had just heard. She wasn't prepared for that.

"What baby?" Michelle's voice cracked.

"I'm pregnant with his baby, Michelle."

Michelle bit her bottom lip as tears filled her eyes. She shook her head from side to side because she didn't want to believe that it was true.

"Why though?" Michelle asked her.

"Because! We're in love and he wanted a fucking baby. That's why! Just leave me alone. You will never understand, Michelle."

Tears fell from Michelle's eyes. She got up to walk away. She looked back before she walked out of the door.

"He should've killed your ass, but I'm sure he'll do that later."

She went back into the waiting room. Tears where falling from her eyes. To say that she was hurt was an understatement. She was broken. She didn't understand what she had done so wrong to deserve all the things that had been happening in her life.

"Baby, what's wrong?" Shirley rushed to her daughter.

"Shara's pregnant with Charles' child."

"WHAT!" Shirley turned to her sister, who had her head down.

"Tell me you didn't know, Sally," Shirley pleaded.

"I just found out today," Sally said sadly.

"Let me just go. This too much." Shirley grabbed her purse. Sally looked sad. The last thing she wanted was for her big sister to be mad at her. This wasn't her fault.

"Don't be mad at auntie, mama. This is nobody's fault but Shara's. I don't even care about Charles, but damn, she's my first cousin. That hurts. I'll get over it though."

Everyone stared at a sad, embarrassed Michelle. She just wanted to lay down.

"Come on Tim, let's go."

***

After flying for twelve long hours, they had finally arrived in Dubai. It felt so good to be so far away from home for the first time. Michelle had never been outside of America, so all of this was new to her. It felt weird that they were in a different time zone. It was 6 o'clock AM back in Boston, and it was 3 o'clock PM in Dubai. That was something that Michelle had to get used to. When they stepped off the plane, Michelle was in complete awe. She had never in her life saw a place so beautiful. The airport was huge and outstanding.

"Wow. This place is so beautiful," Michelle spoke up.

She was happy and that made Timmy happy. He walked her around.

"This is home," Timmy said to her.

"And why did y'all move to America again?"

She, Timmy, and Silence shared a laugh but she was serious. She wanted to know why they would leave a place so big and beautiful.

"Ya mama!" Timmy's mother ran and kissed him all over his cheek. At that moment, it felt like it was just her and her son. She missed Timmy so much and to have him home for just a few days made her cry tears of joy. Even at thirty-three, Timmy was still her boy. Her sons would never grow in her eyes. They were just boys with their own businesses. Michelle smiled and admired how they took each other in.

"Laquad ghab ya abn! (I've missed you, son)" she cried.

"Almashaeir hi' amah almutabadal. (Feelings are mutual ma.)"

Michelle felt out of place at the moment. She had no idea what the hell they were saying to each other, but she did know that they were speaking in Arabic. Silence laughed at Michelle because she looked confused.

"Hey ma! I've missed you!" Silence hugged his mother.

Why couldn't Timmy's ass just speak English? Michelle thought to herself.

Their mother walked up to Michelle and grabbed her hand. She smiled at Michelle then kissed the top of her hand.

"Beautiful girl you are." She smiled. "Just call me mama, Reece, or ma. Whatever you decide."

"I'm Michelle."

They continued to chat while the guys grabbed their bags. On the way to their parents' home, Reece talked the entire forty-minute drive. Timmy and Silence wanted her to hush up but Michelle was loving the conversation. Michelle had already learned that Reece was a cool woman. She was enjoying her company and she made her feel welcomed. Michelle couldn't lie though. She wanted to know how she felt about a woman showing up with a married man. Michelle was still beating herself up about this. What was supposed to be a one-night stand turned into something totally different. When Timmy pulled into *Bromellia Villas,* Michelle's mouth dropped open. She just knew that wasn't their home.

"Close your mouth," Timmy teased her and they all laughed.

"Wow. This is so beautiful, man. I have to take pictures and send them to my baby. She'd love to stay here," Michelle said.

"You should've brought her with you," Reece said.

Michelle didn't want to talk about her daughter. She did, but she didn't want to have to bring up all the terrible things that had been going on with her daughter's health. Right then, she just wanted to feel stress free and enjoy her getaway.

"We're going to bring her back when we come back in a few months," Timmy told his mother. Reece nodded her head. They got out and unpacked the bags.

The residence was so beautiful; Michelle took a thousand pictures. The garden around the front was stunning with all types of flowers. Sitting in the middle of the yard was a beautiful plunge pool. They walked to the backyard and there was a beautiful swimming pool with a spa. There was also a vegetable garden. The place was everything.

"Ms. Reece, this is so amazing. This is a dream home."

"Thank you! My husband and I worked damn hard for it."

The inside was more beautiful. The décor was very different, but it was catchy. The six bedroom 5 ½ bath home was so big and nice. Michelle was beyond tired and she needed a nap. She went into the room that Reece allowed her to pick and laid across the huge bed. The bed was so comfortable. It almost felt like she was lying on clouds.

She was going to call her daughter to check on her but she had to remind herself that it was still early morning in Boston.

Meanwhile, while Michelle was upstairs taking a much needed nap, Reece caught up with her two sons. They hadn't been in the house for a whole hour and she was already pulling things down to cook for them.

"Don't think I'm gone let you slide with bringing a girl here Timmy." Reece cut her eye at him.

Silence giggled.

"Just because I can't stand Patrice's ass doesn't mean that cheating is allowed. You weren't raised that way. I told you in the beginning that marrying that girl wasn't the right decision and you didn't listen to me."

"He ain't listen to me either, ma," Silence interfered.

"Nigga, shut up!"

"I do like her though. She seems like a really good woman. She's down to earth," she said, as she referred to Michelle.

"I'm in love with her," Timmy said honestly.

The room grew quiet, but he didn't care. That's just how he felt.

"When are you divorcing Patrice?" Reece looked into her son's eyes.

"As soon as I get home, I'll have those papers ready for her."

Reece shook her head. She knew things were about to get ugly. She was probably going to go back to Boston with them.

While Reece prepared dinner, Timmy slipped upstairs to go and find Michelle. He crept into the room and noticed that she was sleeping so peacefully. She had to be tired because she still had on her shoes in the bed. He took them off of her and gently massaged her toes. She smiled and moved around.

"Your mama gone get you for being up here." Michelle smirked.

He playfully mushed her.

"I'm a grown ass man. My mama can't get shit."

He slid behind her and planted kisses on her neck. Michelle immediately got wet. He took his hand and rubbed her pussy through her tights. He could tell that she was damp.

"Let me eat that pussy," he whispered in her ear.

Just hearing his sexy voice say that made her want him in the worse way. He roughly ripped the center of her tights and kissed her pussy through her pink lace panties. He slid her panties to the side and sucked on her clit. He flicked his tongue back and forth and that took her over the edge.

"Shit... Timmy!" she cried.

She grabbed one of the pillows and covered her face. The way that he was eating her, there was no way she would be able to be quiet through all of that.

He stuck his tongue inside her hole and down to her ass crack. "How that feel?" he asked her.

She couldn't say anything. She felt herself about to cum... hard... she squirted in his face, but that didn't stop him. He continued to eat her until she was done letting loose. He freed himself from his pants, and his dick was stiff and waiting for her. The veins that were sticking out made Michelle's mouth water. She spread her legs wide as he entered her slowly. She scratched his back and bit his bottom lip. Her pussy gripped his dick like a tight glove. He had never felt something so good and wet before in his life.

"This my pussy." He sucked on her ear. "You hear me, Michelle?"

"Yes," she whispered.

Tears filled her eyes as she came hard. It felt so good to her. He continued to pound her spot and she felt herself coming again.

He laid back and allowed Michelle to sit down on his face. She rode his tongue like she was riding his dick, and when he stuck his tongue in and out of her, that made her go crazy. She lowered herself onto him and rode his entire dick. It hurt so badly, but it felt so good. She needed this. They shared passionate kisses. They were in love with each other. Timmy pumped in and out of her and released all of seeds in her. He didn't care if she got pregnant. He didn't care about nothing but the two of them.

Michelle was at a loss for words. It seemed like every time they had sex, it got even better. He made her feel ways that she never knew about. She was on Pluto when she was having sex with Timmy. He took his time with her body, and she loved it. He kissed her.

"That's what you call real nigga dick," Timmy said to her.

She burst out and laughed.

"Play time is over guys! Come downstairs and eat!" Timmy and Michelle looked at each other and laughed loud. Timmy had totally forgot that they had intercoms all over the house. Michelle was embarrassed. Reece knew what they were doing.

The two of them took a shower and changed into comfortable attire. Michelle acted busy. She didn't want to go downstairs and face Reece.

"Might as well come on. She knows." Timmy laughed.

"Shut up."

They walked downstairs and the table was set up perfectly. Reece was walking around humming and sipping on her red wine. She seemed to be in a happy place. Michelle couldn't wait until she got to that point in her life, where she could be married, stress free, and just happy.

"Y'all heifers ain't slick. Y'all was gone for too long," Reece said.

Timmy laughed, but Michelle didn't budge. She wondered was Reece judging her.

In Michelle's eyes, Reece was the most beautiful Arabian she ever saw before in her life. Her skin was so smooth and beautiful. She had Chinese like squinty eyes and they were dark grey. Timmy looked just like his mother. Even though her hair was wrapped up, she knew she had a lot of hair. You could see her thick curvaceous thighs through her skirt. She had big breast too, and they sat up perfectly.

"No need to be shame, chile." She winked at Michelle and handed her a glass of wine. That made her feel a little better.

On the table was baked salmon, white rice, steamed broccoli, and black beans. It was Timmy's favorite meal. She also had made Silence a strawberry cheesecake. They all sat at the table and begin to eat. The conversation they were having was the bomb. Michelle felt like she knew all of them her entire life.

Chapter Seven

Timmy left his mother and Michelle downstairs in the living room. They were almost drunk, but they were definitely having a good time together. He needed to call Terrance and make sure that everything was good at the firm.

"What's good nigga?" Terrance spoke into the phone.

"Ain't shit, man. What's going on? Everything good?"

"Everything is good. Your crazy ass wife came up here and tried to go into your office, told me you told her to come up there and get some information out your computer for one of your cases." Timmy fell out laughing. Patrice really tried it and she should've known that she wasn't going to be able to pull game on Terrance.

"She wild man. But check this out, I'm about to send you a video, but make sure you delete it right afterwards."

"I got you bro."

"Bet."

He hung up the phone and sent Terrance the video he had of Patrice fucking the P.O. that they knew in their home. Attached to the video was a message: *I'ma eat that bitch alive in court.*

Seconds later, Terrance was calling back.

"What the fuck? That's the P.O. that all the young cats hate. She's fucking that nigga in your house, man? What the fuck?" Terrance was pissed, but Timmy wasn't. He refused to let a bitch get under his skin and right now, Patrice wasn't even that bitch. He was going to simply kill her the right way.

"Yeah, she's a sneaky little bitch," Timmy said.

"I never liked that bitch. I told you that."

"Yeah, I know. But just sit back and watch how this play out. I'ma smart man, nigga. Remember that."

"What we gone do about that P.O. though?"

Even though Terrance and Timmy's hands were clean from that other life, they still had people on their team that was ready for whatever. All they had to do was say the word to Bishop and he would have that nigga knocked off, but Timmy needed to think everything through first. He knew for a fact that he was going to make their lives miserable though. They had fucked with the wrong nigga.

"We'll talk about that later man." Timmy wouldn't dare talk over the phone.

"True. How's ma doing?"

"She good. She loves Michelle."

"Don't we all?" They both laughed.

"Get off my phone, nigga."

"Aye but on the real, tell Michelle to talk to Ciara. She's been giving me her ass to kiss again and I'm close to slapping her ass one good time."

Timmy smirked and shook his head. If he didn't know any better, he would've swore that they had been together for years.

"I got you."

"Alright nigga. Stay up."

"One."

He hung up the phone and got dressed. He threw a simple white t-shirt over his head along with some dark grey sweat pants. On his feet were some simple orange and grey kicks. He was headed to the hospital to visit his father and take him the dinner that his mother had prepared.

Their father, Serri, was a busy man. His schedule was always crazy, due to him being an orthopedic surgeon. Years ago, Serri was a traveling doctor when they were living in America, but he had been working for *American Hospital Dubai* for the last five years. He was a successful doctor and he was a multi-millionaire. No matter how busy Serri was, Reece loved her husband more than anything. He was a faithful man and he worked to make sure that his family was solid. She never got aggravated because when he wasn't working, he always made sure that all his free time went to her. She simply respected her husband's hustle. Being married for thirty-five years meant everything to Reece and Serri. Everyone admired their bond.

He walked downstairs and the ladies were lost in conversation. He went and kissed his mother on the forehead and pecked Michelle on the lips. Michelle was tipsy as hell, so she laughed and covered her mouth. Timmy continued to embarrass her.

"Y'all full of sins," Reece told them.

"We were born full of sins, mama."

"I put your father's food in the microwave. Tell him I love him."

"I will!"

Timmy grabbed the plate then left the house. When he got into the hospital, the ladies eyed him down and whispered in each other's ear. They had never saw a man that looked so good before in their life. He was heaven sent and so many of them would love to suck the skin off of his dick. They never saw a man so built and tall in person before. Timmy walked to the front desk.

"I'm here for my father, Dr. Serri Ralph," he told the secretary.

She licked her lips and eyed him up and down. When she saw his dick through his sweats, she almost choked on her own spit. He was hanging and he wasn't even hard.

She paged Dr. Ralph and let him know that his son was here to see him.

"How old are you, sir?" the secretary asked.

"I'm a grown ass man. How old are you?"

"A grown ass woman who wants to get to know this grown ass man standing before me." She winked and Timmy laughed. He would never give her the time of day, only because she was trying too hard. Timmy liked to do the chasing. He couldn't stand women who thought it was cute to chase men.

Serri came from the back and couldn't believe that Timmy came. That was a big surprise. His mother never mentioned it. They hugged each other tight.

"I'm happy to see you, son! Damn man! This just made my day!"

"I'm happy to see you too, old man." He handed him his plate. "Ma told me to tell you she loved you too."

He smiled. "I love her too. Take a walk with me." Serri patted his son on the back.

They walked throughout the hospital and Serri introduced Timmy to some of the new doctors and nurses that were now a part of the team. Serri loved showing his kids off, and he always made sure they knew that his son was one of the most successful lawyers in Boston, Ma. They walked into his office and took a seat. Serri let out a heavy sigh.

"They're kicking your ass, huh?"

"Yeah man. I've been having so many operations these last few months, it's crazy." He shook his head. "What made you come home?"

"Came to celebrate y'all anniversary with y'all."

That made Serri happy. That was one of the best anniversary presents he could ever have.

"Pop. I need your help with something. I know this is illegal and all, but I honestly need your help."

Timmy had been debating on whether or not he wanted to get in other people's business, but seeing Michelle hurt the way she was hurting about Briana did something to him. He knew for a fact that his father could help Briana survive this cancer.

Serri got up and closed his door and locked it.

"What is it son?" He had his father's undivided attention.

He handed his father the papers he had in his hand the entire time. He had gone into some of Michelle's files and got some of Briana's medical papers. Since Michelle hated talking about the situation and wouldn't open up to him, he figured he could have his father look at a few things to see if there was any hope for Bri.

His father scanned over the papers carefully. "So, she's ten years old with bone cancer and lung cancer, and the doctors are saying she only has two years to live?" Serri asked Terrance.

He nodded his head yes.

"Don't sound right to me." Serri shrugged.

"What you mean?"

He took the X-ray pictures and placed it up in light. Then he took his son to school.

"You see this right here!" He pointed to the picture of her longs. "That right there is a simple blood clot.

There's absolutely no sign of cancer in her lungs." He then placed the other X-ray up to the light.

"Now, this one shows some cancer right there." He pointed to the X-ray.

"So, what you saying?" he asked her.

"I'm saying that whatever doctor she's seeing needs to be fucking fired. Simple as that. The cancer that's in her body can be taken out. It's not that serious, and she DO NOT have lung cancer."

"Damn," Timmy said under his breath.

"Is this the girl's baby your brother told me about?" his father asked him.

Timmy chuckled. Silence could never keep his mouth closed.

"Yeah, it's her daughter."

His father shook her head. "Caught up with two women, huh?"

"I'm divorcing Patrice," he told his father.

"GOOD! When?"

Timmy laughed loud. It was crazy that no one liked Patrice. He wished he would've listened to them in the beginning and he wouldn't be going through all of that bullshit, but sometimes you had to figure things out for yourself.

"Soon," was all Timmy said.

"When will I meet Michelle?"

"Damn, you know her name and all?"

Serri laughed.

"She's at the house now." Timmy smiled. It actually felt good to know that everyone was supporting him and not judging the fact that he was pretty much fucking around on his wife, but shit, she was fucking around on him too, so they were even.

"Well, I have a major surgery to do, so I won't be home until sometime tomorrow, but I'll tell you this. The little girl can be saved. Her cancer isn't that major."

Timmy was so happy to hear that. He knew that Michelle would curse him out for going into her things but he knew that she would be overjoyed with the news he was going to tell her.

"Can you help her?" he asked his father.

"With the consent of her mother, I can. I will do anything for you, son. Remember that."

Timmy stood to his feet and hugged his father.

"Thanks for everything, pops. I'ma get back to the house. Call me if you need anything."

"Your ass better be glad that you found someone because I was ready to put you on one of these fine ass honeys in here."

Timmy shook his head. "They're too thirsty in here."

His father laughed and waved him off.

***

"YOU DID WHAT!?" Michelle was ready to punch Timmy right in the face when he told her that he went through her paperwork. She was furious.

"Calm down, Michelle. The only reason why I went into your things was so that my father could look over everything. I wanted to know if he could help her."

Michelle didn't want to talk about that. Just that fast, she started to cry. She hated thinking about it. She knew that her baby was going to die soon and she couldn't accept it. She tried to put it to the back of her head that her baby had all this shit going on. She even stopped taking her to her doctor's appointments. She finally gave in and allowed her parents to step in.

"How can I trust you if you're going to go through my things? She's dying Timmy. That's all there is to it. She's going to die." Michelle cried.

"No baby. She's not going to die. Listen to me, I took her X-rays to my daddy and he looked everything over from her paper works from the beginning until now. Briana is fine! She doesn't even have cancer in her lungs, just a simple ass blood clot. She does have cancer in her bones, but my father even told me that it isn't anything major. He even told me that he can go in there and catch it before it does get worse. Those doctors that Bri have been going to don't know what the hell they're doing."

Michelle stopped crying and thought about everything that Timmy had just said. She wanted to believe it. She wanted to be happy. But, it sounded too good to be true.

"How does your father know?" Michelle asked.

Timmy looked at her and frowned. "Girl, google my daddy. He's one of the best orthopedics in the world."

Truth be told, Timmy felt a bit offended. He didn't want her to think he was feeding her any lies about something so serious. He trusted his father, just like every patient trusted him. His father was beyond smart and if he said that it was nothing to worry about, then it was nothing to worry about.

Timmy dialed his father's number and he was glad he caught him before he started on the surgery he had to do. After Michelle talked to him for half an hour, she was crying tears of joy and on her knees praying. She called her mother and father and told them the news. At first, they felt just like Michelle. They thought it was too good to be true but after she explained everything to them, they were shouting and praising the Lord over the phone. After talking to them, she called Ciara.

"Friend, please tell me you're not lying!" Ciara shouted into the phone.

"I'm not!"

Ciara began to cry and sob. She knew that God was going to work everything out for her niece. Even though she was mad with her mama, she hung up the phone with Michelle and called her to tell her the good news.

Now, all they needed to do was get Briana to Dubai, so he could start his operation.

***

Patrice stepped off the plane and smiled. It felt too good to be in Dubai. She hadn't heard from her husband in two days and she knew what that meant. He was with that bitch, but that was cool with her because she was ready to come and shut the party down. She knew that Reece hated her and at this point, she didn't give a damn. She was going to prove to them that she wasn't a weak bitch. They had forgot that she could get real hood. She was prepared to slap the shit out of Michelle too. What real woman slept around with a married man? She would always ask herself that. She knew that she wasn't going to be able to stay to Reece's house after what she was about to do, so she made sure to get a nice suite at the *Emirates Towers* hotel. She loaded her things into the trunk of the cab and she gave him Reece's address. When the cab driver pulled up, she sighed and got out. She had to admit that that Reece was a bad bitch. She was living lavish off of her husband and when she said lavish, that's what she meant.

"I won't be long." She handed the driver a one hundred dollar bill.

He smiled and nodded. She had on her tennis shoes, her leggings, and her comfortable t-shirt. She also had her hair wrapped around. She was going straight crazy when she saw that bitch, Michelle.

She rang the doorbell and then gently knocked on the door. She rolled her eyes when Silence opened the door.

"Oh, it's your ass," he said to her.

She welcomed herself into the house.

"Timmy! You're hoe down here! The crazy ass bitch done flew all the way out here to Dubai unannounced."

"No respect." Patrice shook her head.

"I don't have no respect for a hoe!" he told her.

Timmy came downstairs, followed by his mother. They were both shocked, but Timmy was more pissed than anything.

"Why the fuck are you here? Are you stupid or some shit?"

Timmy was beyond pissed because he never cursed in front of his mama. He respected her too much, but that bitch had tried it!

"Where's that bitch at? I know she's here!" Patrice yelled.

"You need to leave my house right now, Patrice," Reece said, while she allowed her heavy accent to flow. They knew that meant she was getting pissed.

She crossed her arms across her chest.

"Girl! Leave my mama's house!" Timmy grabbed her by her arm and pulled her towards the door. She started swinging and hitting him. "Where is she, Timmy Ralph? Tell that bitch to come out. You don't have to hide her for me." She continued to swing, but he held her arms. His blood was boiling and he was so close to slapping the fire out of her ass.

"Hiding her for you? Bitch, I'm not hiding shit! Michelle! Come downstairs!" he yelled.

Patrice almost had a heart attack when she saw Michelle walk out the room with a slight smirk on her face.

"Now. You see her. Go the fuck away."

She slapped him.

"You don't have but one more time to put your fucking hands on me and I swear to God, they gone be sending your hoe ass back cross seas in a body bag. Now, slap me again, Patrice," he dared her but she knew better. She knew he meant every word.

"How could you do this to me?" Patrice asked him

He laughed at her. "Stand right there," he told her. She did as she was told. He came back with his phone in his hand. He showed her the video of her fucking Solem in their home, in their bed, all over their master bedroom. She was stuck. She didn't have anything to say.

"Cat got your tongue?" Silence asked her.

"Let me see that!" Reece snatched the phone and couldn't believe what she was seeing.

"You little bitch!" Reece tried to go after her but Timmy held her back.

"I was good to you, but everyone was right about you. You're a hoe and you never meant me any good. When I come back, your ass better be ready to sign those divorce papers, or else I'm taking you down and you won't have shit."

Patrice tried to swing on him but this time, Michelle came over and put one good ass whooping on her. She pounced on Patrice and punched her in the face, her head, and she even stomped her. As much as Silence wanted to let her kill her, it was getting too bad. Timmy was still holding his wild mama back.

Patrice held her face. Michelle definitely whooped her ass for the old and the new. Once Patrice stood to her feet, Silence pushed her outside and locked the door.

"'Ann alkulbat alquadhira! (That filthy bitch)" Reece spat. She was so upset. So upset, she wanted Patrice dead.

***

A week had gone by and Charles still hadn't shown his face. Even though the police weren't looking for him, he knew that some of Shara's cousins would be. He had been laying low at his homie Young's house. Young was a real ass nigga and he looked out for Charles. He promised Charles that nothing would happen to him while he was with him. He had talked to his mother and learned that some big time doctor said that Briana wasn't dying. He was glad to hear that, but at this point in his life, he didn't care anymore. Hell, even Briana didn't deal with him anymore. He felt alone, so at this point, he didn't give a fuck. He had been talking to Shara and he learned that all she had was a broken leg. He was pissed when she told him that she didn't lose the baby though. He honestly didn't want to have another kid.

"Yo' bruh, come take a ride with me!" Young called out to Charles.

Charles put on a pair of all-black Forces with some black Levis and a black tank top. He hopped in Young's Audi and they cruised the city as they smoked several blunts.

"Where we riding to, bruh?" Charles asked Young.

"Nowhere. I just wanted you to get out that house. Your ass ain't even been wanting to sit on the porch with the rest of nigga. You scared of them niggas or something?"

"Fuck nah, I'm not scared of them niggas. I do love my life though." They giggled.

They pulled into the Gulf Express gas station, and the first person Charles noticed was the lawyer Terrance. His blood boiled as he thought back to how bad he and Timmy beat him in the hospital that day. Charles bit his bottom lip and balled up his fist.

"The fuck is your problem nigga?" Young asked Charles.

"You got your gun on you?" Charles asked him.

"Yeah, what you need with it?"

"Just give it to me."

Young put the .45 in Charles' hand. Charles figured this would be a perfect time to handle Terrance while his back was turned around, especially since there wasn't that many cars outside. Charles crept up behind Terrance while he was pumping gas in his 2015 beamer.

"Aye, nigga?" Charles said. Terrance turned around and before he could defend himself, Charles was beating him in the face with a pistol. He took the gun all the way back and beat him all across his face. Terrance was on the ground as he coughed up blood.

"Fuck ass nigga. You ain't too bad without your right hand man!" Charles yelled.

Young pulled him into the car and sped off.

"That's what the fuck I'm talking about nigga. You handled that shit." They slapped hands. Charles was proud of himself. He was happy he saw that nigga when he did.

***

Ciara sobbed as she looked at Terrance's face. Instead of him going to the hospital, he drove home. He called Ciara and she came right away. When she walked into the house, she could barely tell who he was. His face was swollen, bloody, and his eyes were shut. She cried uncontrollably.

"Babe, who did this?" Ciara cried.

"Your fuck ass brother." He laid back on the couch and rested his head. He had a migraine so crucial, he could've cried like a bitch.

Ciara covered her mouth. She was in disbelief.

"Call up to the office for me and tell Timmy I need him as soon as possible."

Ciara grabbed the phone and called. Michelle answered. "T&T Law Firm. Michelle speaking, how may I help you?"

Ciara cried into the phone and told Michelle everything that she was told. Timmy and her were on their way.

Ciara rushed into his bathroom and got alcohol, peroxide, wet rags, and bandages. She cried as she cleaned him up. His lips were big and swollen but to Ciara, he was still the most handsome guy she ever laid eyes on. She caressed his head.

"I'm sorry he did this bae." Ciara kissed him.

"Don't be," Terrance said nonchalantly. Ciara's heart hurt because deep down inside, she did love her brother, but she knew that he could kiss his life goodbye after what he had done.

When Timmy walked into the room, his skinned turn fire red. He bit on his bottom lip and punched the wall. They had fucked with the wrong nigga. It fucked with Timmy that he wasn't there to protect his brother. Terrance was fucked up pretty bad. As bad as Timmy hated to go back to his old ways, he was going to have to.

"That nigga a dead man walking," Timmy fumed.

Michelle didn't care at all, but she knew that Ciara did. She could tell from the way Ciara was looking.

"You okay, Ciara?" Michelle asked her best friend.

"Yes, I'm fine. He asked for it." Ciara shrugged. Michelle knew that she was only talking, but they would have to talk about that later. Minutes later, Timmy had called one of their personal nurses over to the house to tend to Terrance.

"He fucked him up pretty bad man, but I gave him some Hydro Vicodin. He's going to sleep half of the day, but when he wakes up, he's going to be in a little pain," the nurse informed Timmy. Jake had been on their team since they were in the streets slanging. Whenever something unprofessional went down and they needed medical assistance, they would call him and he'd be right there ready to fix shit up.

"I appreciate you man." Timmy dapped him down and handed him an envelope. Ciara and Michelle were sitting on the couch in silence. The two of them had so much on their minds until it wasn't even funny.

Timmy walked to Terrance's room and sat on the opposite side of the bed from him. He could tell that Terrance was uncomfortable from the way he was moving around in the bed.

"You alright man?" Timmy asked him.

"Sore as fuck, but I'll be good. I want that nigga dead though."

"That's already in play. I just need you to get right though. We have trial next week and you can't walk in that courtroom looking like that.

"Yeah, I know."

The doorbell rung and Timmy already knew who it was. It was Bishop and Carmelo. He went and opened the door for the two men, and Ciara's heart began to thump. She knew that they were there to discuss what was about to happen to her brother. Once they were in and seated, Ciara went into the room and climbed into bed with Terrance. She cried as she snuggled up under him. He pulled her close and held her. He knew why she was crying and Terrance never wanted to hurt Ciara's feelings, but her brother had crossed all lines and he had to get his, and that was just all to it.

After Timmy gave Bishop and Carmelo the full story, Bishop was already on it. After making a few phone calls, they had their whole plan into play. Charles had to go. As nice and easy going as Michelle was, she agreed to it. He had brought her nothing but heartache and pain, then to think that he got Shara pregnant just made her even angrier. The two men left and Michelle walked over to Timmy.

"I have your back through it all Tim." Michelle kissed him.

"I know and that's why I love you."

Michelle blushed. Right there, at that moment, Michelle didn't care that Timmy was still married to his wife. She was comfortable with knowing that she wasn't his side piece. In reality, he belonged to her. She woke up next to him, and she went to sleep next to him every day and night. The only thing that she hated was that she had to hide the relationship she was having with him from her parents. Timmy's parents were probably cool with him committing adultery, but her mother would knock her teeth out of her mouth. Shirley had asked Michelle one time was there anything going on between the two of them, and she swore that it wasn't. Of course, her mother believed her, but if she ever found out the truth, all hell was going to break loose. Michelle had got too far. She was too beautiful and too successful to be settling for a married man. Shirley always told her to be patient. Her dream man was going to come to her sooner or later, but Shirley didn't even know that she had her dream man. A married dream man.

***

Patrice sat in Solem's condo. She was so miserable, even worse now than she was before. She rocked back in forth in his chair as she thought of a master plan. It sickened her that she didn't think smart enough to not creep in the house. She had got way too comfortable with Timmy's good trusting spirit.

"Are you alright?" Solem asked her.

She stopped rocking and looked at him.

How could you be so stupid? Michelle thought to herself. Solem was getting on her last damn nerves. She only agreed to come over because he was willing to help her plot something to take Timmy down. Patrice questioned herself and asked how could she not do Timmy the way he had done her. She knew that he was cheating on her from the very beginning, but she was too busy doing her own dirt. She didn't have time to keep up with him. At the end of the day, she thought both of them were playing around. She knew that they were at a tough spot, so she did her and he did him, but she was never prepared to divorce him so soon. She was sick.

"I have an idea." Patrice stood to her feet.

"What is it?"

"Slap me as hard as you can right above the eye," she told him.

"What?" Solem looked at her like she was crazy.

"If you beat me, I can put it on him. I can make it seem like he's the one who beat me. I'll take it to the media and everything, and his life would be over in the blink of an eye."

Solem wasn't feeling it. Patrice was on some straight psychopath shit and he wanted no parts in it. He was going to go against it but when tears slid down her face, he kind of felt bad for her.

"You actually want me to hit on you? I'll hurt you. I don't think that's a good idea," Solem told her.

"Trust my word."

She stood in front of him and waited for him to slap her. She closed her eyes and balled her fist and took the painful slap to her face. Solem wasn't lying when he said that he would hurt her because that one slap made her beyond dizzy.

"Slap the other eye," she told him.

He slapped her left eye. It stung. Solem couldn't believe that he was doing that shit. He really loved her and would do anything, so if that meant showing her he loved her then that's what it was going to be. An hour later, Patrice was working with two swollen eyes, a busted lip, and a red print on her jaw. Since Timmy wanted to play with her, she was going to show him how to play. She got her phone and took pictures of her face. She got into her car and headed to WCVB news. She wanted the whole world to know what type of man Timmy really was.

Chapter Eight

Shirley, Luke, and Briana sat in the kitchen at the island with their mouths hung wide open. They had their TV on the channel five news and was listening to Patrice Ralph's story about her domestic violence relationship. There wasn't a word being said. What put the icing on the cake was when she announced that Timmy had been cheating on her with his assistant, Michelle. Shirley was hurt, pissed, and embarrassed, but for some reason, it didn't bother Luke at all. It was like he knew. Shirley turned off the TV and faced her husband, who focused on his newspaper and sipped his hot coffee. Shirley snatched the paper from him.

"Michelle has ruined a marriage, Luke!" Shirley said to her husband. "Briana, go to your room please."

"She don't have to go to her room because your ass done said a mouth full already, and my baby ain't ruined no marriage. Just like Timmy ain't put his hands on that damn girl. This is all bullshit." Luke was pissed.

"You saw the girl's face for yourself. He did and the second I get my hands on that daughter of yours, I'm going to knock some sense into her. I can't believe she would represent me like this." Shirley shook her head.

"Timmy isn't that kind of guy grandma," Briana said.

"What exactly do you know about knowing someone little girl? Hush up," Shirley told her. Briana giggled and put her headphones in her ear.

Shirley grabbed her phone and called Michelle, but of course, her phone was going to voicemail. This was way too much for Shirley to deal with. She grabbed her keys and left the house, leaving Briana and Luke behind.

***

Michelle and Timmy sat on her couch in total disbelief. Timmy couldn't express his feelings at the moment. He was hurt, mad, and he wanted to kill the bitch with his bare hands. He couldn't believe that she had went out her way to slander his name like that. He never touched her. Hell, he hadn't saw her since she came to Dubai and acted a fool. He didn't even go to the house because she was still there and he had a feeling that she was going to be on some dumb shit. He knew that he could get out of the situation with a clean face, but just knowing that she did that shit made him furious. Not only did she bash him, but she put Michelle's name in it as well.

Michelle was so mad that she had tears in her eyes. She knew that her mother knew and it was about to be some shit.

"Did you do it, Timmy?" Michelle looked at him.

He stood to his feet and frowned his face. "Are you really asking me that fucking question?"

"Yes. How did she get like that? She's fucked up pretty badly, Timmy."

Michelle loved Timmy and that wasn't a secret, but she had only known him for two months. She fell for him quick; she felt like she knew him but at this point, she didn't know. She knew that Patrice could be a bitch but putting his hands on her like that wouldn't sit well with her.

"I didn't touch that crazy ass bitch. How have I when I've been in your ass every day, all day? I haven't saw her since Dubai. I don't know who whooped her ass but I didn't."

Michelle shook her head. "The media knows about us. I'm gonna be considered a homewrecker."

"Fuck the media! I wasn't happy before we started dealing with each other. You don't have to explain shit because what I'm going to do will solve all of this."

He got up and put on his clothes. The both of them were still naked from when they had been fucking all morning.

"What are you going to do?" she asked him.

"You'll see."

Timmy's phone started ringing back to back. He didn't answer, but he knew that he was going to be harassed all day. The law hated Timmy and Terrance because they were known for getting some of the most serious criminals off in court.

He answered his phone and put it on speaker. "What's up man?"

"Yo', that bitch is straight wilding. What the fuck she got going on?"

"I don't know. I didn't do that shit though. I got to turn myself in though, so be ready to come and get me."

Terrance was back in the office. Even though he wasn't healed all the way, he had to get back to work. This didn't help Terrance's nerves because Carmelo's trial was scheduled in two days, and they really didn't need all the extra distractions.

"Alright man. Bet. I'ma just meet you down there. News reporters are all over the building though, so don't even come here."

"Yeah, they're probably all around my house too."

Michelle started shaking her head. A few minutes later, there was loud knocks on her door. She hoped like hell that the media didn't come there. She looked through the peephole and almost pissed on herself when she saw that it was her mother.

"Shit!" she mumbled.

"Who is it?" Timmy whispered to her.

"It's my mama." She shook her head. Timmy sat down and prepared himself for what was about to happen.

"Open this damn door. Michelle! I know you're in there."

Michelle put on a big t-shirt and a pair of leggings and opened the door for her mother. Shirley was pissed and Michelle knew she would be.

Shirley looked at Michelle, then she looked at Timmy and shook her head.

"How could you Chelle? Huh? How could you go around and sleep with a married man? I asked you good were you seeing this man and you lied to me. I trusted your word."

Michelle was on the verge of tears. She hated that she disappointed her mother. Shirley hadn't been that mad with her since she was fifteen and pregnant with Briana.

"It's not even like that, ma," Michelle said.

"Bullshit, Michelle. It is like that, but if you wanna be talked about and considered a homewrecker then that's fine with me. You weren't raised like that though. It'll be a matter of time before he beats your ass too."

"Mama, you don't even know Timmy," Michelle defended him.

"Hell, your ass don't either. You just met him the day of your graduation and you knew he was married. I don't give a damn because he's a lawyer, I don't care that he comes from money and look good. It's plenty single men that have it like him too," Shirley snapped. She couldn't believe that her daughter had no self-respect.

"No disrespect ma'am, but I've never put my hands on my wife. We have been separated and she can't handle that I'm settling for a divorce. I want Michelle."

Shirley shook her head. "Well, have Michelle once your marriage is finalized."

Timmy wanted to laugh at how serious she was, but he respected her. He knew that she only wanted what was best for her daughter and he could dig that.

"Yes ma'am. I understand."

"Good." Shirley smiled.

Timmy grabbed his belongings and went for the door.

"I'll keep you posted with everything, Michelle. Don't worry about nothing and this marriage is about to be over, sooner than I had planned. I love you." He looked back at her.

Michelle looked at her mother then looked at Timmy. "I love you too, Tim."

She wanted to kiss him so bad, but she didn't want to disrespect her mother. When he was out the door, Michelle sat down on her sofa.

"Why, Michelle? He's married?" Her mother sat next to her.

Michelle began to cry. Her emotions were everywhere. Her mother would never understand because she wasn't dealing with the things that Michelle had to deal with.

"I don't know mama. I'm in love. That's all I can say."

"How did this happen?"

"We started spending time with one another. That's all. He's been there for me through tough times. He held me in his arms when I thought that Bri wasn't going to make it. I fell in love with him, but I did not take him away from her! They were already separated," she lied.

It was true that they weren't at a good place in their marriage, but when Timmy came across Michelle, that only made him want to leave Patrice even more. Michelle showed him how a man was supposed to be treated. She made him feel loved and appreciated. Michelle didn't mind sucking his dick when he was having bad days, and she also motivated him when he was feeling down. It was almost like they were meant for one another. They came into each other's lives at the most perfect time. Even though shit had gotten real bad, they didn't regret their decision. She was going to stand by his side through it all, and she was ready for whatever.

"I think your damn daddy knows because he was so nonchalant about it when we saw it on the news."

Michelle giggled. Luke knew everything and she wouldn't be surprised if he knew, for real.

"This is not funny, Michelle! You know I don't play this type of mess!"

"Yeah, I know and I apologize for lying to you about all of this. I didn't know it was going to get this deep, but I do know that he didn't put his hands on Patrice."

"And how do you know that?"

"The look in his eyes told me so."

Shirley sat in silence. She wanted to tell her daughter that she didn't know a damn thing about that man, but she knew that the two of them were in love. She saw the way they looked at each other. The look in his eyes was the look that Luke always gave her.

"Wow. So, what's up with you and Charles? Have you heard from him?"

"He pistol whipped Ciara's boyfriend at the store a few days ago and messed him up bad."

Shirley mouth dropped. "Shut your mouth and shoot me!" Shirley said.

"Yeah, he did, and he messed with the wrong ones because those boys are going to kill him. Watch and see."

"That boy is really crazy, but can you blame him? Look how crazy his mama is. I'm glad Ciara didn't take after them."

Michelle and Shirley sat there and caught up with one another. Even though Timmy didn't want her to get involved, she had to go and see about him. If he was going to have to turn himself in, she wanted to be right there when he got out. She didn't care. She was in love and that's all that mattered. The media didn't know their story, the media didn't know the truth, so she wasn't going to let them tear down what they had built. She was going to fight for her man, and she was going to beat Patrice's ass one last time for slandering their names.

***

Ciara walked out of the jail with Terrance. They were waiting for them to release Timmy. He was charged with two counts of aggravated assault and two counts of domestic violence. Ciara looked up at her boyfriend and smiled. She admired how close he and Timmy were. Even though Terrance's face wasn't one hundred percent healed yet, he still looked fine. He had a little black ring under his eye and a few scratches but nothing major. Timmy came out and Michelle ran into his arms. She kissed him and he kissed her back.

"Your mama and daddy are on their way here."

"You called them?" he asked.

"Nah, they called me."

"Damn, news travels fast." Timmy shook his head. Timmy and Michelle held hands as they walked on the outside, where news reporters were ready to harass them.

"Here we go," Timmy said.

"Is it true that you abused your wife during y'all relationship? Is this the woman that caused you and your wife's marriage to go down the drain? Why did you feel it was okay to hit her? Is it true?" Questions were coming from everywhere. Timmy wasn't going to respond, but he figured that he would, just for the hell of it.

"I'm an innocent man in this situation and soon, y'all will find out that Patrice is a liar, a cheater, and a manipulator. We were separated when I started dealing with Michelle and that's all y'all need to know. Excuse me."

He pushed through everyone as they followed them and continued to beg for questions to be answered. He was ready to show the world the videos he had of Michelle cheating, and he was going to do it the right way. He first had to pay that nigga Solem a visit.

After hanging out at Michelle's house, Ciara decided that she was going to head home to get some overnight clothing. She had been staying more nights at Terrance's house than she was at her own. She grew close to him and her son loved him, but lately she had been feeling down. Very down. She would walk around looking depressed, and she barely talked. She pulled up to her apartment building and locked her car. When she went to walk up the stairs, she was smacked down to the ground. She could taste the blood in her mouth, and she was aware that her nose was bleeding. She felt like she was seeing stars. She stood to her feet and Charles came from around the corner.

"You hit me?" Ciara screamed.

"I should've killed your ass, bitch."

She cried, but he didn't want to hear it. "Walk into the house," he demanded.

"I'm not doing shit. Fuck you."

He lifted his shirt and showed her the gun that he was holding. Her eyes grew big when she saw that he was carrying a gun. He was on some straight psycho shit and she didn't want to die. She walked into the house with Charles on her heels.

"You're not scaring me," Ciara lied.

"Not yet," he told her.

She looked her brother over and he looked a mess. His hair wasn't cut, his clothes were dirty, and he was stank.

"Why are you here, Charles?" she asked him.

"I just came to talk to my disloyal ass sister. I can't believe how much you would turn on me for a nigga and Michelle's stupid ass." He shook his head.

He stood up and went to her kitchen. He searched the cabinets for some wine glasses then grabbed her bottle of Patron. He sat across from her and poured them both a drink.

"I'm not drinking that, Charles. You need to leave my house now."

For the first time ever, Ciara was actually scared of her brother. She didn't know what he was going to do, and she didn't put shit past him.

"Girl, just drink and shut the fuck up. You're lucky I don't kill your ass," he raised his voice. Ciara's nose was still bleeding and her lip was busted. She couldn't believe that he actually hit her the way he did.

"Can I at least go clean my face? You slapped the shit out of me."

"Yeah, you can." He waved her off. "And leave that phone."

Shit! Ciara thought. She thought she was going to outsmart him and tell someone to get there, but that was out of the equation. She was just going to be nice, so he could leave her alone. Hopefully, someone would notice that she was taking too long and come and see about her. She cleaned up her face and went back to the front.

"You know mama mad with me?" Charles asked her.

"Why she mad with you?"

"Because of your stupid ass. You went off on mama and told her that she was the reason I'm the way I am, and she agreed to that bullshit. You see what you did, Cici? You turned everybody against me. Mama, Michelle, everybody!" he yelled at her. "Drink your liquor and relax. I'm not going to do shit to you."

She relaxed and drunk it. "I didn't turn anyone against you. I simply told my best friend that she deserved more, and she did. Michelle is a good woman, and she deserved more than you. Be honest with yourself, Charles. You weren't there for her and you weren't there for Bri. I would be less than a woman to defend you. Michelle was my best friend before she was your girl and I vowed to never allow y'all relationship come between us."

"Whatever! You just a disloyal ass bitch who's always in someone else business. You've always been that way."

Ciara's head started spinning, and she began to feel weak. She saw two of Charles. She blinked and her vision was blurry, super blurry.

"Charles what did you put in that drink?"

He started to laugh. His phone rang and he answered.

"Come in and finish her, bruh. She's all yours." Ciara began to cry. She laid down on her sofa and prayed that she made it through this alive. *How could I be so stupid and drink that?* She thought to herself.

She sat back up and saw another person standing there. Whatever they were saying, she couldn't hear because they were whispering.

"What's up baby mama?"

Her eyes grew big and she started throwing up. It was TJ's daddy, Trey. The last time Ciara saw Trey was when he came to her mother's house and never came back for TJ. She barely saw him anyways because he had moved to Miami, Florida and hadn't turned back since. Ciara was happy when he left because he was a huge distraction to her and her son's life.

"Trey, you need to leave me alone and leave my house now," she told him.

"Handle your business, bruh," Charles told him.

Ciara began to cry. "Charles! Please!" she cried and begged.

Trey came and kissed her on her neck. He was about to rape her, again. Only this time, she knew what was up. She knew he was about to take advantage of her.

"You missed me?" He came out of his clothes and sat next to her. She hopped up and tried to run but he pulled her back down.

"Lay your ass down!" he yelled at her.

"So, you gone rape me Trey?" she asked him.

"Just how I did your ass back then. Now open up."

She spat in his face and he slapped her. She started crying and kicking, but he was holding her down.

He managed to get in between her legs. He snatched her shirt off, then pulled her panties down. He was glad that she had on a skirt so that he could have easy access.

Tray was in Boston, Ma because his old friend had been killed in car crash. He hadn't been home in about two years and didn't miss it. He owned a few homes and businesses down in Florida and that's where his life was. His family had nothing to do with him and that was fine with him. He was a paid nigga and he was loved in Florida, and that was enough for him. He did still have love for Ciara though. He hadn't met another down ass bitch like her yet. He knew that she hated him with all of her heart and that's why he was about to take that pussy.

He stuck his finger inside of her tight opening. Tears slid down her face. "This pussy still tight. You been giving it away?" He took his tongue and sucked on her clit. Even though she hated what he was doing to her, it felt good.

She figured if she laid there and got it over with, then it would be fine.

He stood over her and put his dick in her face. "Suck it!" he yelled.

"No! I won't!" she cried.

He slapped her back and she cried worse. He slid inside of her and fucked her roughly.

"Please! Please! Stop it!" she cried.

"Shut the fuck up!" She started to bleed and he was disgusted.

"You fucked me better last time." He stood up and put his clothes back on. She was in pain and she needed to get help. She was slumped. He threw a couple dollars on the table.

"Get some shoes or some shit for my son." He left the house. Her stomach was cramped up and she was bleeding really bad. He messed her up. She touched around for her phone, but she couldn't see it. She laid on the couch and cried until she went to sleep.

A couple of hours later, Terrance and Timmy were walking through Ciara's door. After she didn't come back, they felt like something was wrong. They walked into her living room and saw her laid out naked.

"What the fuck!?" Terrance ran over to her. "Ciara, baby, what happened?" She laid there and talked out of her head. Terrance was so mad; he had tears in his eyes.

"What happened Ciara?"

"He came here and raped me," she slurred.

"Who?"

Timmy came back into the front with some towels and a big shirt for Ciara. They called the ambulance to come out.

"TJ's daddy," Ciara cried.

Terrance picked her up and took her to the shower. He turned on the cold water and sat her down. She started to sober up a little bit. She looked at Terrance. "Babe, that's you?" she asked.

"Yeah baby, I'm here for you."

The ambulance got there and carried her away to the hospital. Terrance called her mother and Michelle and told them what was going on. They met her at the hospital.

***

Loretta cried as she rushed to her daughter's hospital room. After hearing most of what happened over the phone, she almost went crazy. Loretta was crazy about her children and even though she and Ciara wasn't on the best of terms, she still loved her daughter with all of her heart.

Loretta came into the filled room. Shirley, Briana, Michelle, Terrance, Timmy, and Luke were all there in her room. They were all looking sad. Ciara held her head down.

"Y'all, let's give them a little space," Shirley told everyone.

Everyone got up and left the room. Loretta sat next to her daughter and rubbed her arm gently.

"Cici, I am so sorry for these last few weeks. Everything you said to me was right. I just didn't want to accept it. I'm so sorry," Loretta apologized.

"It's all good, ma. Despite all the differences we've had throughout life, you've been there for me through it all and I love you."

That made Loretta feel a lot better. "Tell me what happened," Loretta said.

"I walked upstairs to go home and I was slapped down to the ground by Charles. He demanded me to go inside, and he called me everything but the child of God. I tried to relax because I didn't know he would do what he did. We sat down and had a drink. Then I felt dizzy and that's when I realized that he put something in my drink. Minutes later, Trey came in and he allowed him to rape me."

Loretta's heart sunk. Tears fell from her eyes. "No! No Ciara! Please tell me Charles didn't," she cried. They cried together.

"He did mama. He let Trey come in there and rape me."

"Did you tell the police all of this?"

"Yes. I did."

Loretta sat back and shook her head.

"I can't believe it. Charles is evil just like y'all daddy. He has done it though. You need to press charges on him and Trey, and where the hell has Trey been all this time? He just popped up?"

"My first time seeing the bastard in since that day he came and saw TJ."

"I'll be back."

"Where you going ma?"

"To go and call a few people. I'll be right back."

The doctor told Ciara that she would have to stay overnight, so they could run a few tests on her. Terrance was going to be there every step of the way. Even though his head was fucked up after all of this, he was determined to stay focused. They had trial that following day and they had to win the case. It was so much going on at once, he was trying to keep his head on straight. He and Timmy sat in the waiting room with their laptops. They had to make sure that everything was on point for the big day. Terrance had already told Bishop to find out everything about Trey.

He was going to Miami to fuck him up himself. He was going to kill that nigga and not think nothing about it.

Michelle walked into the room with Ciara. She wanted to see how Ciara was feeling after all of this. She didn't know what to tell her. She knew that Charles was crazy, but she didn't know he was crazy enough to allow another man to rape his own sister. The sooner he was dead, the better. She just hoped and prayed that it didn't affect Briana in any kind of way.

"How you feeling?" Michelle asked Ciara.

"Girl, I'm fucked up. I can't believe Charles did that. That nigga really let Trey rape me, and he knew that he did that shit to me back then. I hate them both."

"Me too. Are you still upset about what they planned?" she asked, referring to what Timmy and Terrance planned.

"The sooner they kill him, the better. I hope I'm there to watch the shit."

"Me too."

Loretta stormed back into the room like a mad woman. She stuck her head back out the door and yelled.

"Bring your ass in here!"

Ciara and Michelle looked at each other. They were confused on who it was that she was talking too. Ciara's eyes almost popped out of her head when her father walked in. She was shocked. She hadn't saw her father in forever. He and Charles kept in contact with one another. Charles Sr. had invited Ciara to be a part of his wedding, but she declined the offer. Her father hadn't done shit for her, so she wasn't about to support his ass. She barely spoke to him in public when they would run into each other.

"Look at my baby! Guess why she's here?" Loretta yelled at Charles Sr.

"Why are you here baby girl?" Charles asked his daughter, as he ignored how ignorant her mother was acting.

"Your son put something in my drink and allowed my baby daddy to rape me." Ciara was on the verge of tears.

"Say what now?" He looked from Michelle to Loretta.

"You heard her loud and clear. Your son is sick and his ass is going to jail for what he did! Maybe if your sorry ass would've taught him something, he would know better than this shit! I've done all I can, Charles. You need to talk to him."

"What the hell you want me to do Loretta? He's a grown ass man!"

"What have you ever done Charles? That's why he's the way he is. I've tried! I've done all I can! I can't be a mama and a daddy to that boy, and it's never too late. He's going to end up dead around here if he keeps this shit up, then we'll be burying our son. He had his own sister raped."

Charles sat down and allowed everything that Loretta had said marinate. Charles didn't know a damn thing about being a father to him or Ciara, that's why he left Loretta. She kept pressuring him about being a father to his kids, and he couldn't deal with it. Instead, he went off and found a younger woman who was in her thirties with no kids and married her. Charles Sr. looked damn good for his age, so it was nothing to pull some of the young honeys. When he met his wife, he knew that she had to be his. In all honesty, Loretta was still hurt and bitter behind the way he left her. She was a damn good woman and for him to just up and leave her for a young bitch made her feel less than a woman.

"I'm sorry he did this to you, Cici!" He looked at her.

"Whatever daddy. You don't care and you never did. You've never been a father to us! Even when you were in the same house as us. I don't even know why ma went and got you. You're not my father, you're just a sperm donor. You can leave," Ciara snapped.

"See! That's why I could never deal. They're too disrespectful! Well, Ciara is! I don't know what y'all want me to do. He's a grown ass man with a child. He knew, better than that, but I will have a talk with him and see where the fuck his head was at when he did that shit. Like I said before I'm sorry that he did that and I pray you feel better soon."

Tears fell from Ciara's eyes. The men that were in her life were fucked up. From her father to her brother and her baby daddy. You would think that it would break her, but she vowed to stay strong. She had TJ, her best friend and her mama, and that was enough for her.

"You're a weak piece of shit! Get out!" Loretta pushed him.

She brought him there, but she damn sure wasn't taking his broke down ass back and that was just all to it.

"Fuck both of them," Loretta said to her daughter.

It felt good that Loretta was finally taking Ciara's side. Coming up, she was always taking Charles' side, wrong or right.

Terrance walked into the room and kissed Ciara on her head. "How you feeling?" he asked her.

"I'm okay. Thanks for saving me. You're my everything Terrance!"

"And you're my everything. Everything will be handled soon, okay?"

She blushed. "Okay babe."

Loretta sat back and admired the two of them. They were beautiful and made a great couple in her eyes. She was happy that her daughter was happy and with a decent man.

Chapter Nine

Patrice and Solem sat in front of their TV as they watched the news. They were ready to hear the verdict to Timmy and Terrance's case. Just like the rest of their haters, Patrice was hoping and praying that they lost their case. Deep down in her heart, she knew that they were going to win, but she was praying they didn't. She wished nothing but the worse on Timmy. When the reporter came on the TV, the both of them sat up in the bed.

"Coming to you live outside of Boston courtroom, Lawyer Timmy and Terrance have beat another serious case. Earlier this year, Carmelo Sanchez was charged with murder, drug charges, and a few aggravated assault charges! Instead of taking the plea that was offered to him, they took it to trial and today he walks away a free man."

Patrice threw the remote controller to the TV when she saw Timmy walk out of the courtroom with Terrance and his parents. He was all smiles. He wasn't supposed to be happy in Patrice's eyes. He was supposed to be miserable and unhappy. She should've known better though. Nothing could break Timmy down. She turned the TV off and got out of the bed.

"Where you going?" Solem asked her. She rolled her eyes to the back of her head.

"Out," she told him.

"Listen! I don't know what the hell your problem is but you better get that shit together before you piss me off. Now, I've played your fucking side nigga and do boy all this time, and your ass will not treat me any kind of way."

"Who the hell you think you talking to?" she asked him.

He slapped her across the face. She held her lip. She was shocked. Maybe letting him beat her ass that time wasn't a good idea.

"I'm talking to your stuck up ass. Should I go to the media and let their ass know what kind of games you're playing on this man?" he asked her.

"You wouldn't."

"Try me," he threatened.

She broke down and started crying, but Solem didn't want to hear it. He had played her dummy for too long but not anymore. He was now in charge and she was going to follow his lead. She fucked up when she thought that Solem was dumb. Well, he was at first but now, he peeped what type of chick she was.

"I need to go to my apartment and get more clothes," she lied.

"I'll take you." He grabbed his keys.

"You don't have to."

"What did I say, though?"

"Okay fine! But, I wasn't going to my apartment. I was going to pay his law firm a visit," she said.

"For what?"

"To burn it down."

He shook his head. "I see why you lose all your cases in court. You're not street smart at all. How the fuck are you gonna burn down his place of business on today, out of all days? Girl, you should know that the entire media is going to be there waiting for him to get there."

He made her feel so stupid. She hadn't even thought about that.

"So, how are we going to get back at him?"

"You're not. You're going to let this man go on about his business. He don't want you and you should be glad that anyone wants to deal with you. I'm here trying to love your ass and you won't allow me to. The nigga that you want isn't worried about you. He's on TV flashing another woman. He don't want you. Just accept that."

Patrice waved him off. She didn't care if Timmy wanted her or not, she was going to make his life a living hell if she didn't do anything else.

"Just lay your ass down and relax," he told her.

She didn't know that Solem was crazy. He was crazy as hell. The look in his eyes told her so. She laid back and thought about a smart way to take him down. Making his life hell was something she just had to do.

***

Timmy and Terrance walked into Carmelo's mansion. The house was jammed packed with people. They were having a celebration for Carmelo. They also wanted to reward the two men for working so hard towards his case. Bishop had already wired the two men two million apiece. He was thankful for them. He watched the men come up from little boys in the streets selling drugs to two grown successful business men. He loved how the men worked. No matter how big time they were, they never allowed the money or the fame to change them. They were the same as back in the day. He trusted them with his life. Bishop walked the men through the house and introduced them to everyone. They felt honored to be around so many bosses. Everyone was dressed in white and black attire.

"Rather be at the house with my lady, nigga," Terrance whispered in Timmy's ear. Surprisingly Timmy was feeling the same way. They weren't feeling the big crowd that day. They couldn't remember the last time they got a good night rest from everything that had taken place, so after winning their case, they didn't plan on spending the day with people they didn't know. Timmy's parents were in town so he would rather spend the day with them, and Ciara was just released from the hospital, so Terrance wanted to be under her. His mother wanted him to stop by, but he didn't feel like being bothered with her. She was so negative and he didn't have the time for it. He wasn't in the mood for it either.

"Let's let him know that we're leaving," Timmy told him.

They went and found Bishop and Carmelo and let them know that they were leaving. They still had a lot of unfinished business, especially Timmy. He had to get everything together with his divorce. He hated that that bitch still had his last name. He couldn't wait to expose her for the hoe that she really was. She thought that she was slick, but she should've known that she wasn't slicker than him. You would've thought that she would've handled the situation better than how she did, since he had videos of her fucking another man in their home, but she wasn't that smart.

Terrance and Timmy got into Terrance's car and headed back to town. The both of them were silent with a lot on their mines.

"How you feeling bruh?" Timmy asked.

"I'm good. I'm just ready to handle these two niggas then I'll be all the way straight. How you feeling?"

"Shit, you know me. I'm good, but I'm about to hurt Patrice in the worse way."

"So, what's your plan? What are you going to do about Michelle?"

"I'ma marry her as soon as I get my shit together. She's who I want. The only woman I want, to be honest."

"That's what's up man, I don't even blame you. After how Patrice did your ass, I'm surprised that you even want to think about marriage again. That's good though. Don't let that bitch affect you bruh."

"She thought she was going to fuck me up, but she didn't and she won't."

Terrance pulled up to Timmy's house.

"Alright man. I got to get going. Ciara having one of her fits, so I have to see what's going on with her."

They dapped each other down and took each other in for a hug.

"Thanks for everything man."

Timmy placed his key inside his door and was shocked when he saw Patrice standing there. He hadn't got the locks changed on the door because he knew that she wouldn't come back. What fucked with him the most was she was sitting there with his parents and Michelle, like she hadn't done all the shit that she had did. The look that was on his face explained it all.

"What the fuck is going on here? Why she here?" Timmy looked around the room.

"I asked the same damn thing bruh. She come in here talking about she needed more clothes and shit." Silence came from the back of the house with the Samantha chick. They both were fixing their clothes, so Terrance already knew what that meant.

"I told her she needed to leave son," Reece said.

"Hell, we all did," Serri chimed in.

"By law, this is still my house too. I just came here to talk to you," Patrice said.

"I know your ass better leave MY fucking house now before I slap the shit out of you." Timmy was pissed and that was not what he wanted to run into. He thought today was going to be peaceful. Michelle looked aggravated.

"Why can't you talk to me Timmy?" Tears fell from her eyes.

"He don't want to talk to your ass, Patrice. For one, your ass lied on my son and have the world thinking that he had beat on you, and you know that he would never do such thing, then you're making it like you're this perfect wife and you're not shit. I told my son from the very beginning that marrying you was a very bad idea."

"And I wish I would've listened."

"But you didn't, so now you're stuck with me." Patrice crossed her arms.

"I don't have time for this bull crap." Michelle snatched her purse and coat and went for the door. Timmy went after her and continued to curse Patrice out at the same time.

They got outside and he snatched Michelle up. "Where the fuck do you think you're going Michelle?" She snatched away from him.

"Home, Timmy! I'm going home! This is too much for me. I can't deal with this shit. I should've never messed with you knowing that you were married in the first place. I can't do this. She pops up whenever she feels like it after she starts all of this shit, and I won't deal with that. I have enough going on in my life as it is."

Timmy snapped before he knew it. "What the fuck you mean you can't deal with this? You knew what was up when we first started fucking around. I don't want her, Michelle. I want you and I'm trying to prove that to you."

"How are you trying to prove it to me, Timmy? You're still married to that bitch and you haven't even taken the first step to getting a divorce. Are you still in love with her? Is that what it is?"

"Believe what you want to believe! Fuck it!" Timmy turned to walk away.

"And fuck you!" Michelle yelled.

"Fuck your stupid ass too!" he yelled back.

Michelle got into her car and cried her eyes out. She didn't know what the hell was going on with her, but she needed to get it together. She wasn't about to stand beside a married man and continue to play his mistress. When she graduated, she made a promise to herself that she was going to only focus on her daughter and her career. If she would've never been working for him, maybe she wouldn't have caught so many feelings for him. She had so many things going through her mind. She drove over to her parents' home. She just needed to be around people with happy spirits and was drama free. Timmy had way too much going on.

She walked into the house and it smelled good. She could hear her loud uncle and father. It was a few cars out front, so she guessed that they were having a gathering. She walked through the kitchen and looked into the pots. One pot had crawfish in it, the other one had shrimps, crabs, eggs, potatoes, and corn. They were having a seafood boil and no one didn't even think to call her. She went into the living room and her uncle Tall and her father were standing in the middle of the floor doing karaoke. Briana was too tickled. She stood on the side and recorded them.

"Sing it uncle Tall!" Briana called out.

Shirley and Sally were drinking their beer while they egged the men on. Everyone was having a good time.

"Say hey to Snapchat mama." Briana put the camera to her mama's face.

"Get that camera off of me lil' girl." Michelle laughed.

Michelle waved her mama down. The both of them walked into the kitchen.

"I'm done with Timmy mama."

"Oh Lord, what has he done?"

"I just can't deal. I understand that he's going through a divorce and all that, but I can't deal with all the drama that's coming from his wife. It's aggravating and I have enough going on in my life."

"Well Michelle, you knew that he was married when you first started dealing with him baby. That's why I told you, you shouldn't have messed with that married man in the beginning."

Michelle sighed. She really didn't feel like hearing all the extra stuff. She just wanted to vent to her mama. She hadn't talked to Ciara all day and she had to see what was up with her. When she left the doctor, she didn't want to be bothered with no one, not even her mama.

Shara walked through the back door and Michelle immediately got angry.

"Who invited her?" Michelle asked.

"I don't know, hell… who invited you Shara?" Shirley asked her.

Shara giggled. "I just came to see my mama. I won't be long," she told them.

"She can meet you outside." Michelle rolled her eyes.

"Girl. Bye!" She walked off.

Before Shirley could stop Michelle, she jumped out of her chair and rushed into Shara. She grabbed a fist full of her hair with one hand and punched her in the face with the other.

"Stop it Michelle, that girl is pregnant!" Shirley yelled at her daughter.

They tussled around. Michelle slammed Shara into her mother's china cabinet. She punched Shara repeatedly in the face.

"You like fucking with me?" Michelle asked.

Tall and Luke ran into the kitchen and pulled them apart.

"What the hell is going on in here?" Luke was pissed. He didn't condone in family fighting each other. Even though Shara had done the worse thing ever, Luke thought that she could've handled the situation better.

"She's disrespectful and she shouldn't be anywhere around me or at my mama's house!" Michelle yelled.

"Shara, you came over here to be messy. How did you even know I was here?" Sally yelled.

"Sami told me! I didn't know that I wasn't welcomed."

"Are you crazy or some shit, Shara? You're the most disloyal ass woman I've ran across. You came over here to show off that big ugly ass belly of yours. You know you ain't welcomed here. Take your ass on somewhere!" Tall fussed.

"They're right. Go home. I'll meet you there," Sally told her daughter.

She was tired of defending Shara. Defending her only made her worse. She was going to have to handle that situation on her own. Michelle put one good ass whooping on her. Shara walked out of the house with a ripped shirt, a busted lip, and a scratched up face.

"Briana, get your stuff and let's go home!" Michelle demanded.

"Michelle, baby, y'all don't have to leave," Luke begged.

"No daddy. I need too. This family is so dysfunctional. I need to find myself in peace. I'll call y'all." Briana came into the kitchen with all of her belongings. She kissed Shirley and Luke on the cheek.

"See y'all later," Briana said. They got into the car and headed to her house.

"I'm sorry you had to see me like that Briana," she apologized.

"It's okay ma. I never like Shara anyways." Michelle giggled.

When they got home, the both of them relaxed in Michelle's bed and watched Disney movies. Times like that she would have called Timmy to vent, but she was done with his ass too.

***

Ciara laid across the couch and watched her son play his game. She was in her own world and she wasn't thinking about a thing. Before she was released from the hospital, she was told that she wouldn't be able to carry any more kids. When the doctor informed her that scar tissues were formed around her uterus, she knew that having kids in the near future was a done deal. It broke her heart because she really loved Terrance, but to know that she wouldn't be able to give him any kids bothered her. Terrance was still young, he wanted a family, and he didn't have to deal with that if he didn't want to. She was happy that he and Timmy had won the case, but she couldn't even express her excitement because she was so down.

Terrance walked through the door with bags in his hand. It was clear that he had brought her a few gifts.

"Hey! What's up Terrance?" TJ hugged him.

"What's up with you man? I brought you some new games in that bag." He pointed to the bags on the table.

"What's up Cici?" He leaned down and kissed her.

"Hey," she said dryly.

"What's wrong?"

She tried to hold the tears back but they fell anyways. She wiped her eyes as Terrance pulled her up and led her to the back.

He pulled her down on his lap and kissed her lips.

"What's wrong, Ciara? Talk to me."

She broke down and started crying. "Babe, I can't have kids. It's best you just leave now," she sobbed.

"Damn. That's what the doctor said?"

She nodded her head. "He said that scar tissues are formed within my uterus. Something about it affects the functional lining of the uterus and it'll affect me giving birth."

"God has the last say so though," Terrance told her.

"But what if I can't give you kids? What if I can't give you that family that you want?"

He pecked her lips. "I know you will. I'm not leaving you though. I love you and I'm going to stick by your side. We're gonna try and if we can't have any, we have TJ and we can always adopt."

Ciara smiled. "You love me that much?"

"I do, but your goofy ass think a nigga be playing."

"We fell in love pretty fast though. What if we have a crazy relationship?"

"Man, you think too much. Our relationship is great, in my eyes."

"Yo' mama hate me though. What we gone do about that?"

"Let's do dinner. She'll be alright. She gone have to accept it."

"Okay."

***

Ciara sat at the table at Terrance's house. He had prepared a dinner for her and his mother. He meant when he said that he loved Ciara. He wanted to spend the rest of his life with her and he refused to let his bipolar mother affect that. He loved his mother to death but this was who he wanted, so she was going to accept it or leave him alone.

"How's Timmy doing?" Ciara asked.

"He's good. You know your girl is really tripping though. She's ignoring my boy like crazy."

"She'll come around. She just has a lot on her mind, but I warned her in the beginning and told her that he was married."

"I think they'll be fine once Timmy handle his business. The quicker he exposes that bitch, the better it would be."

"You really dislike his wife, huh?"

"I hate that bitch, never liked her."

He placed the cooked dishes on the table. He had made fried chicken, smothered chicken, and mash potatoes with homemade gravy, sweet peas, and homemade biscuits. That was what Ciara appreciated about him. He was original. Instead of wanting to go out and sit down at someone else's restaurant, he didn't mind getting in the kitchen and cooking himself. She loved that. Terrance was really a nice standup guy. She had never had problems with him when it came to other women, and he didn't have a problem with checking his mother and letting her know that she was who he wanted. Ciara was just praying that things would get better between her and his mother.

There was a knock on the door.

"Show time," Terrance said. "What's up ma?" He kissed his mother on the cheek. Ciara sat up straight in her seat and stood to her feet. She opened her arms for a hug, but Cat acted as if she didn't see her. Ciara didn't trip though. She just wanted to show her respect.

Cat was dressed in long black silk maxi dress. The black and brown chinchilla she was rocking had to cost a good grip. The gold stilettos were off the chain. Her mother had named her Cat because she was born with squinty eyes like a cat. A lot of people always told Cat that she was the singer/actress *Tamela Mann's* twin. She was the same size, she wore her short hair like her, and she had the gap and those deep dimples. She was such a beautiful woman, but her actions made her look very ugly at times. She had the cockiest attitude, and nobody could tell her nothing in the looks area.

She fanned herself and sat down at the table. "It's so hot in here son. You got on the heater?"

"Nah mama. I don't."

"Oh. So, why am I here again?" she asked rudely.

"Come on mama. You know why you here. Today ain't the day for all of that extra mess. I brought you here because you and my soon to be wife need to sit down and have a talk. I've told you over and over that this is the girl that I want to spend my life with and you disrespect her because she's not who you want me to be with. But, you might as well get used to her being around because we're getting married."

"Y'all are what?"

"You heard me right."

Ciara smirked.

"What the hell are you smiling at?" Cat asked Ciara.

"The look on your face was priceless. I don't understand why you hate me though. You don't know me and I've never done anything to you. I don't get it." Ciara reached over and begin to dig into the food.

"I don't want my son with someone who still lives in the projects. He's a millionaire! He needs to be with someone that's in his league. You have a eight-year-old son. He doesn't even have kids, so why should he play step daddy to your son?"

Ciara pushed her plate back.

"First and foremost Ms. Cat, you don't know a damn thing about me, let alone my son. I may not be a rich girl and I may not be perfect but I'm a damn good woman. I live in those projects by choice. I graduated from college and I go to work every day. I don't ask your son for his money. That's not why I'm with him. My son is well taken care of and my bank account looks great. You can't look down on me because you don't know what it's like to be raped, you don't know what it's like to be raised with two parents and only being loved by one, you don't understand any of that because you're too busy worried about all the things that really doesn't matter. I love Terrance and your nasty remarks and shade won't change that. We don't have to be the best of friends, but you will respect me. That's all I ask for is a little respect."

Cat had nothing to say. Even though she was a bitch, she felt for Ciara. She didn't know that Ciara had been through such a thing. She also had to admit that she wasn't born with a silver spoon. Actually, she and Terrance lived in the same exact projects when he was a younger boy. Terrance started selling drugs and she never stopped him because she always wanted to live the life that she was living now. She sat there and thought about everything. Ciara shed a few tears and excused herself from the table. Terrance was going to go after her, but he figured she needed that time to herself.

"You be killing me with that shit ma. Do you remember where we came from and how we got here?" he asked her.

"Yes. I know," she told him. "Look, I'm sorry, okay. I was wrong for how I treated her. If she's the one you want, then whatever. I just don't want to see you hurt behind all of this."

"I'ma grown ass man, mama. I got me."

He left the table and went and got Ciara. Cat stood to her feet and hugged Ciara. She stepped back and took a look at her. Cat was so busy being judgmental that she hadn't even took the time out to look at how beautiful Ciara was. She was beautiful. She cherished her brown eyes and her naturally beautiful caramel skin. Her teeth were perfect and white.

"I apologize, Ciara. I've been so busy judging you and I have no right. Like you said, I don't know you and I can't judge you. I wish you and my son nothing but the best."

"Thank you." Ciara smiled.

"I think this dinner date belongs to you and my son. I'll fix me a plate to go and see y'all later."

Terrance smiled. *Finally, her crazy ass got some sense,* Terrance thought.

When Cat left, Terrance walked over to Ciara and planted kisses all over her face.

"See, she's not that bad, is she?"

"I still don't think she likes me, but that was a start." She kissed Terrance back.

Ever since Trey violated her, she hadn't been comfortable with having sex. Terrance respected her wishes, but he was horny as hell. His hard dick was sticking out of his pants.

"You want me to take care of that?" Ciara asked him.

"Not if you don't feel comfortable."

She snatched his boxers down and admired his nine-inch meaty dick. Her pussy flooded with wet juices when his dick flinched.

She massaged his shaft and spit on it. She dropped to her knees and took his entire dick inside of her mouth. She licked each side and jacked him off. She gently bit his head. Precum oozed out of it. She deep throated his dick without gagging.

"Fuck Ciara!" Terrance groaned. He grabbed a fist full of her hair and fucked her face. She took it like a pro. Once he felt himself on the verge of cumming, he pulled back.

He pulled Ciara's dress over her head and admired her flawless body. Ciara had the fattest pussy ever and the dragon tattoo on her thick fat ass would drive any nigga crazy. Picking Ciara up, they headed to his master bedroom.

Motioning in between her legs, he slowly slid inside of her.

"Mmm…" She bit her bottom lip. He took his time with her. Each stroke he delivered was slow and deep.

"Yessss baby. Right there," she moaned in his ear.

"Fuck man," Terrance groaned.

Her pussy was so tight and he loved how wet she was. His dick was covered with her warm juices. Her pussy was making all kind of noises. It felt really good.

As much as he didn't want to, he busted early, inside of her.

"That was good," she said.

Terrance's dick was still hard. She had to finish him off. They went at it for hours. To know the feelings were mutual between each other was everything. They enjoyed each other.

Chapter Ten

Timmy and Terrance sat back in Timmy's Benz. The both of them were dressed in all-black. Timmy gripped his steering wheel as he watched Charles and Young laugh and joke around. It was only one o'clock in the morning and Timmy had followed them from club *Guilt*. They were some brave ass niggas to even think that they could walk the streets of Boston after what they had done. After talking to Bishop and letting them know that they no longer needed him to handle Charles for them, he stepped back and allowed them to handle the mission. Terrance and Timmy hadn't touched a gun in quite some time. The last time they ever killed anyone was a year before they opened their law firm. After that, they promised themselves that they were never turning back to that life, well only if they had too. Both men were very humble, and it took a lot to make them pull out their guns but Charles had crossed way too many lines. Terrance wanted to kill him for sneaking him at the gas station and also for allowing Trey to rape Ciara. He couldn't understand how a nigga could be so evil. It made him madder every time he thought about Ciara possibly never being able to have kids.

"How long we got to sit out here, man? I'm ready to do this nigga," Terrance barked. He was anxious. Excitement took over him as he thought about what he was going to do to Charles. He thought that Charles was a pussy for sneaking up on him at the gas station. He thought shooting him off guard would've been nice, but he wanted to look him in his eyes when he killed his ass.

"Hold on. I'm trying to peep the scene out," Timmy said.

Terrance let out a frustrated sigh. Young's house was ducked off. It was more in the cut and from the looks of it, no one seemed to be there but them. The area was real quiet.

"Come on! Let's get this over with."

The two of them pulled their ski masks over their heads and put on their leather gloves. Before they got out of the car, they looked at one another.

"I love you bruh," Timmy said.

"Love you too man." They hugged one another and patted each other backs.

"Let's do it."

They silently ran to the backyard. Timmy crept up on the porch and stooped down. He could see through the backdoor window that Young and Charles were sitting at the kitchen table having drinks. Timmy signaled for Terrance to come up on the porch. After he counted to ten in his head, Timmy kicked the door down.

"Oh shit!" Young tried to reach for his gun, but Terrance had already shot him twice in the shoulder.

The two men took off their ski masks.

"Yo', what the fuck man? How'd y'all-" Charles was cut off when Terrance smacked him in the face with the butt of his gun.

"You didn't think you were going to see me again huh?" Terrance laughed.

Charles was scared shitless. He didn't think he was going to see Terrance again, let alone see him like this. He didn't know that Terrance was a gun carrying type of man. He thought those niggas were good boys, but he thought wrong.

"Fuck!" Young screamed out in pain. Timmy stepped on his shoulder with his big Timberland boots. He screamed louder and shed tears.

"Shut up with all that crying nigga. Handle your shit like a man!" Timmy kicked him in the face.

"Please man! I got a baby on the way. I got Bri," Charles begged.

"Nigga, you don't even take care of Bri. Don't put her in this shit!" Timmy yelled.

"You thought it was cool to let that nigga rape Ciara?" Terrance asked him.

"What nigga?" Charles asked.

Terrance shot him in the knee. "Ahhhhhhhh!" he screamed.

"Don't act dumb, nigga. Trey! You let that nigga rape my girl?"

"I don't know what you're talking about man."

A frustrated Timmy shot him in the shoulder. Charles cried and sobbed.

"I don't know what you're talking about man. I would never let a nigga rape my sister."

"So, you're calling her a liar?" He nodded his head.

Terrance pulled his phone out and kept the gun pointed to Charles. He dialed Ciara's number and put the phone on speaker.

"If you say anything, I'ma shoot you right between your eyes," Terrance warned.

Ciara answered.

"Bae? What did you tell me Charles allowed your baby daddy to do to you?" Terrance asked.

"He let him rape me after he put something in my drink," Ciara told him.

"Bet." He hung up the phone.

"Why you lied to me, Charles?

Charles cried and Timmy laughed. He sounded like a bitch. He couldn't believe that Michelle laid down and had a baby from such coward.

"Where do Trey live in Miami?"

"I don't know." Charles laughed.

"Wrong answer again."

Terrance let his gun go. He shot Charles three times in the head and Timmy finished Young off, putting three in his chest.

The two of them jogged to the car and sped off. The two men were silent. As always, they had a lot on their mind. Timmy drove over the *Zakim Bridge* and pulled over to the side.

"Let me see your gun." Terrance handed over his .45 pistol. Timmy tossed both guns in the water and hopped back in the car. His mind drifted off to Michelle. He hadn't heard from her in a week. She hadn't even come in to work. She would do all of her work from home and send it back to them through email. Timmy couldn't lie and say that he wasn't bothered. He basically fell in love with her. He thought that she was ready for everything, but she wasn't. What irked his nerves the most was that she knew what it was from the beginning. He didn't like how she gave up on him when shit got bad though. He was going to give her a few days to herself, then he was going to get his woman.

Instead of going home, the two men got a suite at the *Boston Harbor Hotel*. They just wanted to rest and clear their heads. They walked into the room and laid across the bed.

"I hope that was the last time we had to do that shit," Terrance said.

"I hope so too. It kind of felt good though. I'm not even going to lie."

"Not to me man, that shit brought back too many memories. You know how many bodies we got on our hands? That was supposed to be it for us."

Timmy nodded.

"You talked to Michelle?"

"Nah. Fuck her."

Terrance laughed.

"You hurting ain't you, nigga?"

He not saying anything told Terrance what he needed to know.

"Just go over there, nigga. I'm sure her ole' pretty ass is missing you just like you're missing her. I don't even think she's tripping off the situation. She just got a lot on her plate. You're better than me because when Ciara ignores me, I pop up on her ass."

"I'll go over there tomorrow. I'm a little tired tonight man."

"I agree. Take your tall, big ass to sleep." Terrance goofed around.

***

Ciara held her mother in her arms as she sobbed. Two black detectives had come to the house and gave them the news about Charles and Young being found dead in Young's home.

"I had a gut feeling that something was going to happen, Ciara. I could feel it in my heart. He wasn't living right." Ciara rocked her mother back in forth. Even though Ciara knew who did it, she was still surprised. She shed tears but only for her mother. To see her mother in pain like that bothered her. She didn't feel for her brother at all. If you asked Ciara, he got what he deserved.

Hours later, people crowded around Loretta's house. People were bringing all types of foods, drinks, and cards to show their condolences. Briana and TJ sat under their grandmother and grandfather, who was pretty much under the weather. Family was still coming in from out of town and neighbors hung around. Nobody could believe it. Nobody but Michelle and Ciara. Ciara hated how their father pretended like he was the most perfect father in the world. It disgusted her, but she didn't care that much.

Michelle stood to the side and observed everyone. People felt sorry for her and her daughter but little did they know, Michelle didn't give a damn. She thought about Timmy, who she had been ignoring, and she would rather be with him. She missed him so much, it wasn't even funny.

She pulled her phone out and texted him.

Michelle: I'm missing you Timmy
Timmy: After your baby daddy gone, huh?
Michelle: I don't care about him.
Timmy: Come here with me, then.
Michelle: OMW!

Michelle went into the house and told everyone that she was leaving. Briana decided that she was going to stay with her family. Surprisingly, Briana wasn't as sad as Michelle thought she would be. She didn't know if she was trying to be strong for everyone else, but she hadn't dropped one tear. On her way out, she noticed that Shara had come into the yard. She was crying and causing a big scene. Ciara rushed over to her.

"Do not come over here showing out at my mama's house. You need to leave!" Ciara told her.

"Who she is?" one of the nosey neighbors asked.

"My cousin and Charles' side piece," Michelle spoke up.

"I just came to speak to your mother," Shara said.

"Girl, my mama don't even know you like that. It's a little too late to come around and tell her about a baby that we don't even know for a fact is my brother's baby. Leave before I beat your ass. I don't give a damn that you're pregnant. Leave."

Loretta stepped outside. "What's going on Ciara?"

"Charles' side piece is coming over here trying to start stuff, mama. She's so disrespectful."

"Isn't that your cousin, Chelle?" A confused Loretta asked.

"Yes, that's her."

"Well, why are you here gal?"

"She's pregnant from Charles."

There was so many oohs and ahhs. Loretta's mouth dropped open. She knew it was about to be some shit and she honestly didn't have time for it.

"Baby, please come back another time and another day. I can't talk to you about what you and Charles got going on right now. I'm not in the mood for it."

Shara let out a frustrated sigh and walked away. She was embarrassed more than anything. Ciara and Michelle couldn't believe that she came over there looking the way she did. She had on some grey tights that were spotted with food grease. Her long socks came over her tights and her shoes looked a mess. Michelle was actually ashamed to say that she was her cousin.

Loretta went after Michelle, but she was only wasting her time.

"I'm sorry, Michelle. I really am."

"No need to be sorry. That's just the type of people the two of them are. Go behind your back and do slimy shit. I was hurt at first, but I'm fine now."

Loretta dropped her head.

"I'm sorry you have to go through this, Loretta. I really am. I pray that God heals your heart because I could only imagine how it feels to lose a child."

Loretta shed tears and nodded her head. She didn't even have the strength to say anything. Michelle hugged her tight.

"My mama will be over here to get Bri later. I hope your company keeps you in a good spirit."

"Thank you."

Michelle got into her car and went to her man. The man that was worth the fight and the tears.

Michelle knocked on Timmy's door. It was cold outside. She wanted to be in his arms, she wanted him to make love to her. She wanted everything to be how it was in the very beginning.

Timmy answered the door. He was shirtless and the sweat pants that hung off his waist showed his pretty thick print. Timmy was the sexiest man ever. Michelle stepped inside and traced her hand down his beautiful chest. She looked into his eyes and admired the love that was there. This was the man that she was meant to be with. She didn't care who disagreed. This was the love of her life. The time they spent apart was miserable. She thought about him every day and every night. She had never known good men still existed until she ran into Timmy.

He picked her up and kissed her. "You missed me?" he asked her.

"Yes. I want to be here with you. This is where I belong."

Timmy smiled. "Only if you promise not to walk out on me how you did last time."

"I promise not to do that again."

He carried her upstairs. He was ready to put a hurt on that pussy. It had been so long since he slid inside of that and he was ready to have some fun with her. Michelle hurriedly stripped out of her clothes. She wore no panties and a black lace bra. Her pussy was freshly waxed and pretty. Timmy got on his knees and pulled Michelle to the foot of the bed. Her pretty pink pussy was wet and begging for some of his good attention. He threw both of her legs over his shoulder. As he stuck his tongue inside of her honey pot, she arched her back. The feeling of his thick tongue inside of her was driving her crazy. He stiffened his tongue and licked around her clit in circular motion.

"Shit baby," she moaned.

He stuck his finger inside of her and pressed down on her clit with his tongue. She couldn't hold the orgasm in. She came so hard that she could've sworn she saw stars and the moon and when he continued to suck on her clit, she almost drifted off to sleep. His head was the bomb; it was to die for. Michelle wondered what the hell Patrice was thinking when she stepped out on him. Everything about him was good.

"Bend over," he told her. She got on all fours. "Spread your ass."

Michelle jerked when she felt Timmy's tongue slide across her asshole. Her eyes went to the back of her head and she was glad that he couldn't see her facial expressions. It would've definitely turned him off because the faces weren't pretty.

When she felt his thick big dick enter her, she didn't know what to do. It felt so good. She immediately came on his dick. The more he hit her spot, the more he felt like he was swimming inside of her. Her pussy was so tight. He smacked her ass and pulled her hair. He massaged her nipples and stroked slowly.

"You like that shit?" he asked her.

"Yes! I love it!" she screamed.

He laid on the bed and allowed her to ride him reverse cowgirl style. He didn't know which was the best, watching her beautiful ass bounce on his dick or the feeling of her good pussy. It felt like he was in heaven.

"I'm cumming Timmy," she cried.

"I am too."

They both let off the biggest load ever. Michelle fell over and rested on her arm. Timmy was on her back and covered her with his sweat.

"This is where you're supposed to be. Your ass better not think about leaving either. You and Bri might as well pack up and move in here with me."

"Timmy, you're not lawfully divorced. We're not going that far until you have everything finalized and I mean that."

"Alright, alright. Change the subject before your ass start an unnecessary argument."

She laughed and playfully mushed him.

He pulled her in and they fell asleep right there in each other's arms. There wasn't a care in the world at that point.

***

Instead of handling everything in court like he was supposed to, Timmy decided that he had a few tricks up his sleeve that he wanted to play first. He already knew that once everything hit the judge's desk, he would be a free man in no time, but he wanted Patrice to suffer. He wanted her to look like the biggest skank that walked on earth. He knew that Patrice's mother and sister thought the sun set on her. They believed everything that she said, and they wouldn't dare believe that she was sleeping with another man in their home just from word of mouth. Timmy sat at his desk and uploaded the video of Patrice and Solem making love in their home and in their bed to his email. Timmy was glad that he had went with his first mind and had the cameras installed in their home. He sent the video to her mother, her sister, Patrice, a few news reporters that he knew personally, and he also uploaded it on a few websites under a fake page. He was hoping that would teach her not to play with him.

Hours later, Timmy was receiving emails from all over. The press wanted to hear his side of the story. Patrice's mother and sister had been calling him but he refused to answer. He knew that Patrice was hiding and that was fine too. All he needed her to do was sign the divorce papers, so he could move on. If she had any sense, she would just leave Timmy alone and take losing him as a simple lost. It wasn't that serious to Timmy, so he couldn't understand why it was that serious to her, especially because she was the one that caused all the madness in their marriage.

Timmy was kicked back in his office chair when he heard a lot of noise coming from the front of the building. He jumped up and went to the front.

"No, you're the bitch. You, your mammy, and your sister!" Michelle was in Patrice's sister, Ashley's, face. Terrance had to step between them.

"You're a whore. You home wrecking bitch."

"Girl, fuck you!" Michelle walked off.

"Why are y'all here?" Timmy asked the ladies.

"Nigga, you leaked a video of my sister? Are you fucking crazy?" She tried to hit Timmy but Terrance pulled her back.

"Hey, your wild ass is going to act like you got some sense or you gone get the fuck out of here with that shit." Terrance shook her.

"Fuck you, Terrance. Get off of me."

"I already did, your shit was whack too."

"What's going on? Why would you do my baby like that, Timmy?" Patrice's mother, Linda, asked.

Timmy looked at her like she was the stupidest bitch ever.

"Did you hear the fucking question that you just asked me? Ask your daughter why she would do me the way she did me. She could've ruined my fucking career, my whole life, with that lie she told. I don't give a fuck about her. At least what I put out was the truth."

Linda shook her head. This was just a mess. It was all good when Patrice exposed him and lied, but when he put out the truth, it seemed to be a problem.

"This is some bullshit. We're going to sue the shit out of y'all. Just know that!" Ashley yelled.

"Girl, you're talking to the best lawyer you probably know. You can't sue shit, but let your sister know she better sign those papers I sent her ass, or I'ma do something worse than what I did today."

"Is that a threat?"

"Hell no. That's a promise."

"Come on Ashley. Let's just go."

"Bye whore." Ashley flicked her finger to Michelle.

As much as Michelle wanted to go and beat her ass, she kept her calm. She knew it was going to come to that one day. She always had to tell herself that she wasn't a home wrecker. That home was ruined before she even came into the picture.

"You good bae?" Timmy asked her.

"I'm fine. I wanted to pop that bitch in her mouth though. She better be glad I'm somewhat delivered."

Timmy and Terrance laughed loud.

***

Patrice laid up in Solem's bed. He was talking to her but she wasn't even paying attention. Her phone had been off for the past three days and she had no desire to turn it back on. Her family didn't know if she was either dead or alive. She didn't even care. The entire world knew that she was a whore. She couldn't believe that Timmy would do her like that.

"Are you even listening to anything that I'm fucking saying?" Solem snapped.

"Huh, what did you say babe?"

"I asked you what are you going to do? You can't go back to work, your name is basically fucked up," Solem laughed.

"What the fuck is funny? You think this is funny?"

"Yeah, it's funny because you should've thought before your ass did all of that dumb shit. He knew your ass was cheating the whole time."

Solem disgusted Patrice. The feelings she had for him in the beginning was good and gone. If she could change everything, she would. She didn't feel like dealing with her mother, but she knew that she and her sister was all she really had at this point. Being with Solem wasn't going to work. Nobody knew about him, so he had absolutely nothing to worry about. Patrice watched him as he freshened up for work. He still looked handsome but at that point, looks didn't do anything for her. She wished her husband still loved her. She wished she would've never cheated. She wished for so many things.

"I'll be back as soon as I get off. Get up and do something with yourself. You look a mess."

He left and Patrice took that time to pack all of her shit and get the hell out of dodge. She refused to stay around that man. It was clear that his ass had went completely crazy.

Instead of Solem going to work like he had told Patrice, he headed to his penthouse downtown. He had to check on his wife and his two kids. Patrice didn't even know that she was a side piece herself. Solem was married, and he was actually happy with his wife. He just had to have Patrice when he saw her though. He knew she was a whore and that meant he could have her without even trying. When Solem pulled into his driveway, a black Maybach pulled in behind him. Not sure of who it was, Solem got out and walked towards the car. The windows came down and two men were holding him at gunpoint.

"Whoaaaa! What the hell?" He held his hands up in surrender.

"My name is Bishop and right here sitting next to me is my son, Carmelo. We'd like to take a walk with you inside of your house. We need to talk."

"Can we go somewhere and talk? My wife and kids are on the inside."

"Nah. That's who we need to talk in front of, your wife."

Solem knew that Bishop was the boss of his known cartel, but he had no idea as to why they were paying him a visit. He was so nervous, he was shaking, but he asked for it. He walked into the house and his three-year-old twin sons were running to him. He picked them up and kissed them. Bishop and Carmelo looked around and had to admit that he was living lavish as hell to only be a probation officer.

Solem's wife, Ann, came from the kitchen with a big smile spread across her face. Bishop and Carmelo looked at one another as they noticed that she was pregnant, big and pregnant.

"Oh, hey baby. You have guests. I'm glad I made extras for dinner."

They followed Solem into the dining room and took a seat at the dining room table. Solem tapped on the desk and waited for the two men to tell him why they were there.

"Do you know why we're here?" Bishop asked.

He shook his head.

"Ann, come have a seat because there are a few things that you're going to need to see and hear." Carmelo told her.

She washed her hands and sat next to her husband. She had a smile on her face, but that smile was going to disappear as soon as she heard what they were about to say.

"Are you aware that your husband has been cheating on you with the lawyer, Timmy Ralph's, wife?" Bishop asked.

A huge lump formed in Ann's throat. She looked at her husband. When he didn't give her eye contact, she knew that meant that what Bishop said was true.

"How do you know this, sir?"

Bishop pulled his phone out and showed her the clearer video of Solem and Patrice having sex in Timmy's house.

Ann covered her mouth and began to cry. She stood up and slapped Solem as hard as she could.

"What did I do to deserve that, Solem?" she cried.

"Babe."

She put her hands in his face. "Save it. I told your ass the next time you fucked up we were moving back to Canada with my parents. You can kiss me and my boys good bye."

Carmelo burst out into laughter when he saw Solem shed tears. It was funny to him; he couldn't say the same thing about his father though.

"We need you to confess on tape recording that you were the one that beat Patrice's ass." Solem looked at them as if they were crazy.

"Before you lie to me, think about your wife and your children because I'm a guy that doesn't have a heart. I kill first then ask questions later," Carmelo told him.

"Man, if I confess to that, my entire life will be over. My life, my career, and I'll do time for all of this shit."

"You want that or you wanna die?" Carmelo was starting to grow impatient with his bitching and nagging. They didn't give a fuck about him and his life. They were only here because they were trying to ruin Timmy's life and Bishop would die before he allowed anything to happen to Timmy. Timmy was like a son to him.

"Alright man. I'll confess."

After sitting in the house with Solem for almost an hour, they had the full story as to what really happened. They couldn't believe that Patrice had turned out to be so crazy. Bishop thought the sun set on her, but he wasn't the best when it came to picking out women himself.

Ann had already packed up most of her and the boys' things to take with them. She wasn't trying to hear anything that Solem had to say. He had cheated on her with three different women already and she always told him that the next time he did it, she was leaving, and she meant what she said when she said it too.

They gave Timmy the tape recording and he couldn't thank them enough. He had everything prepared and ready for court. The best part about it all was that he was ready to propose to the woman that he really should've been with. Everything was looking up for him and he was more than excited about it.

***

Shara laid in the hospital bed and cried. While she was there, the rest of her family was at Charles' funeral. She was upset that she couldn't make it. She figured that she was the one that was supposed to be there sitting with the family. Due to her losing so much blood, the doctor made her stay overnight. If she wanted to keep the baby, she had to stay on bed rest. At that point, she wasn't really sure if she wanted to keep the baby. The only reason she wanted the baby to begin with was because she figured that could be a way that her and Charles kept a connection. Now that he was dead, she didn't even care anymore. She was very upset with her mother and sister because instead of them being there for her, they wanted to go to Charles' funeral and be nosey.

Where's the support when you fucking need it? Shara thought to herself.

She was over it all. She couldn't deal anymore.

Chapter Eleven

Patrice walked into her mother's house. After ignoring them for a week, she finally decided to come out. It was now clear that Solem didn't give a damn about her. He had his numbers changed, he wasn't working at the probation office anymore, and he hadn't even been to his place where Patrice had been staying.

"Patrice, where have you been girl? We have been looking for you everywhere!" Ashley said to her.

Their mother ignored her presence. She didn't have anything to say to her. She felt if Patrice could ignore them that long, then she didn't care about their feelings. They had been worried sick about her and even went as far as putting in a missing report.

"I had to get my head straight," Patrice told them.

She kicked off her shoes and sat next to her mother. She didn't know what to say. She was hurt. She wished that she could make it like it was. Everything she did came back and slapped her in the face. Patrice started crying. She couldn't hold it in anymore. Ashley felt sorry for her, but her mother didn't. She couldn't believe that Patrice went out of her way to do all of that and she was the one who started everything.

"It's gonna be okay, sis." Ashley rubbed her back.

"I'ma just sign the papers and move on with my life. I've done enough."

"What!? You're not going to allow him to win and take everything. He cheated on you too."

Patrice shook her head. Ashley was just like her. A manipulator, but she wasn't about to fight with him.

Everything was basically Timmy's anyways. The money, the cars, everything was his She had nothing to worry about when she was with him because she was basically living off of him. Throughout their marriage, they kept separate bank accounts. She never paid a bill and never had to come out of her pockets. When she sat back and thought about it, her husband was good for her. She allowed jealousy to take over her. She was jealous because he was more successful than her.

"I did him worse, Ashley. This is all my fault." She shook her head.

"I never knew you was that type of young lady, Patrice. You're a disgrace to me!"

Patrice wiped her tears.

"Mama, you cheated on daddy for years, so don't act like you were a good role model in my life," Patrice snapped and Ashley's mouth dropped open. Patrice had never talked to their mother like that.

"You're damn right. I stepped out on your father when he stepped out on me! Was it right? No, but he led me to it. You did it because you never thought all of this would fall back on you. You could never compare our situation."

"Whatever!" Patrice snapped.

"I'm just going to sign these damn papers so that the divorce is finalized. I'm thinking about moving back to Florida as well. Nothing good has happened to me up here."

"Don't blame it on Boston. You had a good life until you started acting like you didn't have any sense," her mother snapped.

"You're crazy as hell though. I would fight his ass."

"Fight with what? I have no proof that he was cheating on me, even though I know he was. I didn't think to bust him how he busted me." Patrice shrugged. She grabbed her phone and texted Timmy.

Patrice: I'm ready to sign the papers. You won.
Timmy: That's a good girl. ☺
Patrice: Fuck you!

She threw her phone and cried. She never thought about the consequences that was coming with everything. She didn't even know if she was going to face charges for everything she had done.

***

Two months later, Timmy walked out of the courtroom as a free, happy man. He and Patrice was lawfully divorced and all charges were dropped on his end. Due to Patrice and Solem being charged with perjury, the both of them would have to serve time. Since Patrice lied under oath, she was charged with three years state prison time and two years federal probation, which caught everyone by surprise. Patrice was thinking if she gave up on everything that she would walk away free, but the judge proved her wrong. Only because Solem confessed to the judge and they had the recording of him telling the truth, he was sentenced to one year in the Boston prison with three years of probation. His wife had already moved back to Canada with her children and they were going through a divorce as well. Patrice's mother was devastated that her daughter had got in so much trouble. Patrice was shipped to The *Department Of Corrections Women's Facility* in Rhode Island. Her mother and sister decided to move there, so they would be close to her. Leaving everything behind wasn't easy for them, but they had to be there for her.

Timmy and Terrance had rented out the entire *Whiskey Saigon Club*. The night was still young and they wanted to celebrate Timmy's freedom, his divorce, and most of all, the success of their business. Michelle and Ciara had spent hours in the *Copley Place Mall* finding something nice to wear that night. Michelle's navy blue half-shoulder lace dress and black pumps were purchased from Jimmy Choo, and the gold balloon print jumpsuit that Ciara purchased came from Louis Vuitton. She already had a closet full of shoes so that was her least worry. They both were ready to step on the scene and kill shit. The men, of course, were wearing their suits. The entire city was coming out and it was going to be epic. As much as Briana wanted to join the adults, she had to stay home. Michelle wasn't having her in no club. She promised her to send plenty of pictures though.

Lately, Briana's health had been good. Before Serri could do his operation on her, she had a surgery that had to be done at the children's hospital in Boston first. Even though Serri didn't agree with her having so many operations, it was a procedure that had to be done. Everyone had faith that everything was going to be okay.

Michelle and Ciara had a scheduled appointment at the Lovely Nails and Spa. Their hair was already done, so they were going to take that time to relax. Once they both were seated, they had a little girl chat.

"Are you excited about everything?" Ciara asked.

"I am. I'm just glad that the bitch is out of our lives and got what she deserved. Timmy is happy, so I'm happy."

"Are you and Bri going to move in with Timmy?"

"Yeah. He purchased a townhome over there on Mount Vernon Street. It's real nice. He wanted it though. I told him I didn't have a problem with staying at the mansion."

"Is he selling the mansion?"

"That's what he said."

"You selling your condo?"

"Hell nah, I'm not selling my damn condo. My uncle paid for that condo in cash and he will have a fit. Besides, me and Bri love that place."

They caught up and finished getting pampered. The two ladies where at a very happy place in their life. They were just thankful for growth. Ciara had been spending a lot of time with her mother. She still couldn't accept the fact that her son was killed, and they still hadn't found the suspects.

Michelle walked into her parents' home. The two of them were dressed and ready for the party. Yes, Luke and Shirley were going to be in the building too. Briana and TJ were spending the night with Loretta. They were prepared to keep her company.

"Y'all look good," Michelle complimented them.

"Thank you baby." Shirley blushed.

"I came to see if you had cooked, but I see you've been lazy today," Michelle pouted.

"Yeah, me and your daddy went to Red Lobster. I get tired of cooking for y'all asses. Cook for me sometimes."

"I just cooked for your big ass last week," Luke joked with his wife.

Everyone laughed.

"Y'all are a mess, but I will see y'all later tonight."

On her way to the house, she decided to stop by Krispy Kreme doughnuts. She had been craving some glazed doughnuts with a large Carmel Latte. Lately, Michelle hadn't been paying attention to her weight. Whenever she was hungry, she ate, and whatever she craved, she would have it.

At twelve o'clock that night, the couples walked through the crowded club. Cameras were flashing and people were reaching for Timmy and Terrance, not caring that the two ladies were right there by their side. Neither of the men gave the women any attention. They were there with the women that they wanted to be with.

The DJ shouted them out when all of them noticed their presence. The women bartenders walked through the crowd with sparkling Champagne bottles. They sat down in VIP and enjoyed the scene.

"Look babe! There's the camera!" Michelle pointed at one of the photographers. They smiled for all the pictures that were taken.

The men walked around the club while the women sat there and took shots. They were feeling and looking good. Random women were looking at them, wishing that they were the ones that were sitting there with Timmy and Terrance. The groupies considered the ladies as blessed.

The women danced on the dance floor with their glasses in the air. They were turned up. They were celebrating for the old and the new. It felt good to have a good time without any worries and any drama. The women were living the good life. They dreamed of times like this and now since they had it, they didn't know how to act. When Future's song *Stick Talk* blasted through the speakers, the entire club was hyped. Timmy walked up on Michelle and kneeled down and pecked her sexy soft lips.

She had to give her man props. He looked so good with his fresh line up. His navy blue boss trim fit solid wool suit was cleaner than a mother fucker. On his feet, he was rocking a pair of Black Jimmy Choo Alaric Black Shiny lace up shoes. The Rolex on his arm was shining bright. He and Michelle were matching. Everyone had to admit it. The two couples were perfect matches.

The music stopped and everyone in the crowd booed the DJ.

"Kill the DJ!" everyone started yelling.

Michelle and Ciara thought that was the funniest thing ever. Well, everything was funny to them. They had been drinking Patron straight and it had them feeling good and happy. Terrance passed the mic to Timmy. The security came and made everyone move to the side. Michelle was so tipsy, she didn't even realize that she and Timmy were the only two in the middle of the dance floor. The scene was beautiful, the disco ball shined down on the two of them. Timmy licked his lips and smiled at Michelle. She gave him a big smile back. She knew that she loved the man. She was in love with him. Her heart started thumping and she was breathing heavy. She loved him for showing her what it was like to be loved. He never disrespected her. In every way, he made sure that she and Briana had everything that they needed. She felt so secure with him and Briana loved him simply because he made her mother happy.

When Shirley and Luke walked on the dance floor, Michelle grew excited. She had been looking for them the entire night, and when Serri and Reece came out, she was surprised. Nobody never told her that the two of them were in town.

"I got something I want to ask you," he spoke into the mic.

Michelle smiled and tears filled her eyes. She already had a gut feeling what the question was. Timmy got down on one knee and reached into his pocket. Michelle began to cry. He pulled the black box out of his pocket and revealed the 14k white gold princess cut ring. It was beyond beautiful. The most beautiful ring that she had ever saw in her life. "Michelle, will you marry me?"

She couldn't control the tears.

"You gone marry a nigga or nah?" Timmy asked again, which made the audience fall out from laughter.

"Yes, I will marry you, Timmy!" Michelle yelled in the mic. She was so excited. She jumped around when he put the ring on her finger. He lifted her up and kissed her passionately. Ciara ran to her best friend and hugged her. She was genuinely happy for her friend. Ciara had been there through Michelle's entire journey and she always wanted her friend to meet someone who was going to give her the world, after she noticed her brother wasn't the one. They took pictures, danced around, and had a good time. Michelle sent Briana a picture of her ring and pictures of all of them together.

Briana: So happy for you mama. You deserve it and you look beautiful.

Michelle: Thank you Bri! I love you!

Briana: I love you more ma. *Smooches*

That was for sure a night to remember.

***

Everything had gone back to normal. Terrance and Timmy were back in their office with their clients. They were more famous now than they were before, thanks to

Patrice. She tried to bring them down, but she only helped them out more. They were literally never not working. Michelle was still assisting them. They kept her busy, but everything flowed smoothly. Everyone loved Michelle, much more than Patrice anyways.

As busy as they were in the office, Terrance had to handle what he had been waiting so long for. Bishop had got links to Trey in Miami. Timmy wanted to go with him so bad, but there was too much work to be done for both of them to leave and besides, Terrance wanted to have a little fun with Trey. They were sure that Trey thought all of it was over, so that was going to be the beauty about Terrance's unexpected visit. Ciara begged Terrance to leave it alone, but that was something that he couldn't do. He had to handle it.

After a long day of work, Terrance went home and packed his bags. His plane was leaving in two hours. He was prepared to be gone for two days and two days only. He was coming back in time to be there when Briana had her surgery. He lied to Ciara and told her that he was going to meet with a client. The two of them had moved in together. Terrance had gotten a bigger condo and they weren't too far from Timmy and Michelle.

"Do you have to leave today, babe?" Ciara stuck her hands in the front of his pants. He laughed.

"Yeah, I'll be back in two days."

Ciara would've asked to go with him, but she had to work. As much as she hated to see him go, she had to remember that he was a businessman.

Terrance's grew hard. He looked at Ciara and then his hard dick. "Handle that for me." He licked his lips.

Without having to be told twice, Ciara dropped to her knees and got to work. Allowing the wall to hold him up, Terrance leaned back and fucked Ciara's face. That mouth of hers was something serious. It turned Terrance on when she slapped his dick over her lips. She was a naughty girl. That's what he loved about her the most.

"Fuck Cici! You gone make me nut!"

"Do it then."

He busted the biggest load down her throat. He almost went crazy when she continued to suck him off after he came. He got weak in the knees.

With no time to have sex, Terrance washed up and changed into his comfortable attire. Ciara was dropping him off to the airport. The entire ride there, Ciara talked about how good of a man Timmy was for Michelle, and Terrance had to agree. He felt the same way about Timmy how Ciara felt about Michelle. They both didn't have the spouses they deserved in their life, so when they met, it was like clockwork. They met right on time.

Ciara pulled into the airport and she grew sad. She had gotten so attached to him that she didn't want to be away from him, let alone two days. He looked at her and smiled. She couldn't help but to blush. His smile was so beautiful to her. It was something about that look that he always gave her that did something to her.

"Gimmie a kiss?" he asked her.

"Only if you take it."

He kissed with so much passion. He loved that girl. It was something about her eyes that made him yearn for her.

"Two days! I'll be back! I love you!"

"I love you too, babe. Call me as soon as you make it."

"I will."

Terrance followed Trey around in *The Lincoln Road Mall.* He began to get aggravated because this nigga shopped in almost every store. Bishop had so much connections in Miami, that's how they were able to find out who Trey was so fast. It was never in Terrance's plan to have to kill two people, but Trey was with a woman.

"Dumb ass nigga," Terrance said under his breath. He could tell that Trey was spending all his money on the chick. Her appearance screamed *Gold digger!* Once the two of them were finished shopping, they got into Trey's Rolls Royce. Terrance had to admit that the nigga was living pretty nice. He looked like new money. Staying a few cars behind, Terrance made sure that he kept up with Trey. When Trey pulled up at his penthouse, Terrance was determined to kill him fast and get it over with. Once the coast was clear, Terrance got out of his car and made sure that he had two guns tucked in his belt. He looked down at the paper that Bishop had given him. They were at the right address. Terrance wondered why Trey was living so lavish and didn't do for their sons. He also wondered why Trey wanted to take advantage of Ciara when he had so much pussy around him. He had a lot of questions, but he wasn't going to overthink everything.

Terrance walked to the door and covered the peep hole with his hand. He gently knocked on Trey's door.

"Who is it?" the woman gently asked.

"Delivery. We need you to sign."

She opened the door and Terrance mushed her. Before she could scream, Terrance pointed the gun to her face. She threw her hands up in surrender and tears fell from her eyes. She was nervous.

"Who the fuck was it?" Trey yelled.

Terrance grabbed the chick by her hair. He pointed for her to guide him where Trey was. When they walked into the bedroom, Trey almost pissed on himself.

"Yo, what the fuck?" He jumped up.

"Lay your ass back down, nigga." Trey did as he was told. Trey was pissed and scared. Out of all the nights he told himself not to bring his gun from his other home, this was the night a nigga wanted to rob him. Little did he know that this wasn't a robbery.

"Why are you here man? I can give you money. Money ain't an issue," Trey begged.

"Nigga, you think I'm here for money?" Terrance pushed the girl and shot her twice in the chest. She was dead in no time. Terrance got mad all over again when he thought about the night he found Ciara naked and bloody from where he had violated her.

"Why the fuck you shoot her for, nigga?" Trey cried.

"Why the fuck you raped my lady?"

Trey was confused. He wasn't sure which lady Terrance was talking about because he had raped so many.

Terrance shot the gun, missing him on purpose.

"Who the fuck are you talking about?"

"Your baby mama, nigga."

Trey's eyes grew big when he thought about it. It was the lawyer nigga that Charles had told him about. It was Ciara's boyfriend. He couldn't believe that he came back for him.

"Yo', Ciara's lying man. I swear to God I never raped her. All she's ever done was lie man."

"You lying nigga! That's why you got to go!"

"Wait man!" Trey put his hands up.

"I got three million under the bed man. Take it man. Y'all will never hear from me again."

Terrance shot Trey twice in the head. He went under the bed and got the duffel bag that was filled with money. He pulled his hat over his head and took the stairs. Once he was in his car, he laid back and watched the law enforcement rush into his house. Terrance wasn't sure if there were any cameras around, but he was most certainly sure that he wasn't going to get caught. When he got back to his room, he called Bishop.

"It's done."

"Good. Make sure that you're out of Miami first thing in the morning. Stay ducked off as much as possible."

Terrance chuckled. "Bet."

***

It was the day of Briana's surgery and everyone was sitting in the waiting room. They had sent prayers up, and everyone was in good spirits. Terrance made it back in time enough to be there to support everyone. Timmy and Michelle were in their own world. The family had taken pictures with Bri before she went upstairs for her surgery. The procedure would only be for three hours. They were all ready for it to be over with. Shirley and Luke was glad that everything was almost over. After that surgery, everyone planned on flying out to Dubai, so Serri could work his magic. They believed in God and they knew that it was all in his hands.

"I got something to tell you all." Michelle stood to her feet. The smile on her face made everyone anxious to hear what it was that she had to tell them so.

"Spill it already girl, shit," her uncle Tall said.

Everyone laughed at him.

"I'm four months pregnant."

"What?" Timmy jumped up and hugged her. It was a lot of oohs and ahhs going around the room. Timmy was so excited; the whole family was. He was having his first child from the woman that he dreamed of having all of his kids with. He didn't know why he couldn't tell that she was pregnant. She was always hungry, she gained a few pounds, and now that he paid attention to it, she had that glow.

Ciara blushed. She was happy that she didn't have to hold that secret in for so long. She wanted to tell the world, but she had to wait on Michelle first.

"My second grandbaby." Shirley rubbed her daughter's belly. "I pray y'all have another girl. I wanna spoil her rotten, just how I got Bri."

"I want another girl, too," Timmy agreed.

Michelle didn't care what she had, she was just happy that she was pregnant with another child from such a wonderful man. She was more excited about it than anybody else in the room. She had gone to the doctor and found out right before Timmy proposed to her. Ciara looked over at Terrance to see if he was bothered. He wanted kids, but she wasn't going to be able to give them to him. Luckily, he was just happy for Timmy at the time. Ciara felt very low. She wanted him to be happy. She wanted him to be able to have his own kids with her, but that was only wishful thinking.

"Are you okay?" Terrance asked Ciara.

"I'm fine," she lied.

"We'll talk later. Don't be upset Cici."

"I'm not."

Everyone sat around and enjoyed each other's company. Three hours later, they were on pins and needles as they waited to hear the good news from the doctor. When he walked into the room, he didn't look happy.

"Well?" Tall broke the silence.

"I'm so sorry to say this, but Briana didn't make it through the surgery."

Michelle closed her eyes and closed them tight. She knew that what he said to her wasn't the truth. Matter of fact, she knew that what he said was just a joke.

"Nah man. Nah," Tall said.

"Briana Brundage is who we're talking about doctor," Michelle said.

"Yes. I'm so sorry. The operation was going perfectly fine and her heart just stopped beating. I'm so sorry, Ms. Salson."

Michelle broke out with a loud scream that pierced everyone's ears. She fell on the floor and cried. She wasn't expecting that news. No one was expecting that news.

"Please. Not my baby. Please." She cried. Timmy tried holding her but she pushed him away. Shirley and Luke couldn't comfort their daughter because they were an emotional wreck themselves.

"She was here with me. She was just smiling. She was happy." Michelle cried.

Ciara tried rubbing her back but she flipped out on everyone. She couldn't stand the pain. Just that fast, her happiness was snatched away from her. Michelle wondered how God could do her like this. How could he snatch away her pride and joy?

"My baby! It wasn't her time." Michelle cried.

"Come on Michelle." Her mother and her father pulled her up.

"I have to see her, daddy."

Everyone was in complete shock. Who would've ever thought that Briana would go into surgery and not come back out alive? Everyone was heartbroken. It broke Timmy's heart because he had begun to build a bond with her.

Walking in to see Briana, Michelle rushed to her bedside. She rubbed her face and kissed on her cheeks. Everyone felt so bad for her. She wouldn't let go of Briana's hand.

"Briana baby, talk to me. Please. Come to me, Bri." Michelle cried.

"Oh my God!" Ciara broke down into Terrance's arms. She couldn't deal.

"Lord, this my baby. My world. What am I gone do without you Bri? Huh?"

"Come on Michelle baby. It's time to go." Shirley pulled her.

"No!" Michelle yelled.

Tall had to walk out. He had never experienced something so emotional and heartbreaking before in his life, not even his wife's death.

After rolling Michelle downstairs in a wheelchair to the car, they thought she would've calmed down, but she got worse. She screamed and cried and begged God to let it all be a dream. She just wanted to hear Briana's voice. She wanted to see her smile one last time. That's all she wanted.

Timmy laid her on the back seat. Ciara got back there with her to hold her. With her head in Ciara's lap, she cried and thought about the good times. She was happy that she told her baby that she loved her, she was happy that Briana was in good spirits when she went into surgery.

But what ruined her the most was when she thought about it all. They had told her that Briana didn't have long, but she wouldn't believe them. She also thought about when Serri told her she didn't need to go through with that operation, but she did anyway.

"She was just a baby, Ci. My baby hadn't even lived her life yet." Tears fell down to her ears. "She was such a good girl." She cried. "My baby was a good girl."

"It's gone be okay friend. It's gone be okay."

Michelle shook her head. "No, it's not," she sobbed.

Ciara's mother called her phone, as much as she didn't want to answer, she did.

"What's going on, Ciara? Shirley called me screaming and crying in the phone," she said.

Ciara didn't say anything, but Loretta could hear someone crying in the background. Her nerves were all over the place.

"Ciara!" she screamed.

"Briana didn't make it out of her surgery, ma."

Loretta dropped the phone. She wasn't going to believe it. Ciara could hear her mother scream. Between her and Michelle, she didn't know who was crying the worse.

They pulled into Shirley's and Luke's house.

"Come on bae." Timmy opened the door. Michelle shook her head and rocked from side to side. He scooped her up. She held her chest. Every time she thought about Briana's lifeless body lying on that bed, she thought she would die. She wanted to die. There was no purpose for her to be here on this earth. She wanted to be on that bed with Briana. Walking into the house, Tall was trying to console his hurt brother, Luke. Shirley cried and shook her head as she prepared her some hot tea. She called her pastor and begged them to come over and pray for her daughter. She didn't have it in her.

Timmy laid Michelle in her old bed. He got in with her and looked into her hurt eyes. He didn't know what to say. There was no way that she was going to be okay. She had just lost her daughter. Timmy rubbed her stomach and wiped her tears.

"She was so happy for me, Tim. She was happy that I found someone. She was happy. I didn't even get to tell her that I was pregnant. I was waiting until she came out of the surgery." She cried.

"She's still happy, Chelle. She's happy babe. She's going to be our guardian angel."

Michelle shook her head. "My baby ain't dead," she talked out of her head.

For the first time in a long time, Timmy cried. He sent a text to his mother and father, and they promised to be on the next plane. He held Michelle close and squeezed her as hard as he could. She wouldn't stop crying though.

Shirley walked into the room with a few men and women. Out of respect, Timmy got out of the bed. Michelle was so broken and torn that she didn't acknowledge any of them. She just laid there and stared at the ceiling.

"Michelle baby, Pastor Brown and some of our deacons and mothers are here to pray for us." Michelle cried. Her mother climbed in the bed and laid next to her as the pastor started praying and rubbing Michelle down with holy oil. The more they prayed and praised God, the more the family broke down and cried.

The bad part about it all was Briana was turning eleven in the next three days. Michelle's life had changed forever on that day.

Chapter Twelve

Michelle and the rest of her family watched Briana's light pink casket as it lowered in the ground. Everyone walked up to Michelle and hugged her, showing their deepest sympathy, but it was like she wasn't even there. She couldn't make herself believe that she had lost her one and only daughter. She had spent so many nights praying and begging God to not take her daughter from her, and he did it anyways. Her life would never be the same without Briana. She didn't even have the strength to live at that point. The rest of her family had been telling her that the baby that God blessed her and Timmy with was going to be their miracle child. The child that would make up for all the pain she had from losing Bri, but she had already told herself that the baby that was growing inside of her could never make up for her first born. Michelle felt that some people didn't realize that Briana was more than just her daughter. She was her best friend and her motivation. She couldn't focus without thinking about Briana. Every day, all she thought about was Briana. She looked down at the casket and dropped her red rose on top of it. Tears fell from her eyes, and she felt a little light headed. Timmy squeezed her tight and she let out a loud scream. She sobbed in his chest and begged Timmy to tell her it was all a dream. Timmy believed that this was God testing their faith. He figured that something good was going to come out of it all. Even though Michelle had been shutting him out the last few days, he wasn't going to give up on her.

"I don't know what I'm going to do without her." Michelle cried.

"We gone get through this baby." Timmy kissed her forehead. She shook her head. Timmy couldn't feel what she was feeling. It was so easy for him to say that it was going to be okay. He had no idea what it felt like.

"You ready?" Timmy asked her.

"No. I just need to sit out here for five more minutes." Michelle wiped her tears away. She cried and shook her head. She had never experienced anything like it before. Everyone stood back and allowed her to grieve over her baby. Watching her cry and ask God to please let Briana come out of that casket and go back home with her broke everyone's heart. Ciara couldn't take it, so she had already left and got back into the family limo. Shirley didn't go to the gravesite because she couldn't take it. Everything was so crazy. Everything was so unexpected. Serri and Reece admired their son for being there for Michelle the way he had been. Michelle had been cursing everyone out and Timmy was the only one that could pretty much calm her down, and they applauded him for that.

"I just want my baby, Timmy. I just want her to come to me. I want to squeeze her little chubby jaws." Michelle cried. "My baby was a good young lady. She was supposed to bury me. She wasn't supposed to die like this."

"I know babe, I know." He held her. "We gone get through this."

When Michelle got into the limo with the rest of her family, she felt some type of way. Everyone was staring at her, and she wasn't feeling it. She just wished that everyone would let her grieve in peace.

"I wanna go home." Michelle rested her head in Timmy's chest.

"It's people at your mama them house, Michelle," Timmy told her.

"I know! I just can't be around anyone right now, Tim. I just want to lay down and sleep. Please, just tell the driver to take me home."

"I understand. Just go and get some rest baby girl." Luke rubbed her back.

She managed to smile. Her daddy and Timmy had been everyone's soldier through it all. When Michelle walked into her condo, she went straight to Briana's room. Her heart broke as she stared at Briana's pictures on the wall. She rubbed the picture frame of Briana and her doctor. She was going to miss that smile. Tears dropped. Timmy stood in the doorway and watched her.

"Come get in the bed, Michelle."

She jumped. She didn't even know he was standing there watching her. She turned back around and stared at her pictures.

"I'ma sleep in Briana's bed."

Timmy shook his head. He didn't know what to tell her. "I think you should come in our bed, babe. Just for today."

"No!" Michelle yelled. "I'm gonna sleep in my baby's bed until she comes back to me. I'm gonna wait on her right here." She cried.

Timmy's eyes watered. It hurt him to see her like this. Instead of saying anything, he just held her tight and planted kisses all over her. He wanted her to know that she had him. He wasn't going anywhere anytime soon.

Michelle hugged him and inhaled his Versace cologne that she had purchased him. His big arms felt so good around her. He was warm and cozy. Tears continued to roll down her face. No matter how much she tried to think about something else, her mind would always drift off to Briana.

"I want her," Michelle sighed.

"I know you do, Michelle. We'll see her again one day but right now, I need you to be strong for the baby." He rubbed her belly. She rolled her eyes.

"I'm not even strong enough for this baby right now."

"That's why you have to get strong. I need you to focus. We don't want anything to happen to the baby, Michelle."

"Maybe having this baby was a bad idea."

Timmy stepped back and frowned. He understood that she was going through something, but now she was just talking crazy.

"So, what you saying Michelle?" he asked her.

"I don't want this baby is what I'm saying," she snapped.

She caught Timmy off guard. He wasn't expecting that. There was no way he could hide his frustration. He had been dealing with her and her rudeness all week long, but she did it then. She basically said, in so many words, that she didn't give a fuck about his baby. She really hurt him when she said that.

He bit down on his bottom lip. "I'ma just take that cause I know you're going through something right now," he told her.

"I meant what I said. This shit is stupid. My life has been ridiculous, since I met you. Maybe this is my karma for messing with a married man. I got pregnant, I lost my daughter. I'm considered a homewrecker. This whole engagement is wrong. We had no business dealing with each other in the first place." Michelle cried.

"Oh yeah?" Timmy voice cracked.

"Yes." Michelle wiped her tears. She took the beautiful ring off of her finger and handed it back to him. He looked at her with sad eyes. Was she really doing this? Was she really blaming him for all of this?

"You can leave."

"For real, Michelle? You gone put all this shit on me?"

Timmy was hurt. He couldn't believe none of this shit. The silence answered his question.

"You know what Michelle? Fuck you, man. You're the most inconsiderate heartless bitch I've ever met. I've done nothing but try to love your stupid ass, and you wanna make this shit about me? That's your fucking problem, you're always blaming people for shit. I've done nothing wrong, and you knew I was married when we first starting fucking around. Now you wanna take your frustration out on me? Fuck you!" he yelled.

"Fuck you too, Timmy! Fuck you!" Michelle screamed. She picked up a vase off of Briana's dresser and threw it. When she noticed that it was Briana's handmade vase she had made at school, she flipped out. She started swinging at him.

"See what you made me do!" she yelled.

"I didn't make your crazy ass do shit."

"Just get out!"

"Let me get my shit and I'll be gone for good!"

Michelle was so confused that she didn't know what to do or what to think. She had sat there that entire time and accused that man, but watching him stuff all of his belongings in a garbage bag almost drove her insane.

Is this nigga really about to leave me? Michelle thought.

Once he went to the door, he looked back at her. Her eyes begged him not to leave. She wanted to beg him to stay and tell him that it was just her hormones that had her acting like this. It was just her emotions. She wanted to snatch the ring back. She wanted him to make love to her. She didn't want him to leave.

"I tried Michelle." Timmy left her house key that she had given him on the dining room table and left the house. Michelle went crazy. She couldn't deal with it all at once. She ruined the entire house. She broke almost all of her dishes and she broke any picture frame that didn't have Briana's picture in it. She was torn, and she didn't even know that Timmy listened from the other side of the door. He shook his head. He knew she was hurt, but he wasn't going to stick around and allow her to treat him like shit when all he ever did was tried to show her what it was to feel real love from a real man.

***

Reece handed her son a cup of hot coffee. She sat down and plopped her head in her hand. She watched him while he drunk and she actually felt really bad for her son. She knew that it was hurting him how Michelle had went off on him, but she, as a woman, knew what Michelle was going through.

"Rubbama yjb ealayk nadeu laha, taymi." (Maybe you should call her, Timmy.)

"La! Faealt hdya ya 'amaha!" (No! She did this, ma!)

Shirley threw her hands up in surrender.

"I do miss her though." Timmy shook his head. "She said she didn't want my baby, ma. That shit broke my heart, man. She basically said if it wasn't for me, this wouldn't have never happened. She said this was her karma for messing with a married man."

Reece shook her head. Timmy sat there for hours and said the same thing over and over. She just wanted him to know that Michelle was only hurting. Reece loved Michelle. She knew a real woman when she saw one. She would rather him with Michelle over Patrice any day. She was so glad that he got away from Patrice.

"Son, I don't know how many times I have to tell you that she loves you. She's just hurt. It's not easy losing a child. She's broken right now. You need to call her and make sure that she's okay. Remember that she's still pregnant with your child."

"If you bring your crazy white ass over here, I'ma lay your ass out. For real." Silence came into the kitchen as he yelled in the phone. "I don't give a damn. I told your stupid ass not to come here. Who the hell you think you is? Coming all the way to Dubai with that stupid shit."

Reece and Timmy laughed. They knew it was Samantha on the phone. The two of them were always going at it with one another. Reece didn't understand how women could deal with Silence. He was so ruthless, and he was a man whore. That's why she cherished Timmy so much.

"Your white ass ain't my girl, so you can't be popping up on me and shit!"

"Silence, cut it out!" Reece told him.

"Nah mama. She needs to respect me. She done came all the way out here unexpected."

"I don't know why that nigga always flexing, mama. He loves Snow White," Timmy told her.

"Nigga, don't ever try me on no shit like that. I don't love Samantha," he whispered.

That tickled Timmy. He knew his brother more than he knew himself and he knew that he had more than just feelings for Samantha. Timmy had to admit that Samantha wasn't that normal white chick that would irk your nerves. She was down to earth, she stayed high, and she was pretty.

"Is she here in Dubai?" Reece asked Silence.

"Yeah, she's here."

"Tell her to come over for dinner tonight."

"My mama said you can come over tonight, but I won't be here."

"Put me on the speaker," Samantha told him. Once he told her she was on speaker, she spilled all his business.

"Mrs. Ralph, I would love for you to know that your son has another woman pregnant in Boston. I found out two days ago. He got another woman pregnant on me."

Reece's mouth dropped wide open. Silence's eyes widened, he didn't know she was going to say that.

"What?" Reece yelled. Timmy fell over laughing.

"Why would you say some shit like that Samantha? You know damn well that baby isn't mines!" he yelled in the phone. "Don't bring your ass over here, for real now. You full of shit for that one."

Reece shook her head. She hoped like hell that Silence hadn't got anybody pregnant. He wasn't ready to be a father. He was still an immature little something in Reece's eyes.

"Somebody's at the door." Timmy answered it and it was Samantha. He laughed and shook his head.

"Silence, you got company!" Terrance yelled. He picked Samantha's bags off the ground and put them by the door.

As much as Silence wanted to front, he was happy that Samantha had come. He actually smiled.

"He in love mama," Timmy called out.

"I already know," Reece said.

"Hey y'all. I hate that I came unannounced, but sometimes that's how I have to pop up on Silence when he's in town."

"You're fine. Come on, let me show you to the guest room." Reece grabbed her bags.

"What the hell she going to the guest room for? I got a big ass bed in my room," Silence argued.

"Y'all aren't married."

"And neither was Michelle and Timmy, but they slept in the same room."

Terrance laughed. Reece wanted to argue with him, but he was right.

"Whatever. Just don't have sex in my house!" Reece yelled as they disappeared upstairs. Timmy felt a little salty. He saw how Samantha had made Silence's day and he was still sitting there miserable, as he thought about Michelle. He was missing her something terrible, but he didn't want to be the one who gave in first. Michelle said some real hurtful things to Timmy that he couldn't get over. He just wished like hell she hadn't pushed him so far away. He twirled her ring in his hand and remembered how happy she was when he slipped it on her finger.

"Just call her son." Reece smiled and handed him the phone.

***

Michelle sat on the floor of Briana's room. She smelled some of her clothes and her scent was still there. She teared up. It seemed like the more the days went by, the more pain she felt in her heart. She had made up her mind and staying in that condo was something that she couldn't do. The entire family was over, helping her pack up her things. It was too many memories of Briana in that condo. She thought that it would hurt her uncle Tall's feelings, but he understood. In no time, he had met with a realtor and purchased Michelle a new condo. It was bigger and better. Michelle thought that he was doing too much when he told her that the apartment was a little over nine million dollars. In Michelle's eyes, her uncle spent good money on unnecessary things. Between his wife's insurance and his business money, he was filthy rich and he treated Michelle to anything that she wanted and needed, but she figured that he should save that kind of money for hard times. He snuck and did that because Michelle was considering moving back in with her parents. She needed the company, since Timmy was done with her. It had been two weeks and she still hadn't talked to him. She cried herself to sleep every night and wished that she hadn't said some of the things that she had said, but what was done was done. She wasn't going to sweat it. Life was too short and she wasn't going to dwell on the bad things.

Ciara walked into the room with two glasses of Patron in her hand. She handed one to Michelle and she threw it all back with one swallow.

"You okay?" Ciara asked her.

Michelle nodded. "I feel better today. I'm just glad that y'all are here to help me."

"We're always trying to be here for you, your ass just always shutting us out." Michelle laughed. Ciara was telling the truth.

"I know, and I am sorry."

"It's okay, Chelle. I'm just glad that you're still in your right mind. I thought you were going to die, friend."

"It felt like I was going to die. You know how much Briana mean to me."

"Yeah, I know."

Ciara picked up one of Briana's sweaters that she had brought her.

"Briana used to love the hell out of that sweater," Ciara said. She and Michelle laughed. Everyone was familiar of her pink and green sweater.

"I miss him, Ciara." Tears fell from Michelle's eyes.

Ciara had already told Michelle how she felt about the way she handled the Timmy situation. Ciara loved Timmy and she knew that Timmy was a good man. He really didn't deserve what Michelle did or said to him.

Ciara handed her the phone. Michelle looked up at her and she nodded.

"What if he don't want to talk to me?"

"Girl, we grown ass women. We ain't in high school. You and I both know that nigga missing you just as much as you're missing him, and you were wrong, so you really need to call him."

Michelle stared at the phone and took a deep breath. When she dialed Timmy's phone number, she sighed.

"Here we go," Michelle said out loud.

"Hello?" Timmy spoke into the phone.

When he answered, she got stuck. She didn't know what to say, so she just closed her eyes.

"Timmy, I love you," she blurted out.

Ciara thought that was the funniest thing ever. But, Michelle meant it. That's how she was feeling. She wanted him to know.

"I know that I said some things that I shouldn't have said, but I didn't mean it. You didn't deserve it baby. I need you though." Tears fell from Michelle's eyes.

"I wanna see you," Timmy said softly into the phone.

"I'm at the house."

"I'll be there, once I wrap up this meeting with my client. I love you, Michelle."

"I love you too." She smiled.

Once she hung up the phone, she laughed. That one simple conversation brought her so much joy. She didn't know why she had pushed him away in the first place. Timmy pretty much completed her. She needed that man.

Ciara was happy. Whenever Michelle was happy, she was happy.

"See, that wasn't hard was it?"

Michelle shook her head.

"Y'all alright in here?" Luke stuck his head in the door.

"We're fine daddy."

"Okay, we're about to take some more of your things to the other apartment."

"Thank you, daddy."

Luke noticed the smile that was spread across Michelle's face. He hadn't saw that smile in a while.

"What the hell am I missing?" he asked her.

"She talked to Timmy." Ciara smiled.

"That nigga must have the juice or some shit? Hell, even I haven't been able to make you smile like that." Everyone laughed.

"Get out daddy!" Michelle threw a pillow at him.

Luke was so happy to see his daughter in such a good spirit. He went into the front and told everyone about her smile and her mood. Shirley was happy. She and Loretta had even been getting along lately.

Later that day, the apartment was completely empty. Everyone had left, and she enjoyed the peace and quiet time. Michelle sat on the floor of the apartment and nursed her drink. She wanted to spend her last day in the apartment remembering the good times. She looked around and wished that Briana was there. She closed her eyes and wiped the tears from her face.

"Babe!"

Michelle jumped. She didn't know that Timmy was standing behind her.

"How'd you get in?" she asked him.

"I had a spare." He winked.

She stood to her feet and walked to him. She didn't know what it was, but it looked like he looked better, he looked sexier than he did before. His hair had grown out and his full beard turned her on. He wore a tank top that showed off his beautiful muscles. Michelle rubbed his arms and looked into his beautiful eyes. When he licked his lips, she had to kiss him. She poked her lips out and he kneeled down. Slipping his tongue in her mouth, she helped him out of his shirt. She planted soft kisses on his chest. She missed that man. She had every intention to fuck his brains out.

"I'm sorry," Michelle whispered.

Timmy slipped his hand under her dress. He grabbed her soft ass and poked her dimples. She had the softest body ever. He couldn't stop touching her. Pulling her panties to the side, he gently rubbed her clit. She was already soaking wet.

"Mmm…" she moaned.

He picked her up and she wrapped her legs around his waist as they tongue wrestled. He sat her on the counter and pulled her dress over her head. Her beautiful titties were sitting straight up. They were begging for some of his attention, so without second thought, he sucked on them. He stuck his finger inside of her tight opening and she couldn't take it anymore. She needed to feel him inside of her. She laid back on the counter and rubbed her clit. Timmy enjoyed watching her please herself. Stepping out of his slacks, he massaged his shaft.

"Put it in Timmy, shit," she begged.

He slid her to the edge and pushed himself inside of her. She was so tight that he couldn't go to work how he wanted to. She closed her eyes and gripped his arms tight. She knew he was about to shove his thick dick inside of her. He stroked her slowly. He couldn't believe that pussy could be so good. She was tight and she was wet. He pinned her legs all the way back and went deeper. It hurt really badly, but it was so much pleasure there. Tears slid down her face. He pressed down on her clit, which cause her to squirt. It was the sexiest shit ever.

"Ohhhhhh Timmy!" she yelled.

The more he hit her spot, the more she tried to push him out of her, but he couldn't do it.

"Move your hands," he demanded.

He picked her up and threw her arms around his neck. She bounced up and down on his dick. That position made her much wetter.

"Fuck, Michelle! Slow down!" That only motivated her to go faster. She felt herself cumming again.

Timmy bit down on her neck. "Bend over." He put her down. Touching her toes, Timmy had an eye full of her fat cat from the back. He had to taste it. When he licked her from the front to the back, she almost fell to the ground. He just had that touch. Every time he stroked her from the back, it felt like she was going to cum. He massaged her hard belly gently and slowed it down a little bit. She could feel his balls every time he shoved himself all the way into her.

"Oh shit, Timmy! I'm cumming again!" she screamed.

Seconds later, Timmy came. Naked, Timmy laid on the ground and Michelle laid on top of him. She felt complete and so did he. He rubbed his fingers through her wild bushy hair.

"How you feeling?" he asked her.

Michelle thought that was funny. You would've thought that would've been the first thing he asked her when he walked into the house, but they both wanted sex.

"Better, but my heart still hurts a lot," she said honestly.

"We'll get through it together. I never want you to feel like you're in this shit alone, Michelle. Just know when you're hurting, I'm hurting. I loved Briana too."

Michelle nodded and wiped the tears that threatened to fall from her eyes. She didn't want to cry anymore, but she couldn't help it. She missed her daughter, and she was pregnant and emotional.

"Have you been to the doctor?" he asked her.

"Yes. We should find out the sex next week."

Timmy smiled. "If we have a girl, what do you wanna name her?" he asked her.

"Ashanti." Michelle smiled.

Ashanti was Briana's middle name. Because she couldn't name her Briana, she wanted her next daughter to at least share a piece of Briana in some kind of way. Even if they didn't have a girl, if they ever had any more kids after the next baby, they were going to keep trying. Michelle would've really felt happier if God blessed her with another girl though.

"I'm all for it." Timmy kissed her. He stood up naked as the day he was born and went to his pants and pulled the ring out. Michelle felt better, but he would feel better once she had that ring back on her finger. He kneeled down on one knee.

"Michelle. Do you still want to marry me?" he smiled.

She smiled as the tears fell from her eyes. "Yes Timmy. I will marry your handsome ass."

He slipped the ring on her finger and kissed her. "Let's go home. This hard ass floor is not what's up." They laughed.

***

Shara had just hit eight months and she was already ready to have her baby. Her mother and sister rushed to the hospital to be there with her. She had been having complications throughout her entire pregnancy and she couldn't wait another month to have the baby. Shara was surprised that the baby hadn't come earlier than now. The baby weighed only five pounds and three ounces.

Sami and Sally walked down to Shara's room. She had been crying a lot. Of course, Sally felt bad because that was still her daughter, but Sami felt nothing. She couldn't believe that her sister had turned out the way she did. Coming up, everyone always knew that Shara was the jealous one, but they didn't know she would stoop so low. Almost the entire family was shocked.

"Where the baby?" Sami asked her.

"Why are you here?" Shara yelled.

"Oh bitch, I can leave." Sami turned to leave, but her mother pulled her back.

"Can y'all just cut it out and act like sisters? This is beginning to get on my nerves," Sally fussed.

"She's just so disloyal, mama. I don't wanna deal with her!" Shara said.

"I'm not disloyal. Your ass just mad because you're a snake for sleeping with your cousin's baby daddy. I call it how I see it, and you're a snake. Simple as that."

"You can leave," Shara told her. Sami waved her off.

"Where's the baby?" Sally asked.

"They should be bringing her back in, in a few minutes."

"How are you feeling?" Sally asked her.

"I wish Charles was here to see her."

Sami sighed and shook her head. She didn't understand how her sister felt comfortable to talk about him around them. She talked about him like he actually belonged to her. She couldn't understand it.

Sally shook her head. "You know Shara. I love you, but I really have to ask you this. What's wrong with you baby?"

"You can't help who you love mama," Shara said.

"Yes the hell you can. You should've never started loving his ass in the first place. Talking 'bout you can't help who you love."

"Sami, shut up please." Sally grew aggravated with her.

The nurse knocked on the door before wheeling the baby in. Sami jumped up and rushed to the baby. She just wanted to see who the baby looked like.

Sami snatched the baby blanket back and burst out in a laugh. That was the ugliest baby Sami had ever saw and she didn't think that baby was Charles because Charles was handsome as hell. She knew it was a little early to tell, but that baby looked like neither of them.

"What the hell is funny?" Shara snapped.

"That 'lil ugly baby does not look like Charles, Shara. You need to find your baby daddy."

The nurse's mouth dropped.

"Can you please tell security to come up here and make her leave?" Shara asked the nurse.

"I will," the nurse said.

"Oh, you don't have to do that, boo. I just came up here to be nosey anyways. Call me when you ready for me to come back up here and get you, mama." Sami took one final look at the baby and laughed again. "I'll be damn," she said before she left the room. She couldn't wait to tell everybody about that shit.

"You can leave, mama," Shara said. Shara was really broken. She couldn't believe that her own sister hated her so much.

"I'm not gone leave. I'ma sit here and spend some time with my grandbaby." Loretta picked the baby up and cooed. In Loretta's eyes, the baby was the most beautiful little thing she had ever laid eyes on. Sami was only trying to make Shara feel bad, but the baby didn't look like Charles. That baby was dark skin with dark brown eyes and a big ass head.

"Who this baby daddy for real, Shara?" Sally asked her.

There was another knock on the door. Shara covered her face when Silence walked in. He wasn't supposed to come while her mama was there.

"Where's the baby at, Shara? I know that baby ain't none of mines anyways," Silence said out loud. When he and Samantha walked around the corner, Sally couldn't believe what she was seeing and hearing.

"Who is he?" Sally asked.

"I'm the nigga that's supposed to be the baby daddy. Can I see the baby?" Sally moved the blanket over and showed him the baby.

"Hell nah, man! That baby full black, Shara! No fucking sign of Arabian, no curly hair, nothing. Who fucking baby is this, cause it ain't mines?" Silence yelled. Shara was so embarrassed.

"Excuse my language ma'am, but I'm pissed. Shara actually tried to put this baby on me," Silence said.

Samantha laughed so hard, her face turned red. "This is what you get for fucking anything that walks," Samantha said to him.

Sally put the baby in Shara's arms and grabbed her purse. She couldn't stand to be in the room any longer.

"Mama, wait!" Shara called out.

Sally had to leave. She had never been so embarrassed and shame before in her life. That was the craziest shit ever.

"Who fucking baby is this, Shara?" Silence asked her.

"I don't know." Shara cried.

Before they could turn to walk away, Serri, Timmy, Michelle, and Reece walked in the room with balloons and all kind of gifts.

"Y'all might as well turn around. This ain't my damn baby," Silence said.

Michelle almost stopped breathing when she saw who it was.

"Shara!? What the hell?"

"You know Shara?" a confused Silence asked.

"That's my cousin that was supposed to be pregnant from my baby's daddy."

Silence's mouth dropped open.

"What the fuck? So, you been playing everybody huh?" Silence asked Shara.

"Get out! Just get the fuck out!" Shara called for security.

Once they left out the room, Serri and Reece asked everybody for an understanding because they were clearly confused. After Michelle gave them the run down, all they could do was shake their head and go off on Silence. Samantha was so happy that baby wasn't his. Michelle couldn't wait to tell her mama about the crazy chaos.

***

Ciara and Terrance laid at the top of their bed, while TJ laid at the bottom of it. They were enjoying the rainy day in the house. They were watching *Django* on Netflix. It was TJ's favorite movie.

"Watch how he blows all of them up, mama," TJ cheered.

"Calm down TJ. I've watched this movie with you one thousand times." Ciara and Terrance laughed.

Ciara looked at her phone and rolled her eyes when she saw Trey's mother calling her. She was a sweet woman, but Ciara really hated anyone who had anything to do with Trey. He was a snake and a creep.

"TJ, your grandma is calling." She answered the phone and put it on speaker. "Here." She handed TJ the phone.

"Hey grandma," TJ said dryly.

"Hey TJ! Where's your mama?"

"Right there. Hold on."

"I don't wanna speak to her!" Ciara whispered and waved TJ off. He giggled.

"She's not in the mood to talk right now grandma. You want me to tell her something?"

She started to cry in the phone. "Tell her it's an emergency."

Ciara snatched the phone. "What's wrong with you, Pearl?" Ciara asked.

"Trey was found dead in his apartment today, Ciara." She broke down.

Ciara didn't feel anything, but she did notice the sad look on TJ's face. "What happened?"

"Someone shot him. They killed my son," Pearl sobbed.

"I'm so sorry, Pearl." Ciara shook her head and looked over to a nonchalant Terrance. He got out of the bed and went into the front. He figured the two of them needed that time together.

"He wanted to be cremated, so we're going to have a small service at this Saturday. Are you going to be able to bring TJ or will I need to come up there and get him?"

"Y'all gone have to come and get him," Ciara said.

"Okay. Tell TJ I love him and we'll be there to get him on Thursday. I love y'all, Ciara."

"Yeah." She hung up the phone.

"You okay TJ?"

"Did the police kill him?" TJ asked.

"What makes you ask that?"

"Because the police is killing up all the black men. I used to be scared for my daddy, a lot," TJ said sadly.

"No, TJ. The police didn't kill your father. Are you okay though?" Ciara rubbed his little back.

"I'm fine. I'ma just go into my room and play my game. He was barely around anyways, but I did love him, ma."

"I know son."

TJ left the room. Ciara knew that he was going to go in his room and cry. TJ was a strong kid and ever since he was little, he never liked people to see him cry.

Ciara got up and went into the kitchen where Terrance was on the phone. She crossed her arms and stared at him.

"Hey. Let me call you back later, man," Terrance said into the phone.

He had just got off the phone with Bishop. He had updated him on all the news that he had about Trey. They had just found him in his apartment dead, and they didn't have any leads to who had done it, which was a good thing. Terrance had absolutely nothing to worry about.

"You did it, didn't you?" Ciara asked through gritted teeth.

Terrance didn't say anything, but he gave her a look that told her she was right. She was so upset with him.

"You told me you were going there for business, Terrance."

"I did go there for business," he told her.

She shook her head and stormed off. She didn't understand why he had to go and kill him. His days were numbered and she wanted someone else to handle him. She had so many questions she wanted to ask him, but she was too pissed to ask. She went into the room and slammed the door behind her.

Terrance came in. "You fucking mad with me about that nigga?" Terrance asked her.

"Why did you do that Terrance? What if it comes back on you?" Ciara's eyes watered.

"It's not, so stop fucking tripping. I would've been a coward ass nigga to allow that nigga to live knowing he did that to you."

She shook her head. "You should've left it alone," she said.

"Well, it's done now. So get the fuck over it."

"You need to go in there and check on my son. He's hurting."

Terrance nodded. "I'ma talk to him. Are you okay though?"

"I'm fine."

Terrance pecked her on the cheek and left out of the room. He knew that Ciara was pissed, but he honestly didn't care. He had to do what he did to Trey. He didn't deserve to live. He was a deadbeat ass daddy anyways.

Chapter Thirteen

Today marked thirty-two weeks for Michelle. Time had flown by, and she was definitely excited. She was excited because she needed to feel complete again. She was hoping and praying that she could find that connection she had in Briana with the new baby. Instead of the doctor telling her and Timmy what they were having, they wanted to be surprised. They didn't know why they told Silence, out of all people, to keep the secret, but he had done pretty good. The family was setting up for her baby's shower at *The Tiffany Ballroom; The Four Points by Sheraton Norwood.* The day was kind of bittersweet for Michelle. As she sat in her living room and allowed Sami to do her makeup, she was in her feelings. She wanted Briana to be there with her so bad.

"Girl, your big ass is going to sweat all the makeup off your face before you even get to the damn baby shower." They laughed.

"Shut the hell up. It feels like my face has a thousand pounds of this shit. I hope you laid my eye brows, too," Michelle complained.

"Oh honey, you know I did." Sami put the mirror in her face and she had to smile. The Berry Black lipstick made her entire face pop. It looked really good on her. She loved how she shaded her eyebrows two different colors. Her lashes were full and just the right length, and her eyebrows were thick and pretty. She loved the look and Michelle wasn't the makeup type of chick. She pushed herself out of the chair and wobbled in her room with Sami in tow. Sami watched her as she picked from the two outfits she had laid out on the bed.

"Why are you looking at me like that?" Michelle giggled.

"Because you're so beautiful, cousin. Even pregnant, your ass is pretty."

"Aww thanks, Sami."

"I never thought we'd be so close. I always thought your ass was going to be boogie and shit. You're really cool, and I'm so happy that you're still carrying that smile. You've been through so much and I really love you."

"Aww, Sami. I love you." Michelle eyes watered.

"Uh-uh, Michelle. Don't come with all that emotional shit. You know I'm not the crying type, and I will sit there and stare at your ass if you break down in here."

Michelle burst out and laughed. "Girl. Thank you! I love your ghetto ass! You were always much cooler than your sister. I appreciate you for always being honest and real. For real."

"That sister of mines is a piece of work, but I honestly pray her crazy ass gets better. I do. I love my sister, but she's crazy as hell."

"Tell me something I don't know."

Ciara and Shirley walked into the house. Shirley had her hair in big rollers, and Ciara's hair was still wet.

"Ciara, really? The shower starts in another hour and your hair isn't even done," Michelle fussed. Just that fast, she was pissed off. She had told them that she didn't want to be late. She wanted to show up on time, but no! That wasn't going to happen.

"I know, Michelle, but that lady at the salon messed my hair up. Girl, I made her wash that crap out my head and I didn't pay her either."

Michelle's mouth dropped.

"I was so embarrassed." Shirley shook her head.

"I don't know why. You know she messed my hair up, Ms. Shirley. Then she had the nerve to say that wasn't her best set of work. I wanted to slap the taste out of her mouth."

Shirley laughed, but Ciara was really pissed. Right when she thought she was going to have her naturally hair in curly twists, the beautician at the salon proved her wrong, so now she had to slap a simple bun on her head. She was so upset.

"It'll be okay, friend. The makeup will make up for the hairdo."

Everyone laughed.

"No, I was serious," Michelle said.

Timmy walked through the door and Michelle smiled. He allowed his curly hair to grow out in a small afro and it looked so good. He wanted to cut it, but Michelle insisted that he didn't. She loved that look on him.

"How y'all doing?" he greeted everyone. He walked over to Michelle and kissed her on her forehead and rubbed her belly.

"Why are you not dressed?" he asked her.

"Trying to decide on which outfit I wanna wear. Come in here and pick one for me real quick. You got good taste." She pulled him into the bedroom and closed the door behind her.

She tried taking his shirt off of him and he laughed.

"You think your ass slick. You want this dick, don't you?" He laughed.

"Just a quickie." She smirked.

He snatched his *Father To Be* shirt off of him and placed it neatly on the chair next to their bed. Michelle pulled her skirt up and stretched out on the bed. Timmy got on his needs and put his face in between her thick juicy thighs. Once he began to tickle her clit with his tongue, she was about to go crazy. She grabbed a pillow and put it over her face. She didn't want her family to hear them get their freak on. He licked every spot and every crack. As always, he made sure that he pleased her clit with his fingers. He was a beast for sure.

"Ride my dick," he told her.

She sighed. "Ugh!"

"Your lazy ass!" He slapped her ass. She climbed on top of him and went all the way down on his meaty dick. It felt so good to her. Timmy watched as she bounced up and down on it. It amazed him on so many levels how wet Michelle could get. He watched her do her. He leaned up and sucked all over her breast. He even left hickies.

"I'm 'bout to bust," he warned her.

She kept going until he emptied all of his seeds inside of her. They both were tired after that quickie and honestly, Michelle didn't even feel like attending her own shower. She wanted to tell Timmy to just go by himself and Facetime her the entire thing.

Coming out of the bathroom with a wet rag, he washed between her legs. She admired how he took his precious time with her. He was such a standup guy.

"Get your lazy ass up." He pulled her off of the bed.

"Which one?" she asked, referring to the outfits.

"I like the gold and blue dress. It matches my outfit."

She smiled. "It does."

Once she was done getting dressed, she sat down on the bed and let Timmy brush out her curls. Michelle thought that was too cute.

"Thank you baby." Michelle pecked him on the lips.

When she went into the living room, everyone was taken back on how beautiful she looked. She was glowing and that handmade dress that her college friend had made her was too gorgeous. The blue, gold, and pink dress was simple, yet cute. The top of the dress said *Praying for a princess,* which was really cute and different. The words were covered in gold glitter. Her gold strap sandals were pretty. Her pedicure was stunning, thanks to Timmy. He had attempted to do her toes the night before and it turned out really good. She felt beautiful, even though she was huge. It felt like she was carrying two kids instead of one.

"You look so beautiful, my baby." Shirley kissed her cheek and snapped a few photos of her.

"I'm so hungry. It's really a shame!" Michelle sighed.

"That makes two of us." Timmy rubbed his stomach.

"Okay, I'm ready." Ciara came into the living room. She looked amazing. Everyone was wearing blue and pink. Michelle just really wanted to know what it was that she was having.

On their way to the shower, Michelle opened up Briana and her text messages. She don't know why she did it because it only made her emotional, but it also made her smile.

You are beautiful, and you are amazing, ma. One day you will be happy. I just want you to be happy because you deserve it. Hopefully it's with Mr. Timmy. I like him a lot.

Michelle burst into tears and Timmy slammed on breaks. "Michelle, what's wrong?" he asked her.

She handed him the phone and he read her message. He looked at her with sad eyes. He knew it was coming sooner or later. He reached over and massaged her shoulders.

"Just know that she's happy baby. She's looking down on us right now smiling."

Michelle nodded. She knew what Timmy was saying was right, but it would've been so much better if she was there with them. She would've loved that she was gonna have a sibling.

When Timmy pulled up to the building, he went over to Michelle's side and opened the door and helped her out.

Everyone came outside and admired the couple and how beautiful they looked. Pictures were being taken from left to right. Michelle smiled and waved as she and Timmy walked into the building. The professional photographer was getting great pictures. Michelle was more than surprised when she looked at the gift table. It was overflowing. The decor looked so beautiful. It was a boy or girl theme, where they had blue on one side and pink on the other. Serri and Reece was almost more excited than Shirley and Luke. They were finally about to have a grandchild.

"Oh my God, Silence. I want this so bad." Samantha rubbed his arms.

"Well, you can forget it because I'm not getting your ass pregnant," Silence tried to whisper. Reece slapped him upside the head, and Michelle and Timmy couldn't hold back the laugh.

"He's always talking," Reece rolled her eyes.

"My bad mama."

The night was going by fast and it was so much going on at one time. The place was packed with people from church, the neighborhood, and the family. Like always, uncle Tall was the center of attention and everyone loved him.

After playing games and enjoying everyone's company, all of them walked outside so they could find out what gender they were having. Everyone knew, but Timmy and Michelle. She was so anxious and nervous that she was on the verge of tears.

"Alright. The couple has waited a long time to find out what they're having and in this box is a balloon. It's either blue or pink. Blue for the boy and pink for the girl," Silence spoke into the mic. "Y'all ready?"

The crowd yelled "Yes!"

Michelle and Timmy had their fingers crossed. They were so excited.

"Y'all ain't ready man." Silence playfully walked away.

"Oh, stop playing and open the damn box, Silence!" Reece yelled and the crowd laughed.

When he opened the box and the pink balloon came out, Michelle jumped up and down as she held her stomach.

"Wait a minute!" Silence yelled and shook the box. Another balloon came out and it was another pink balloon.

Michelle screamed as tears fell from her eyes. "Twins? I'm having twins?"

Timmy smiled and pecked her. She didn't even know that Terrance had already ran his mouth and told him she was pregnant with twins.

Michelle cried and everyone surrounded her. "I just wish my baby was here, y'all." Michelle cried.

"Hey, hey, hey! We've come so far. It's gone be okay." Shirley and Loretta rubbed her back as the other women rubbed her stomach.

The day was bittersweet. Everyone walked back into the building and enjoyed the rest of the day. It was so many gifts that they weren't able to open them all, and the games brought out all the fun in the day. Overall, Michelle was really happy. She had no idea that she had two little human beings growing on the inside of her, even though she thought of it. Timmy's family was so excited. They had come all the way from Dubai just to celebrate with their family. You would think since most of them were Muslim, they would be weird, but they were very down to earth, and Michelle's family got along with them very well.

"She would've been so happy today babe," Michelle whispered to Timmy.

"I know. She's still happy though." He pecked her on the lips.

"Yes. I can feel it," Michelle agreed.

Once everyone prepared to leave, Michelle sat down at the table with her mother, Reece, and Ciara as she ate cake and ice cream while she watched Terrance, Silence, Timmy, Luke, and Tall clean the building. They were surprised when Terrance's mother, Cat, came. She had been better since Terrance got on her. Her gifts to Michelle was Louis Vuitton baby bags with the matching strollers, and plenty of name brand clothing for the babies. She had gone all out. Michelle was happy. For some type of reason, Cat had never come off as a bad woman to Michelle. She loved her vibe.

"I'm so thankful that my son found Michelle. He hasn't been this happy in so long," Reece told them.

"I'm happy as well. Even though I didn't agree with the way they got together, I'm glad that they're free. That drama they went through was something serious. I was mad as hell with my daughter," Shirley said.

"I knew it was going to come to that, but I'm just glad he got away from that Patrice. She was something else." Reece held her chest and laughed.

"Yeah, that woman was crazy. She had me thinking Timmy had beat her ass for real." Everyone laughed.

"I knew my son didn't do it. I know my child. I had told him that she wasn't meant for him though. I guess that's what the mean when they say sometimes you have to learn for yourself." Everyone agreed.

Once the guys were done cleaning the building, everyone was ready to part ways. Michelle didn't want everyone to leave though. When they all were around, she felt complete. Her mind wasn't on Briana as much when everyone was around. She told herself that she wasn't going to keep crying about it though. Crying wasn't going to bring her baby back, and she now had two kids that she had to be strong for. She just prayed that they didn't have to go through what Briana had went through at such a young age.

***

The guys spent their day at the *Jumeirah Golf Estates* with Serri. They were currently on vacation and they were trying to do as much as they could while they were there in Dubai. Serri was excited that Timmy and Terrance were able to come at the same time. They would usually be so busy with their cases that both of them couldn't have vacations at the same time, but they had finally had the chance. Serri was on vacation for a whole month, and the entire staff at the hospital was already missing him. The feelings were mutual though.

Silence joined them in the court. They were all dressed in comfortable golf attire. The men goofed around as they puffed on cigars and drank expensive champagne. They were enjoying the sunny day in Dubai. It always felt good to be there.

"I got you and Michelle something," Serri told Timmy.

"What's that?" Timmy asked.

"I'll show you later."

"I'll be damn man. That tall cocky ass nigga always getting gifts and shit. Y'all always treated that nigga like he was the youngest," Silence fussed.

Serri waved him off. Silence was way too spoiled and that was always his problem. He was spoiled, and he didn't have a care in the world. Serri always saluted Timmy because Timmy never used his parents having money as a reason to depend on them for everything. Even when he didn't have too, he went out in the streets and got his money.

"Me and Michelle don't need no more gifts, pop," Timmy told him.

"Yeah. Their asses already got it all," Terrance agreed.

"Give it to me and Samantha then," Silence puffed on his cigar.

"You and Snow White will be broken up next week and your ass talking about giving y'all something. Shut the hell up, Silence," Serri said.

"Yeah, you're right. I'm already ready for her ass to go home, pop." Terrance and Timmy laughed. You had to love Silence.

Meanwhile, on the other side of town, Reece, Ciara, Michelle, and Samantha were taking a tour around the city. They still couldn't believe how nice the city was. This was the best getaway for Ciara. She was excited, just how Michelle was when she first came to Dubai.

Reece was so glad to have the girls' company. She showed them so many new things. The chauffer drover them around.

"Takhudhuna 'iilaa almasjid alharam min, fadlik," (Take us to the Grand Mosque, please.) Reece told the driver.

"What exactly is it that you speak, Mrs. Ralph?" Ciara asked her.

"Arabic. My husband and my sons know how to speak it too." Reece smiled.

"Timmy speaks it too?" Ciara asked, surprised.

"Yes. They don't like it though. They're just like their father."

"So, how does it go in y'all relationship? You know? You're Muslim, your husband is a Christian."

Michelle got aggravated.

"You're asking so many questions, Ciara. God lee!"

"They said ask if you wanna know," Samantha said.

"We simply respect each other's beliefs. You see, I was raised here in Dubai with my mother and father and the both of them were Muslims, but when we moved to Boston, I ran into my husband. Oh girl, my parents couldn't stand him, and they punished me a lot because I was in love with a man who didn't share the same belief as me. I never understood why you couldn't love who you want to love because of a belief, so I went with my heart and stuck it out with my man."

"What's so bad about a Muslim and a Christian being together though?" Ciara asked.

"In Islam, men are allowed to marry people of the book, Christians and Jews. But, Muslim women are not allowed to marry outside their faith."

"Ohhhh ok, ok! I see! That's so interesting. Y'all are the perfect meaning of real love." Ciara smiled.

"I love my husband. I don't care that he's a Christian. We both respect each other and that's all I care about. When I said *I do,* I knew that I didn't make a mistake. My parents didn't agree when they were alive, but my sisters support me. I'm happy."

The women were amazed. They were so happy to hear about Serri and Reece's love story. Hell, Reece loved to tell it. She was glad the girls wanted to hear about it.

They pulled up into the Grand Mosque and got out of the car.

"Come ladies."

Ciara and Samantha looked at one another like they were confused. Michelle was all in. She wanted to know more about her fiancé's culture.

"This here is where I worship my Allah." Reece smiled then bowed and said a prayer in Arabic. "This Mosque was originally built in 1900. They demolished and rebuilt it in 1960. They added more in 1998. Isn't it beautiful?" Michelle nodded.

The entire day, the ladies visited some amazing places. They went to the Dubai zoo, The Dubai mall, and they even walked the Kite Beach. They had never had so much fun before in their life, but they couldn't do too much in that one day because Michelle was pregnant and of course, she got lazy fast.

The ladies walked into the house and surprisingly, the men had prepared them a big dinner. The table was set up and they greeted the ladies at the door.

"Wow! Y'all did this for us?" Reece kissed Serri.

"Yeah. I had to show these young men a few things in the kitchen," Serri said.

"Nigga, you barely cooked a damn thing," Silence said. Everyone laughed.

"Yeah, he's telling the truth, pop," Timmy agreed.

"Whatever man."

"This is nice y'all. Thanks." Michelle hugged Timmy. He kissed her forehead and then her stomach. He was so happy that Michelle was happy. For the first time in a long time, Michelle hadn't talked about Briana. She simply was enjoying herself.

The men had prepared Shrimp Kabsta Stuffed Bell Peppers, Spaghetti with Yoghurt and Meat, and Blueberry jam slices for desert. Reece was really pleased. It was her favorite dishes and they almost did better than her in the kitchen.

"The food was delicious y'all, but it's a must I go upstairs and get me some rest. I'm big and tired."

"Good night friend, Facetime me if you get bored." Ciara hugged her.

"You're so silly." Michelle laughed.

After Michelle took her shower, she put on a comfortable nightgown and stretched out over the bed. Timmy walked into the room shirtless. Lord knows that he was the finest man that she had ever saw. He laid in the bed with her and pecked her lips. Michelle caressed the side of his handsome face.

"You're the most gorgeous man that I've ever saw before in my life."

Timmy chuckled. "And you're the most beautiful woman that I've ever met before in mines. You're so beautiful and you don't even try to be." Michelle blushed.

"I thank you for this vacation, babe. I needed this." Timmy put his finger over his lips.

"I love you." Timmy kissed her with so much passion.

"I love you more, baby. Thanks for being so amazing. You came into my life when I needed you the most." Tears slid down her face. "You're the most amazing guy that I've ever dealt with. You took all of my heartache away and even when your wife tried to ruin us, you wouldn't allow it. I thank you for supporting me with my baby. She loved you. I'm just glad that God placed you in my life."

Timmy felt like the man. He showed off his pearly white teeth. "I'm sure you already know that a nigga loves you to pieces. I knew from day one, you were going to be mines. I just kept telling myself to be patient, and I got your ass how I planned too." The both of them laughed.

"I wonder am I still considered a homewrecker?" Michelle asked sarcastically.

"You were never considered one in my eyes." Timmy shrugged.

"I kind of was though. We were fucking before you were divorced, and I hate to think that I came on to you first." Michelle covered her face.

"That pussy was good when I first got it too."

Michelle cried as she laughed.

***

The trip had come to an end so fast. Everyone wanted to stay, but Michelle was kind of home sick. She couldn't wait to see her mother and father's face, and it was nothing like home. They all had one final stop to make before they went flew back to Boston, Ma. Timmy and Michelle had to wear blindfolds since it was their gift. Once they pulled into the Al Barari private community, everyone got out the car but Michelle and Timmy.

"Yo', what the hell? This is their engagement gift?" Silence asked. Michelle was ready to snatch off her blindfold.

"Y'all can take them off now," Serri said.

Michelle and Timmy got out of the car and looked at the home they were standing in front of. Michelle's mouth dropped open, and she could feel the babies moving. She held her stomach as she ran in the yard.

"Is this for us, pop?" Timmy yelled. Serri nodded and handed him the set of keys.

"My goodness, Serri. This is beautiful babe." Reece hugged him, she had no idea.

"Damn man? That's their engagement gift? If that's the gifts you giving out, I need to go ahead and propose to Samantha's ass." Everyone laughed, but Silence was serious.

"Shut up, man. You talk too damn much." Serri handed Silence and Terrance a set of keys.

Silence's eyes widened when Serri pointed to the mansion on the left and the right. "Oh shit! Oh shit! Pops, is this my shit?" Silence jumped up.

"Mr. Serri? You got me a house man?" Terrance asked. He was so excited that he didn't even see that Ciara had already run towards the house.

"Yes. These are my gifts to you hard working men. It took two whole years for my men to pull this together, and y'all better like it because all these houses together cost as much as I make in one year."

Terrance almost shed a few tears. He had never had that father figure in his life, but since he was a young boy, Serri always made him feel like he was his own.

Timmy's Villa sat in the middle. It was the biggest and prettiest on the block. The villa had six bedrooms, nine bathrooms, and an infinity private pool. It was a cement home. Silence's house was much smaller, but it was beautiful and big enough for him, and Terrance's home was almost the same size as Timmy's. The beauty of it all were that they were neighbors. Even though Silence or Terrance wasn't engaged or married, Serri couldn't gift one without gifting all. He had spent a lot of days and nights operating on people to make sure that they would have days like this. He went hard just so his family could have it all one day, and it was days like this that made him understand the long nights and early mornings in that ER.

Reece was crying. She was so thankful for such a wonderful, family oriented husband. She had prayed to Allah for days like this since she was a little girl.

"This was so amazing, Serri. I can't believe you pulled this one off without me knowing." Reece wiped her tears.

The two of them hugged and kissed each other. All of the couples were beyond excited and happy. Everything was so beautiful. Michelle couldn't believe it and neither could Ciara. Just to think, Ciara still had her apartments in the projects and Terrance wanted her to share the Villa in Dubai. Life was great and it was definitely something to thank God for.

Chapter Fourteen

Timmy slammed on breaks in front of the ER at the Massachusetts General Hospital. He blew the horn for help. Michelle was sweating and blowing her breath as she rubbed her huge stomach. She was in panic mode. The babies were finally ready to come. She was due to have the baby that week, and they were finally ready to come.

"Timmy, help me! They're ready to come out!" Michelle screamed.

"I'ma get help, bae. Stay right here." Timmy hopped out of the car and rushed on the inside. He was more nervous than Michelle. He came back to the car with a wheelchair and nurses in tow.

Michelle was crying. "Lord, my stomach hurts so bad." Michelle cried.

Once Timmy picked her up and put her into the wheelchair, they rushed her on the inside. "Ahhhh!" Michelle yelled.

"Hold on, Michelle!" Timmy rubbed her hair back. It bothered him that she was in so much pain.

Once the doctor came into the room, he looked at Michelle and giggled.

"What the fuck is funny?" Timmy asked the doctor.

The doctor ignored Timmy and washed his hands. "Ms. Salson, I'm Dr. Henry and it's going to be okay. We're going to need you to sit up for just a second."

"Why?"

"It'll actually be better if you stand up and exercise a little bit. That'll stop the pains a lot," he told her.

Michelle leaned her head back and sobbed. "Can't you just get these big ass babies out of me? I'm in pain."

Shirley and Luke rushed into the room. The two of them were very excited about their grandchildren.

"We came soon as Timmy called, baby. How are you feeling?" Shirley caressed her daughter's face.

"I just wanna die, mama. I wanna die." Michelle cried. Shirley wiped the sweat off of her forehead. They couldn't stand to see her like that.

"It's gone be okay, baby."

"She cursed me out the whole ride here, Ms. Shirley," Timmy told her. Luke laughed.

"Where is Uncle Tall?" Michelle asked, right before a pain shot down her back. "Ahhhhh!" she screamed.

"He's downstairs at the gift store," Shirley told her.

The doctor came back into the room. "We're gonna get you ready. You're almost at 10cm. Will this be your first one?"

"No. I had a daughter."

"Had or have?" he asked.

"Man, that's another story for another day." Timmy waved him off. He nodded.

Once all the nurses walked into the room, they washed up. Michelle was very nervous. She was really scared to push out two big stubborn babies, but she would rather do that and get it over with.

They prepared for the delivery. Due to Serri and Reece not being able to be there, it was Timmy's responsibility to record the entire thing. He had never witnessed anything like this before, so he was for sure shaking in his boots. The doctors started their procedure and it was the most disgusting thing to Timmy.

In less than thirty minutes, Michelle gave birth to two identical beautiful little twin girls, Briann and Ashanti Ralph. They couldn't tell who the happiest parent was,

Michelle or Timmy. Timmy shed more tears than Michelle. Michelle was almost numb to everything. She was still shocked that she had given birth to two little girls.

In less than a year, her entire life had changed. She lost her daughter, her baby's father was killed, she found her fiancé who she loved with all of her heart, and she gave birth to two babies. She was almost numb to all the pain that she had went through. Even though she missed her daughter, she was finally at a point where she didn't cry when she thought about her, talked about her, or heard her name. She got back into church and that filled the void a lot in her heart. She was almost complete again.

***

Ciara stared in Terrance's eyes as he slipped her wedding ring on her finger. Ciara was happy and full of joy as the two of them stood before her pastor at the John Adams Courthouse. The wedding was very last minute, but the couple figured that life was short and they were in love with each other. Ciara couldn't express the love that she had for Terrance enough. He was everything that she could ever want in a man. She had never been so happy before in her life. The wedding ceremony was really small. Michelle and Timmy was there, Shirley and Luke, Loretta, TJ, and Cat, and Serri, Reece, Silence, and Samantha. Those were all the people that they needed there.

Ciara looked so beautiful in her *Ivory Organza Vera Wang Bridal Gown.* Her Wavy Malaysian versatile sew-in was pulled up into a simple ponytail. She looked absolutely beautiful. Terrance was so excited. He was finally married and he didn't regret his decision.

"You're so beautiful." Terrance kissed her one final time.

The crowd cheered them on as he picked her up and walked out of the courtroom. Even though Terrance wanted to have a peaceful private wedding, the press wasn't going to let that happen. It was reporters all around the courtroom waiting for them. Thankfully, Terrance was in a good mood and he didn't curse anyone out. Ciara smiled and showed off her $100,000.00 ring. She felt honored to be married to such an amazing man. She had never felt so happy before in her life.

"I'm happy for you, son." She rubbed the side of his face.

"Thanks, ma." He kissed her cheek.

"We're out man. Newlyweds!" Terrance yelled and threw up his deuce signs as they got into the car.

"Go best friend, that's my best friend, that's my best friend!" Michelle yelled out. Everyone laughed.

"I want this one day, Silence," Samantha whispered in his ear.

"Your ass is always wanting something." He smiled at her.

Ciara didn't want a reception, so she and Terrance decided to head straight to Dubai for their honeymoon. She was more than ready to have a good time with her husband.

The two of them got on the private jet and was ready to take off. They hadn't even changed clothes. Terrance laid back in his seat as he smiled at Ciara. She couldn't help but blush.

"How does it feel to be Mrs. Shield?" Terrance asked her.

"So far, it feels the same, I just have on a big ass gown and a fat ass ring." They laughed.

"Seriously though, it feels really good, Terrance. I'm so happy to be your wife. I just pray that our marriage is forever solid. Your ass is stuck with me forever."

"I already know. A nigga is happy with you, always know that. I know that our marriage will be solid. You've made me happy since day one, and that's all that matters to me. We in this together."

"I never knew your mother would be so happy. She was crying and everything," Ciara said excitedly.

Terrance giggled. "Cat is a true drama queen, and I knew that she would come around. She told me so many times that you remind her of herself when she was younger."

Ciara sighed and smiled. She looked out of the windows and into the clouds. She never in her life thought that she would get married. Everything happened so fast and unexpectedly. She knew that she had went through a lot in her life just to get to where she was at right now. Her son loved her, her mother loved her, and most of all, her husband loved her. She also had a supportive best friend and two god babies that she loved with all of her heart. She was so thankful for it all.

She and Terrance had so much planned for their honeymoon. They planned to be gone from home for two whole weeks. The beauty of their trip was being able to be at their own home in Dubai. They both were happy. They planned to enjoy themselves with no worries. Ciara was happy, but she had one more thing to clear up before they rolled over into the New Year.

***

Michelle cried as she stared at her two babies at their christening. It was the most beautiful thing ever. Both babies were the most beautiful kids she had ever laid her eyes on. Briann was much darker than Ashanti. Ashanti had light brown eyes, and Briann's eyes were much darker. The mothers at their church were crowded around the babies. They couldn't believe that Michelle had two gorgeous kids. The babies were so cute; they could be on one of those worldwide baby pages on social media.

Timmy and Michelle both were dressed in all white.

"That's my stanka." Michelle kissed over Ashanti's face.

"Let me get a picture of y'all," Shirley demanded. The beautiful family took the best picture ever. Timmy leaned down and kissed her.

"You alright?" he asked Michelle.

"I'm fine. I'm just sleepy."

"Let's get you home then."

Michelle walked over to her mother and told her that they were leaving. Knowing Shirley, she would be there for two hours talking to everyone in the church, and Michelle just wasn't in the mood for that. She was thankful that everyone had come out and joined her at her babies christening, but lately, all she wanted to do was lay around and chill with her daughters. She was so in love with them. She was nervous at first because she thought dealing with two kids would be a bit much at one time, but with Timmy's help, everything was flowing perfectly fine. Since she had the kids, she had been a stay at home mom. She didn't mind that at all because it was very relaxing, but she did want to get back to work soon. Whenever she felt that she was getting a bit overwhelmed with everything when Timmy was out working, Shirley and Luke would come and take the kids. As always, Michelle loved and appreciated her parents.

Michelle walked on the porch and there was a huge box in the front of the door. She smiled when she saw that it was something from Reece. She missed her so much and she couldn't wait until they went there for their vacation. They hadn't been back to Boston since Ciara and Terrance's wedding. Reece could come anytime she wanted to but she chose to wait so that whenever Serri could take off, they could come together. Reece wanted them to pack up and move to Dubai, but Michelle just couldn't see herself moving that far from home so soon. Maybe in the future, but not at that moment.

When they got into the house, Michelle opened the box.

"Aww babe... look!" Michelle held up the handmade knitted dresses that Reece had made for the girls. Both of the dresses were pink, but they had their name in both of them. It was very creative.

"Yeah, my mama knows how to be creative when she wanna be," Timmy said with pride.

"I love them. I have to call her and thank her for these."

"Come sit down, Michelle. Let me talk to you." She followed him into the living room and sat on the couch.

He patted his lap, so she could throw her feet over him. She laid back and allowed him to massage her feet.

"Are you happy?" he asked her.

"Huh?" She was confused.

"Are you happy? I just wanna know what's on your mind. I've been so busy lately and I just wanna make sure that you're okay. I know that so much has happened in so little time, but I just wanna know how you feeling? What's on your mind?"

Michelle smiled and pecked Timmy on the lips. He was more than confused when her eyes began to water.

"Why you wanna cry?" he asked her.

"I don't know." She shrugged. "I'm just so happy, Timmy. I honest to God didn't think I could ever be happy after losing Briana, but God has a way in making things work. You were sent to me for all the right reasons. As soon as my life started going left, you came into my life and helped me every step of the way. You gave me two beautiful little girls, and you're always making sure I'm satisfied. I'm always happy, babe. Always." They kissed each other with so much passion. Timmy felt the same. He honestly never loved a woman the way he loved Michelle. She was everything to him, and he loved her even more because she was the mother of his two kids.

"Guess what?" he asked.

"I took off for the next two weeks, so we can go out to Dubai."

"Shut up!" Michelle said with excitement.

"For real."

Michelle jumped up from the sofa and started doing the Bobby Shmurda dance. Timmy laughed so hard, his stomach was almost hurting.

"Shit. I'm tired." Michelle flopped into the sofa.

"Your ass is wild, man. I needed that laugh though." Michelle giggled.

"I'm happy. I miss your parents, and I can finally get out of this house."

"Yeah, Reece really miss y'all too. We'll leave in two days."

"Good! Let me go and get dinner started." She got up. Timmy admired her.

"Aye bae!" Timmy called. Michelle stopped and looked back.

"Yes?"

"I love you." He blew a kiss as she blushed and walked away.

***

Ciara hadn't been back home for a whole week and TJ's teachers continuously called her about his behavior, but Ciara had enough. When the principal called her at her job and told her that TJ was in in-school detention for rubbing a young lady's private part from the back, she couldn't wait to put her hands on him.

She walked into the school's office with the meanest look on her face. She was furious.

"Hey, may I help you, ma'am?" the school secretary asked.

"I came to meet with the principal. I'm Trey Jones' mother."

"Oh, Ok. You can follow me."

When Ciara walked into the office and saw her son sitting there, he immediately lowered his head. He knew an ass whooping was coming his way.

"Hello! How are you?" Ciara spoke to the principal.

"I'm fine. I'm so sorry that we had to disturb you, but we had to call you. This is the second time that we've gotten a complaint about Trey touching another young lady in class. Her two parents came in this morning and complained, saying that their daughter was being touched by Trey."

Ciara was hurt. That was all. She looked at her son with tears in her eyes. She said a silent prayer, asking God to please not let her son turn out like his perverted father.

"Why Trey?" Ciara asked him.

He didn't say anything.

"So, now you can't talk?" TJ didn't answer.

"Ma'am, is it possible if you can walk me and TJ to his classroom?" Ciara asked the principal.

"Oh sure. You all can follow me."

TJ walked slowly behind his mother. She turned around and snatched him by his arm.

"Don't walk slow! Walk fast!" Ciara yelled.

When they got into the classroom, Ciara greeted everyone and the teacher. All the students were quiet and waited to see what was coming. They thought it was quite funny that TJ was the class clown, but wouldn't even hold his head up in front of his mother.

"I came here today to talk to you students. I'm TJ's mother."

"Yeah, we remember you. You used to be at all our football games!" one of the students yelled.

"Look kids. Never come to school and embarrass your parents. We send y'all to school to get your lesson, not act like clowns, touch on your classmates, and disrespect your teachers." She looked at TJ. "When I drop my son off to school every day, I make sure we talk about these things because TJ knows I don't play the mess he's been doing. I work every day to make sure he has every new game system, shoes, clothes, anything he asks for, he gets it. But, why should I reward a child who don't respect his classmates, his teacher, or his mother? Why should I reward you TJ?" she asked him.

"Man, whatever," he mumbled.

That's when Ciara lost it. She took the leather belt out of her purse that she had waiting for him. She held his arm up and beat him with the belt. The class was going crazy. Students were recording with their phones, and the principal and students didn't interfere simply because most parents needed to do what Ciara was doing.

TJ was crying, his nose was running, and he was embarrassed.

"Look at me? Do you take me as a joke, little boy?" she asked him.

"No, ma!" He wiped his face.

"You must do because you know damn well I don't play this. Go to that little girl right now and apologize."

The class was still hyped and was still recording, but Ciara didn't care. She wanted TJ to know that what he was doing was not right. He was going to be a respectable young gentleman, not a thug like his dumb ass father.

"Sorry," he said to the young lady.

Ciara walked to him and swung the belt again, which made him flinch.

"Say it like you mean it before I beat you again!" Ciara yelled.

"I am sorry for touching you, Amanda. It will never happen again."

"Apology accepted Trey." The girl hugged him.

All the young ladies in class clapped while all the young men clowned Trey. He was pissed, but he knew better than to show it in front of his mama.

"Now, apologize to your teacher and your principal."

"I'm truly sorry," he said to the both of them.

"I am so sorry for all of this. I pray that y'all forgive him for this, and I will love to talk to the young lady's parents. You all will not have any more problems out of this one. Ain't that right, Trey?"

He nodded.

"Get your stuff and let's go."

"This goes nowhere," the teacher said to the class.

The entire ride to her mother's house Ciara cried like a baby. Trey didn't understand what his mother had been through. She didn't want him to disappoint her.

"I'm sorry ma," Trey said. It really hurt him to see his mother like that.

She pulled into the yard and cut off the car. "TJ, you can't go in these streets touching on female private parts and shit. Do you know that kind of shit will get you killed or put away in jail for life? What were you thinking?"

"I wasn't."

"That's shit perverts do. You wanna be like your daddy?" Ciara covered her mouth. She didn't mean to let that slip.

"You don't have to cover your mouth. I know." He lowered his head.

"How?"

"I heard when you and uncle Charles were arguing a while back. You said he put something into your drink and took advantaged of you."

Ciara wiped her eyes. "He did." Ciara nodded.

"I hate that nigga, ma," TJ said.

"Don't say that TJ, but you see that's why you can't go around doing shit like that. I didn't know that you knew though. I really didn't."

"Yeah, that's why I didn't take his death hard. I mean, he was barely around and when I heard that, I didn't care anymore." He shrugged.

Ciara looked at her son. She admired the young man that he had become, despite the dumb shit he had been doing lately. He was very tall to only be nine years old. He had just had a birthday and most people thought he was ten or eleven.. He was skinny, but he was very handsome.

"I'm sorry about that ma. You have a point. I shouldn't have been acting that way. I was tripping."

"You were, but when we go home, I need your game systems, your TV, and that hoverboard. You're grounded for a month until I get your report card."

That pissed TJ off all over again.

"And we're going to Miami in few days. We got a few loose ends to tie up."

"Yeah," TJ said.

Ciara didn't care that he was mad. Hell, she was still mad. She did have mixed feelings about him knowing that his father raped her, but he was old enough to know. He needed to know.

***

"You sure you wanna do this?" Terrance asked Ciara.

She nodded her head. "I have to. I need to be done with this."

Terrance, TJ, and Ciara walked into the *Crazy about you* restaurant in Miami, Florida. They were meeting with TJ's grandmother, Pearl. There were a few things that Ciara needed to get off of her chest and after that, she was leaving her past in her past.

"Hey, Ciara! Hey, little Trey," Pearl greeted them, but she didn't greet Terrance. He didn't give a damn though. He was only there to support his wife.

"You could've greeted my husband too," Ciara said.

"Hi."

Terrance nodded his head. *Fuck her old ass,* he thought.

"So, what is it that made y'all fly all the way out here to Miami?" Pearl asked.

"I've been holding something in for so long that has affected my life, and I just want you to know because after today, I plan on never looking back."

She had Pearl's undivided attention.

"When I got pregnant with TJ, Trey raped me. It was never my intentions to get pregnant. He seduced me, then raped me."

Pearl immediately jumped to her dead son's defense. "You will not lie on my son, Ciara!" she yelled.

Tears fell from her eyes. "I'm not lying." She shook her head.

"I don't think she is either grandma," TJ spoke up.

"How come you're just waiting to say this then?" Pearl asked.

"Because I was crazy in love for a long ass time, but not only did he rape me when I got pregnant with my son, but he raped me a little bit before he was murdered. My brother allowed him to."

"What?" TJ yelled. That was something that he didn't know. Ciara looked at him and nodded her head. TJ excused himself from the table, and Terrance went behind him.

Pearl shook her head. She didn't want to believe it.

"I wouldn't lie about something like this, Pearl. Trey was crazy. That's why I didn't attend his funeral. I hated him so much." Tears fell from Ciara's eyes. "But I don't anymore. I'm glad he did that because I learned from it."

"Honey, I am sorry. That's all I can say. I am so sorry. I wish I would've known before he was dead though."

"I'm sorry for not telling you, but I had to get it off my chest. I wanna be happy. I don't wanna think about that."

"I respect that."

Ciara rubbed Pearl's hand and smiled. "Thank you for believing me. God bless you, Pearl."

Ciara grabbed her purse and went outside. Terrance was having a man to man talk with TJ. He needed it and Ciara was thankful that TJ still had a man's guidance in his life.

Terrance kissed Ciara. Ciara rubbed TJ's back.

"It's all good, son. Your mama is a strong woman. Don't even sweat it," Ciara told him.

"How you feeling?" Terrance asked her.

"Free! I can finally live my life without holding on to something I can't control. I just wanna focus on my family."

Terrance smiled and kissed her.

"I love you, girl."

"I love you too." She hugged him.

Ciara felt like a weight had lifted off of her shoulder. At that moment, she knew it was her new beginning.

Epilogue
One Year Later

Michelle stood next to her husband in her long beautiful peach and cream diamond studded Nicole Miller wedding dress. Their reception was being held at the most beautiful building in Boston, *The State Room.* It was beyond beautiful. Serri, Reece, Luke, and Shirley paid all the expenses for the wedding and reception, and they had spent over five hundred thousand dollars. She held Timmy's hand and giggled. She was the happiest woman on earth and nobody could take her joy away. They were on the dance floor waiting for the DJ to drop their favorite songs, so they could do their couple's dance. They had practiced their routines over twenty times, and they were more than ready to show off their stuff. Michelle thought that she would be nervous, but she had enough shots where she was comfortable.

Once the DJ played the *Whip, Nae-Nae* song, the entire crowd went crazy when they started dancing. It had gotten so fun that they didn't even do their routine they made up, they just went along with each other's flow. Everyone was recording and taking pictures of them. It was the most beautiful wedding you'd ever see, and the best part about their wedding day was that it was on the twins' birthday. They were finally one years old and bad just didn't describe them. They were spoiled brats. Everyone thought it was so cute when the twins ran out on the dance floor and joined their parents.

Michelle and Timmy could've gotten married sooner, but they figured that there was no need to rush marriage. The two of them were really in love with each other.

It was over three hundred people who attended their wedding. All of Timmy's family from Dubai and Boston was there and all of Michelle's family. Members from the church came and some of Timmy's clients from work.

"Go head and dance baby!" Tall got on the DJ mic. Uncle Tall was still the same uncle Tall. Funny, blunt, and full of life. Shirley and Luke watched the newlyweds and were almost in tears. They had never thought their daughter would be so happy. It warmed their hearts. The devil tried so hard to steal Michelle's joy, but he did not win.

Soon, everyone joined them on the dance floor when the DJ played the slow music.

"Look at her baby. She's so happy," Shirley said to Luke. He nodded and smiled.

"I prayed for this day," Luke said.

"Me too." She pecked his lips.

Ciara and Michelle went to the table and had more shots. Their friendship was truly unbreakable. Every day they thanked God for one another.

"I love you so much, Ciara." Michelle threw her hand over Ciara's shoulder. She was almost drunk.

"I love you more, friend. Remember when we were little girls and we used to play in y'all backyard? We said it was going to be like this. God loves us." They laughed.

"He sure do."

Ciara was the happiest she had ever been. She and Terrance were still married, and they were blessed to have each other. Even though she couldn't have her own kids, they went through with adoption. They had a two-month old baby girl that they loved like she was their flesh and blood. Ciara was happy because Terrance was happy. He never got frustrated and upset when they tried to have a baby and didn't succeed. That made her love him even more. The two of them opened one of the biggest fashion boutiques in Boston, and it was amazingly successful. Of course, Terrance was still doing what he did best in the court, but he loved his side hustle with his wife. They were beyond rich and whenever they weren't in Boston, they were in Dubai living the good life.

Michelle had opened up her own printing company. She was known all over the world, but she was so excited about the connections she had in Dubai. Every month she was at a different interview in a different state or country. Whenever she and Timmy were too busy to go to important business meetings away from home together, they would leave the babies with Shirley and Luke. Every two weeks, Michelle would visit Briana's gravesite, just to talk to her and get a peace of mind. She always said that going out there was her therapy. Instead of it making her sad, it made her happy. She had finally come to accept the fact that God could love Briana more than she could, and even though she wasn't fully over Briana's death, her heart didn't hurt how it used too. She always thought of that beautiful smile whenever she felt like giving up. That smile brought peace to everyone's heart.

Timmy and the rest of the guys were turned up to the music at the reception. Everyone was having a good time and that's all that mattered to everyone.

Shara walked up to Michelle and hugged her. It took a whole lot of prayer and time, but Michelle had forgiven Shara for what she had done to her. Michelle felt sorry for Shara. She didn't know who her first child's father was, and she was pregnant again by God knows who.

"I'm happy for you." Shara smiled.

"Thank you... cousin..." They hugged.

"Congratulations, sis! I'm happy for you. You know my mama and daddy ain't gone spend this much money on my wedding when I get married and shit. They always liked that tall lanky ass nigga more than me," Silence said. He was drunk, but it wouldn't be him if he wasn't goofy.

"Shut up, Silence." Michelle laughed.

"Nah, real shit though. I'm happy for you and my brother, man. You're the best that nigga ever had, and you know I'd tell you the truth."

"I know Silence. Thank you so much. Hopefully you and Samantha is next."

"Hell nah!"

"Silence! I know you saw me waving you down!" Samantha wobbled over.

"See, you talked her aggravating ass up," Silence sighed. "I did not see you waving me down," he lied.

"Go fix me some more food please."

He shook his head and walked away. That tickled Michelle's soul.

"Y'all are a fucking mess." Michelle took another shot.

"That's your brother-in-law. He's such a fucking jerk." Samantha shook her head and stormed off.

Silence and Samantha finally had a baby on the way. She was six months pregnant and they were having a little boy. As much as Silence loved Samantha, he honestly didn't think they would ever work out for a relationship. She was just too difficult for him, and she always used the baby just to get on his nerves. He was excited about his baby, but he could do without her. He was also tired of dealing with her racist ass family. They hated his guts. He had already moved back to Boston permanently so he wouldn't have to be back and forth throughout her pregnancy, but he was missing home something terrible. Reece missed him so much because whenever Serri would be working a lot, Silence was always there to have a great time with her. She was in America much more now.

Earlier, before their wedding, Timmy received a letter from his ex-wife, Patrice. As much as he didn't want to open the letter, he did anyways. He was surprised when she wished him the best of luck in his new marriage. She was still doing time in prison, but her letter made Timmy feel like she had learned her lesson. He laughed his ass off when he read in the letter that she was now gay and her girlfriend's name was Coco. She and Coco had plans to get married and move to New York when she was free. Michelle was even happy that she had reached out to Timmy. She even thought it would be nice if he sent her some canteen. He wasn't feeling it though.

Timmy went up to the booth and grabbed the mic.

"Thank y'all for making me and my wife's day amazing. I'm drunk. I'm drunk as hell, but me and my wife gone have a good ass time tonight. Briann and Ashanti, we love y'all but we need a break from y'all bad asses." Everyone laughed. "But seriously, I love my wife man. I'm so thankful for her. We've been through the worse together and she stuck by my side."

"I love you too baby!" Michelle yelled.

When their slide show played on the projector, Michelle cried like a baby, especially when they showed Briana's pictures. Everyone helped her cry then. It was pictures from the beginning of their relationship, up until that moment. Beyoncé and Jay-Z's song, *Forever Young*, played with the slide show. It was magnificent.

In less than two years, everyone found themselves, even if it took breaking them down to get to that point.

They learned to love, forgive, accept, and be happy. With strong supportive friends and family, everyone could finally say they were happy and at peace in their life, and they gave it all to God. Life was truly amazing.

"Cheers to the Ralph's!" the DJ screamed.

Everyone put their glasses in the air and threw their shots back. The definition of the "GOOD LIFE" was right there in that building.

The End

CPSIA information can be obtained at www.ICGtesting.com
Printed in the USA
LVOW10s1752170316

479611LV00016B/521/P